Anonymous

The Knights of the Frozen Sea

A narrative of Arctic discovery and adventure

Anonymous

The Knights of the Frozen Sea
A narrative of Arctic discovery and adventure

ISBN/EAN: 9783337285890

Printed in Europe, USA, Canada, Australia, Japan

Cover: Foto ©Andreas Hilbeck / pixelio.de

More available books at **www.hansebooks.com**

FALLS OF WILBERFORCE.   P. 141.

30   120   11

E

Polymia Isles PARRY
Clintock
ck I
on I. Melville Isl
C Russell
Str: Liddon Gulf
C Dundas
C Hay
Merry Parker Pt
Russell Id MELVILL
WS Pr of W
Collinson Pt
Pt ALBERT Ld

Coll

Wollaston Victoria L.
Union Str
York Archip
CORONATION GULF

Bathurst Inlet

Augustus

Contwoy to L. L Bea

Sussex L

L Aylmer

Providence Artillery

Lake

L Athabasca

L Wollaston

Pierre au Calumet

Methye L. & Ft
Clear L
Buffalo L
La Ronge Ft

I

A MAP TO ILLUSTRATE THE SEARCH FOR THE NORTH-WEST PASSAGE.

THE

KNIGHTS OF THE FROZEN SEA.

A Narrative

OF

ARCTIC DISCOVERY AND ADVENTURE.

BY THE

AUTHOR OF "HARRY LAWTON'S ADVENTURES."

WITH A MAP,

AND FORTY-FOUR ILLUSTRATIONS.

NEW YORK:

D. APPLETON & Co., 445 BROADWAY.

1867.

CONTENTS.

LIST OF ILLUSTRATIONS.

KNIGHTS OF THE FROZEN SEA.

CHAPTER I.

EARLIEST ARCTIC VOYAGES.

THREE centuries have now passed away since a celebrated old English navigator declared that 'the only great thing left to be done in this world of ours was the discovery of the north-west passage to India.'

It was a singular idea, yet one which has been taken up and thoroughly worked out by a succession of ardent spirits, down to our own times. They did not, it is true, consider it the only great thing remaining undone; but they thought it a sufficiently great one to occupy all their best energies, and to justify the risking of their own and many other valuable lives.

Only in our own times has the discovery been made, after all; and now that it is made no one at present knows what to do with it; for the dangers are too great, and the Arctic summers too short, to allow of vessels going that way.

This is not, however, the place in which to discuss the utility of the object, or the prudence of those who went or sent forth to seek it. We have to tell our tale; and that tale, we venture to say, will be found as full of interesting, romantic, and instructive incidents, as any which the many volumes of voyages and travels about the globe can furnish.

When the tale is done we may, perhaps, be in a better position to say 'what good has come of it all.'

It is at least one which, in many ways, reflects glory on our country; and few, except Britons, have any part in it: for this particular field of discovery seems long to have been regarded as our own special ground, and other nations have almost entirely resigned it to us.

England has, indeed, always been forward in the work of discovering new shores; and though once by no means so enterprising as some of the other European nations, she yet began early; and her naval spirit, as well as power, has been increasing down to the present time.

It was in the reign of our great Alfred that Englishmen made their first voyage of discovery — at least, the first of which we have any record; and that one was in a northerly direction.

At that time the Venetians were the first maritime power in Europe, and its great carriers. They traded with all the rich products of Turkey and

India, bringing the latter by the overland route; and of this traffic they were determined to maintain the monopoly. So that if an English or French vessel ventured into the Mediterranean it was immediately seized, either by the Venetians or the Moors, and the crew carried into slavery.

But besides this, heavy taxes, intended for the support of the Romish Church, crushed the commerce of England. These, therefore, the king repealed; and feeling that it was useless to think of rivaling the Venetians on their own coasts, he determined to try to find another way of reaching those far Eastern countries from whence they drew their wealth.

The field which he entered was one since chiefly occupied by the Russians, namely, the search for the *north-east passage.*

In the early chronicles we read of a commission given by him to a certain Simon Otho, or Ochter, to take under his command 'the goode ship Adelgitha,' and with her to sail across seas, to discover lands unknown, all 'for the glorye of God, the honour of his kinge, and publique goode of his countrie.'

It was only the southern parts even of Norway and Sweden that were then known to Europe, nor did any one presume to say how the land lay beyond a very moderate latitude; but there was an impression that, somehow or other, ships might sail in a north-easterly direction until they reached India on the other side.

Simon Otho seems, therefore, to have been the

first to attempt the north-east passage; and taking
his instructions from a Danish pirate he set forth,
imagining that, about latitude 55° north, he should
find a sea which washed the northern shores of Europe and Asia, and by which he might sail round to
the desired haven.

Knowing nothing of the peculiar dangers of the
Baltic, he soon reached that sea; and almost immediately his ship struck on a rock, now known as
Falsterborn Reef; and he and his crew were placed
in great jeopardy.

However, the 'Adelgitha' was got off, and after
being repaired at what is now probably the town of
Elsinore, she was brought back to the North Sea;
and they continued their voyage along the coast as
far as latitude 68° north, where, getting among the
numerous rocky islands of that part, the 'goode
ship' again met with much damage, and her captain's
courage cooled; so that, satisfied that no one had
ever been so far north as himself, he turned and
came back home again. This is one account. But
another says that he reached as far as to the river
Kola, if not to the White Sea itself.

The narrative drawn up by King Alfred, from
Otho's own story, speaks of whales and reindeer,
and describes the Fins. It has called forth the
praises of modern writers on account of its remarkable clearness; so that, perhaps, the difficulty of
deciding on the limit of the voyage arises from the
misrepresentations of later chroniclers. The undertaking does not appear to have been followed up,

for troublous times succeeded; but in this, as in many other things, the reign of Alfred seemed to give a sort of picture of England's future character and condition.

There can be no doubt that the first to enter on that field of discovery, which has obtained the honour of knighthood for Ross, Parry, Franklin, and so many others, were the old sea-rovers of the North. And very probably, if the riches of the southern countries of Europe had not so strongly drawn them in that direction, their roving disposition might have long ago led them on to the point which we have only so recently attained, and which to a Northern people, and a very hardy one, would have proved so much less difficult to reach.

As it was, they no doubt sometimes wandered for the very sake of wandering; and the first-fruits of their discoveries was the island of Iceland, at first named by them Snowland, on which some of them were driven by a violent storm, about the end of the ninth century, and which they soon decided to colonise, making it a refuge for all who were oppressed at home.

A century passed, and the Icelanders received into their body a powerful Norwegian chieftain, who had been banished for homicide. His son Eirek, surnamed Rauda, ' the Red,' from his sanguinary disposition, soon followed him; and finding no occupation in the colony which suited his tastes, and being, possibly, obliged to leave it, he resolved to make a voyage of discovery to a land on which one

of his countrymen had been driven by a storm ; and
so he set out westward, A.D. 982.

Soon two lofty mountains met his view, and
these he called Huitserken and Blaarserken—White
Shirt and Blue Shirt—one being covered with snow
and the other with ice. He landed on a little island,
just south of Cape Farewell, and spent the winter
there.   In the spring he explored the mainland, and
happening to find one part covered with verdure,
he called the country ' Greenland,' because he said

Scandinavian Vessel.

that ' a good name would induce people to go and
settle there:' though, as an old writer says,* ' Greenland is a place in nature nothing like unto the name:
for certainly there is no place in the world yet known
and discovered that is less green than it.'

So Eirek, the Red Hand, both discovered and
named Greenland ; and what is very surprising, when
we think of the scanty provisions generally carried
in those days, we read that he remained there
three years, and returned to Iceland only to describe

* Purchas.

to his countrymen its wonderful advantages; and then the next year he went back with numerous followers, and settled on a creek which was named after him, Eireksfjörd, which soon became an important colony.

A few years after this, Eirek's own son, Leif, visited the first Christian king of Norway, was converted himself, and soon went over to the new colony, taking a priest with him to preach Christianity to the colonists.

In A.D. 1121 their first bishop was consecrated, and for three centuries the colony and church continued to flourish. But after that, strange to say, both went to ruin, and very soon altogether disappeared. Of this extraordinary circumstance many writers have tried to discover the cause; and some have supposed that, owing to the hindrances thrown in the way of their trade by the mother-country, they were really starved out: but, in fact, it is a mystery which no one has yet explained. All we know is that these colonies did exist, and are gone.

There is reason, however, to believe that Greenland was not all of the new hemisphere discovered by the Northmen. It is said that a son of one of Eirek's companions, wishing again to winter at the paternal hearth, fitted out a vessel and tried to follow his father. But not knowing the land, or how to reach it, this Bjarni was much driven about, and at last saw land, which did not answer to the descriptions which he had heard of Greenland. When at length he reached his father's dwelling, this wonderful voyage of his was much talked about, and the consequence was that about A.D. 1000 Leif, the son of Eirek, of whom we have spoken, fitted out a vessel and started on a voyage of discovery. He soon made the land described by Bjarni, a rugged plain of broad flat rocks, which would appear to have been Newfoundland; and next came to another part, the description of which answers to that of the north coast of Nova Scotia, where he and his companions built houses and passed the winter, returning to Greenland next spring laden with timber and grapes, after naming the country in which they had been staying Vinland — the land of the vine.

They visited it from time to time, but seem never to have attempted to colonise it.

Besides what we have related above, we have a very mysterious account of a voyage said to have been made in the twelfth century by Madoc, prince of Wales, to some part of the American continent; but little can be made of it. A citizen of Marseilles also performed a voyage to the north in those early times; but where he went we do not know, as he only tells us that 'his progress was at length arrested by a barrier of a peculiar nature, being neither earth, air, nor sky, but something composed of all three, through which he could not penetrate!'

Another account of a north-western voyage, that of the two Zenos, has become more generally known, and certainly produced great results, as we shall see as we go on.

Nicolo Zeno and his brother were two Venetian travellers, who, on a voyage to one of the western countries of Europe, were caught in a storm, and cast away on a strange coast, which some suppose to have been Greenland, some an island nearer home. In the old records it is called 'Engrone-land.'

Leaving all these early attempts, we will now pass on to sketch the history of those which, beginning in the reign of Henry VII., have been followed by others in a constant succession down to our own 'age of travelling.'

The discovery of America by Columbus had set many a man longing to share in his honours, by being the first to bring to light some other unknown and new land; and though England had missed this honour, her spirit was aroused when she found that not only had Spain been before her here, but that Portugal also was boldly launching forth her vessels on the ocean, and that Vasco de Gama had found out for her the passage to India round the Cape of Good Hope.

So, when Sebastian Cabot proposed to attempt to outdo Portugal by finding another passage of half the length round the north-west coast of North America, the idea was entertained even by Henry VII. himself. This Sebastian was a Venetian, and the son of an adventurous navigator then residing, as a merchant, in Bristol. He himself is said to have been born there; and very early, he tells us, he 'felt in his heart a great flame of desire to do some notable thing.'

He is said to have been the first to attempt the North-west Passage; and a bold scheme it was for those times, when so little was known of the new continent at all.

But he does not seem to have expected to be obliged to steer very far to the north before he found the ocean across which he intended to sail direct for 'the land of Cathay'—that mysterious country of vast and unknown treasures. 'Understanding,' he said, ' by reason of the sphere, that if he should sail by north-west he should, by a shorter track, come to India,' he 'caused the king to be advertised of his device, because all men thought it a thing more divine than human to sail by the west into the east, where spices do grow;' and the king quickly ordered two caravels to be prepared, with all things necessary for so long a voyage. In the summer of 1496 he set sail; but when he found that, instead of quickly finding the upper coast, he was forced to continue his course more and still more to the northward, because the land went on, as it appeared, interminably in that direction, he became greatly disheartened, especially as the coast of Newfoundland, at which he touched, promised no such riches as Spain had found in the south.

A cold, dreary place it seemed to him; and the people he described as 'like to brute beasts in their behaviour, dressed in beasts' skins, and eating raw flesh;' so, after taking away from thence three of the poor Esquimaux as specimens, he sailed southwards, and soon came in sight of Florida. Then, his victuals failing him, he departed and returned to England; where he stated, that in the month of July he had found in those seas 'such great heapes of ise' that he 'durst passe no further: also, that the dayes were very long, and in maner without nyght, and the nyghtes very clear.'

Sebastian Cabot has consequently been generally considered as the discoverer of these two countries, Newfoundland and Florida; though some suppose that his own father, John Cabot, had previously visited the former, even at an earlier date than that in which Columbus discovered the West Indies and South America. Had the great Alfred, instead of the mean and sordid Henry, been then on the throne, the records of these events would have been regarded as matter of some interest, and would have been more carefully kept, and not allowed to 'moulder in one of the lanes of the metropolis.' But men sailed then in search of gold; and such discoveries as these were of little account.

Sebastian Cabot returned to find England in a great ferment, on account of the rising of Perkin Warbeck and the preparations for a war with Scotland; and seeing his design overlooked, he some time afterwards entered the service of Spain, and made many voyages under the auspices of the Spanish king.

But though the report of these new lands was little thought of in England, yet Portugal, then the greatest maritime power in the world, eagerly followed it up.

By her discovery of the passage round the Cape

she had struck a fatal blow at the power of her great rival, Venice; and her sons were not slow in pursuing their advantage. Multitudes of them were flocking to the New World; and now that another part of it was laid open, they made ready to enter that also.

In A.D. 1500, only two years after the return of Cabot, Gaspar Cortereal, a gentleman of high birth in the court of King Emmanuel of Portugal, sailed from Lisbon, and after touching at the Azores, pursued his course in a north-westerly direction, until he came to the coast of Labrador, to which he gave the name of Terra Verde, and which some have therefore confounded with Greenland, though Sir John Barrow shows that this is a mistaken notion.

Gaspar Cortereal, like Cabot, was the son of a naval adventurer; and his father also is said to have been in these northern seas before him. Gaspar explored the coast for some hundreds of miles, and took home with him some specimens of its inhabitants, who, according to the opinion of a Venetian ambassador, given in a letter to his brother after Cortereal's return, were 'admirably calculated for labour, and the best slaves he had ever seen.'

That 'might is right' was certainly the prevailing maxim of that day: nor did many persons then seem to feel themselves bound to 'keep their hands from picking and stealing,' except in their own native lands. On this principle had Alonzo Gonzales, twenty years before, suggested that the poor Africans might be appropriated by civilized nations, and even built the fort of D'Elmina for the purpose; thus earning for himself the infamy of being the originator of the African slave-trade. And so it was planned to use the mild and laborious Esquimaux, though, happily, that scheme fell to the ground.

Next year Gaspar was sent out again, and endeavoured to penetrate still further north. A storm, however, arose as he was entering a strait, which was probably Hudson's; and he was never heard of more. When the other vessel which had accompanied him returned with the news, his brother Michael set off in search of Gaspar; but of him also no tidings ever reached home: and the king, who had brought the brothers up, and was much troubled at their loss, positively refused to allow the third to risk his life. He sent out armed vessels himself in search, but they met with no success; so the land, which Gaspar had named Terra Verde, was, after them, called 'the land of the Cortereals.'

It was in 1524, the year before the battle of Pavia, that France followed the example of her neighbours, and fitted out four vessels for an Arctic voyage.

The command of the expedition was given to a Florentine named Giovanni Verazzano; and he must have been a man of great energy and ability—well suited to the trust; for we read that he coasted along the whole of what is now the United States, as well as a good part of British America. But when he returned and found Francis a prisoner, the French army destroyed, and his country half-ruined, he did not, it may be supposed, meet with all the honour or encouragement which he had so well earned; and ten years passed before the French made another attempt.

Jacques Cartier was then sent out; and he made two voyages, in the course of which he circumnavigated Newfoundland—'the land of Cod Fish,' as it had been called—discovered the Isle of the Assumption, explored the Gulf of St. Lawrence, which he also named, ascended the river St. Lawrence, and got into friendly relations with the natives, who brought their paralytic old king, Agonhanna, to be touched and cured, as they hoped, by the Admiral.

The French party remained some time at Hochlaga—or Montreal, as it has since been called, from the French name, Mont Royale—and learnt from the Indians not only a cure for the scurvy, from which they suffered much, in a decoction of the leaves and bark of the North American white pine, but also became acquainted with tobacco. And great was their amazement when they first saw the natives 'suck it so long, and fill their bodies so full of smoke that it came out of their mouths and nostrils, even as out of the tunnel of a chimney!'

But as no gold or silver had been found, the French king was not particularly well satisfied with their expedition, and cared not to undertake the expense of another; nor was it till four years after that Cartier was enabled to revisit the country, by joining in the private expedition of a French nobleman who wished to settle there.

Had he not most disgracefully, on the first occasion, rewarded the kindness of the natives by carrying off their old chief, Donnaconna, into France, they might easily have done this. But now Cartier was very differently received; and they had to build a fort for their own defence on the site of the present city, Montreal.

But to return to English enterprises.

Cabot began his Arctic researches, as we have seen, in the reign of Henry VII. In the reign of Henry VIII. there appear to have been two Polar expeditions; and both were made by Englishmen. Of these, however, the records are but scanty.

The first was undertaken by a merchant of Bristol of the name of Robert Thorne, who, having long resided at Seville, where he had heard much of the treasures pouring into the Spanish coffers from the New World, as well as from India, memorialized the king on the subject.

He urged on his attention that, by sailing northward and passing the Pole, they would get at the East Indies by a much shorter route than that lately discovered round the south of Africa; and, besides, that three-fourths of the world being discovered by other princes, this remaining one was the only way open to glory: and so enthusiastic was he in the matter, that he even persuaded himself that men had overrated the severity of the cold in the extreme north; and maintained that the danger probably lay only some little way before the Pole is reached, and after it is passed. 'After which,' he said, 'it is clear

that from thenceforth the seas and lands are as tem-
perate as in these parts!'

Two ships were, it appears, at length granted to
this eager man; one of which was cast away on the

Caravel: time of Henry VIII.

coast of Newfoundland, and of the other there is
no record.

The other expedition was undertaken by a Lon-
doner, a certain Master Hore; who is described as 'a

man of goodly stature and great courage, and given to the study of cosmography.'   He took with him a hundred and twenty persons, thirty of whom were gentlemen who belonged to the Inns of Court, and sailed to the coast of Newfoundland, where they got into such fearful distress that they had begun to kill and eat one another, when a French vessel arrived, of which the English contrived to make themselves masters; and out of which they took provisions enough to carry them home.   The French followed, and complained of the outrage which had been committed on them; but Henry was so touched at the tale of his poor subjects' sufferings, that, though he well repaid the French for their loss, he refused to punish those who had done the wrong.

Henry, however, took very little interest in any of these voyages: but of his young son, Edward, we are told, that 'naval affairs had seized his mind as a sort of passion;' and that 'while yet a child he knew all the ports and harbours in his dominions, as well as in France and Scotland, how much water was in them, and what was the way of coming into them.'

Sebastian Cabot returned to England, which he regarded apparently as his native land, in his old age; and his worth was soon discovered by the young king, by whom, it is said, he was created Grand Pilot of England, with a pension of 250 marks, or 166*l.* 13*s.* 4*d.* of our money, 'in consideration of the good and acceptable service done by him.'

It is at least certain, that he was placed at the

head of a company of merchants, who were making preparations for a north-eastern voyage of discovery.

Sir Hugh Willoughby, who, if not much of a sailor, is described as a most valiant gentleman, was appointed to the command of this expedition; while Richard Chancelor, a 'man of great estimation for the many good parts of wit in him,' was captain of one of the three ships fitted out: and Cabot drew up the instructions for their guidance.

Notwithstanding the ill success of various previous voyages the present adventurers started in high spirits, dropping down to Greenwich, where the court lay in a kind of triumph, and being met there by a rush of courtiers and common people, who flew to the banks as they passed, and gave them as hearty a cheering as if they were returning in full success, instead of only setting out on a most perilous, and, as it proved, a very mournful expedition.

At the North Cape, Chancelor's ship got separated from the other vessels in a storm; and they never met again.

Willoughby and the third ship continued their course to Nova Zembla, and even tried to reach a more northerly latitude, but were soon obliged to turn; and at length the two crews, consisting of sixty persons, got shut up by the ice on the coast of Russian Lapland, where they all perished miserably. Sir Hugh Willougby's body was found frozen to death by some Russian fishermen two years after. A journal lay beside him; and his last entry told how parties had been sent out several ways in search of some human habitation, but without success.

An attempt was made to bring home the bodies of the adventurers in their own vessels; but they sank by the way; and thus those who were conducting them were also lost.

Chancelor, meantime, had been more fortunate. He had resolutely held on his way until he came to the White Sea, and landed at Archangel, where he learnt from the fishermen that he was in the dominions of a great sovereign, named Ivan Vasilovitch, who held his court at Moscow, six hundred miles away.

At once he determined to visit this monarch; and although they had to travel the whole distance over the snow in sledges, he carried out his purpose, and thus laid the foundation of our commercial intercourse with Russia. The company of merchants, who from thenceforth were known as the Muscovy Company, were so well pleased with his success that they soon sent him out again, both to trade and to make fresh discoveries. On his return from this second voyage he brought with him an ambassador, who had been sent by the emperor to visit the court of Philip and Mary; but a storm overtook them at sea, and Chancelor, with many of his crew, was lost, though the ambassador escaped, and was graciously received by the king and queen.

Meantime, another Russian expedition, commanded by Stephen Burrough, had been sent out by the same company, in which the ' goode olde gentleman, Master Cabote,' took such interest, that before they set out he gave a great banquet, at which, ' for very joy that he had to see the towardness of their discovery, he entered into the dance himselfe amongst the rest of the young and lusty company.'

Burrough, however, made no very particular addition to the knowledge then possessed of those northern coasts.

CHAPTER II.

SIR MARTIN FROBISHER AND HIS SUCCESSORS.

WE have come now to the reign of Queen Elizabeth, a reign so rich in great characters that it is not surprising that amongst the list we find several who have distinguished themselves as naval adventurers, and as adventurers in those parts of the ocean which come within our province. First, we have Martin Frobisher, a name generally known, perhaps, chiefly in connexion with the defeat of the Spanish Armada; and yet he was in his day a well-known man long before his share in that great event gained him the honour of knighthood.

Very early in life he had set his heart on the same design which had so much occupied the mind of Sebastian Cabot, namely, the discovery of the North-west Passage; and so convinced was he of the importance and practicability of the scheme, that for fifteen long years he went about agitating the subject before he succeeded in gaining a hearing.

But fame was his object; and as he conceived that 'no other great thing remained to be done in the world,' and that, therefore, this was the only road to it, he persevered, until at length, in 1576,

Ambrose Dudley, earl of Warwick, took up his cause, and he was enabled to equip three vessels of 35, 30, and 10 tons respectively, with which he sailed down the Thames, the Queen standing at her window at Greenwich as he passed, and waving her hand as a parting greeting; while a gentleman despatched by her went on board to wish them 'happie successe,' and to 'make known her goode likings of their doings.'

The voyage was tolerably prosperous; and in July the vessels arrived at what Frobisher took for 'the Friezland of Zeno,'—an imaginary country on which that old Venetian traveller is said to have been wrecked, but which really appears to have been the southern coast of Greenland. They tried to land, but a violent storm arose, in which the pinnace, with her crew of four, was lost; and then the crew of the 'Gabriel,' 'mistrusting the matter, privily conveyed themselves away,' and reached England safely soon after.

But Frobisher's courage still kept up. When others had been faint-hearted during the violence of the late tempest he had distinguished himself by his calmness, and encouraged them by his quiet self-possession and presence of mind; and now that his own vessel was left to battle alone with the fury of the elements, and often in danger of being crushed between the enormous masses of floating ice, he still bravely determined to persevere.

Finding it impossible to land on the Greenland coast, he turned southwards, and after many days reached what seems to have been the dreary shores of Labrador. There, the vessel becoming shut in on the outside by an impenetrable barrier of ice, at length entered a strait to which Frobisher gave his own name. Along the banks of this strait they soon perceived some strange beings whom, at first sight, they took for porpoises, but who turned out to be

Esquimaux with their Kajaks.

Esquimaux, in their kajaks, or boats; and they hastened to make acquaintance with them.

No doubt these people were, in all respects, much the same as their descendants of the present day. 'Salvage people,' he described them, 'like to Tartars, having long black hair, broad faces, and flatte noses; and the women being marked on the face with blewe streekes downe the cheekes and round the eyes,' and wearing 'bootes made of seal skinnes, in shape somewhat resembling the shallops of Spain.'

But the loss of a boat's crew of five men soon cut short any attempts at a nearer acquaintance with these people; for when 'they had often in vain called them back by the sound of trumpets and the firing off of falconets,' Frobisher, taking it for certain that some wrong had been done them by the natives, in revenge enticed one of them to the side of the ship by the tinkling of a bell, and then 'pluckt him up, boat and all;' and, with him on board, set sail for England, the poor fellow, in his rage and despair, biting his own tongue in half by the way.

At home the captain was well received, and treated as a person who had done great things, notwithstanding that he had failed in the main object of his voyage; but it was a little accidental circumstance that turned the nation's hearty welcome into a perfect frenzy of enthusiasm, and made him the lion of his day.

Most of his party had brought some little memento of the land from whence they had come — some flowers, some grass, or stones; and Frobisher had taken possession of one of these stones, in order that he might have something to show his friends. It was black, and remarkably weighty; and when one of his acquaintance asked for a piece of it, he willingly bestowed it on her. By some accident this piece of black stone got thrown into a fire, where it burned for some time, and when taken out and 'quenched in a little vinegar, it glistened with a bright marquesset of golde.' Instantly curiosity was awakened about it, and when some gold-finers of London, to whom it was shown, declared that the ore contained much gold, men immediately thought that a golden land had been discovered, and that heaps of treasure would soon be pouring into the country.

Some offered immediately to accompany Frobisher back to search for more, while many others went privately to the queen to seek for the privilege of holding the new land on lease.

She, too, shared in the excitement, and warmly entered into the matter, directing that another voyage should immediately be made, and giving 'her loving friend, Martin Furbisher,' very full directions for his guidance, some of which are extraordinary enough.

Taking it for granted that he would again touch at this 'Friezland of Zeno,' she desired him to take with him on his 'viage' certain condemned persons, whom he was to land on that shore, with what food and weapons he could conveniently spare, and there leave them, duly instructed ' to conduct themselves well, and so as to gain the good-will of the natives.'

A cheap way this of disposing of criminals! However, it is fair to say that, if possible, they were to speak with them on their return.

A few of the natives also were to be brought home, to serve as specimens; and that their consent was not to be asked we gather from the caution, that 'as they were never to return, and it was desirable to conciliate the natives,' he must 'be careful how and where he took them.'

An Esquimaux Youth.

Frobisher himself seems to have been caught by the golden vision, and either turned by it from his original design, or else he felt himself obliged to yield to circumstances. The next voyage appears to have been entirely devoted to collecting the supposed golden ore, which was found chiefly on a little island named by them the 'Countess of Warwick's Isle.' They took back with them about 200 tons of the mineral, and were rapturously received on their return.

The queen, delighted to find that 'the matter of the gold ore had appearance, and made show of great riches and profit, and,' as she said, though we see not for what reason, 'that the hope of the passage to Cathaia by this last voyage greatly increased,' gave the name of 'Meta Incognita' to the newly-discovered country, and determined to colonise it.

A hundred persons of various trades and callings were appointed as the first settlers, and fifteen vessels were prepared to carry them across the ocean, Frobisher being made commander-in-chief of the expedition.

Of these, twelve ships were to return laden with the ore, and the other three were to remain with the colonists. And in a few weeks they reached their destination, though only after passing through fearful dangers and distresses. One vessel, indeed, which carried a large wooden house, intended for the immediate occupation of the colonists, had been crushed between the icebergs, and had immediately foundered; and another had, under cover of night or of one of the fogs, turned her helm and sailed for England; but the rest of the fleet continued to knock about in the midst of ' incredible paine and perill,' until a fresh breeze sprang up, and, driving the ice before it, left them an open sea through which to sail.

Then their spirits revived, and, nothing daunted, they set to work to repair the damage which they had sustained; and resolving, as they expressed it, to push on ' towards the inward,' they soon had sight of land, which they supposed to be some country on the north-east of Frobisher's Strait.

But new troubles awaited them; for in a short

time the whole fleet was enveloped in thick mists and fogs, and the ships, becoming separated one from another, again beat about at random, amidst the horrible noise of the ice grinding and crushing against the ships' sides, not knowing where they were, or in what direction they were moving.

When at length the sky became clearer, and some communication could be held between the vessels, the pilot declared that the strait was one which he had never seen before; but Frobisher, though from the first he had probably known this, to still their minds insisted that they ' were in their right course and knowen straits.'

It was, as is now believed, Hudson's Straits—an opening, as he saw, in the right direction. And it is reported that he afterwards said, that ' if it had not been for the charge and care he had of the freighted ships, he both could and would have gone through to the South Sea, called Mar del Sur, and dissolved the long doubt of the passage which we seek to find to the rich country of Cathaia '—a large way of talking, which did very well for a time, when men were running mad after the honour and glory of westward adventure, but which would hardly increase our confidence in a naval commander in these more cautious times.

To found this colony, however, was now the first object, and many attempts to land were made; but neither could they succeed in this nor in establishing friendly relations with the natives; so at length Frobisher proposed that they should give up that design and attempt some discovery: but the commanders of the other vessels objected; and, as the provisions were running short in consequence of their losses and disasters, it was eventually concluded to abandon the enterprise and return home. This was an inglorious ending to an expedition prepared at such great cost, and sent out with such high expectations, and one which caused much disappointment in the country.

Frobisher, however, does not seem to have relinquished his scheme; and although for a time he fell into neglect, we read that a fourth expedition was proposed by him, and that it was approved by the great Sir Francis Drake: but it does not appear ever to have been carried out.

Other exciting events, or plans, no doubt turned the current of public attention; yet still men lived under the impression that a golden land existed in the northern parts of the New World, if only its treasures could be obtained. Nor was it until some time afterwards that the supposed golden ore was found to be only a micaceous sand; and so the dazzling vision was altogether dissipated.

But as the thirst for gold, and the sordid desire for amassing wealth, had not been the motives which originated the first enterprise of Frobisher, so neither did the spirit of adventure and the romantic desire for fame which he had helped to nourish in his countrymen, die out with his failure. Englishmen are not easily daunted in any undertaking on which they have set their minds: and a happy thing it no

doubt was for our country that no such treasures
fell to her lot, as had both sharpened and debased
the Spanish and Portuguese appetites.

Trained, for the most part, in that spirit of
intolerance which was even at that very time causing
rivers of blood to flow, both in the Spanish Peninsula
and in the Netherlands, as well as in the pomp and
luxury of a proud and prosperous country, the sons
of Spain and Portugal went out with two unworthy
aims—to amass wealth, and to force men to become
Christians, either by fair means or by foul. No
wonder, then, that the story of Spanish colonisation
is a dark one.

But our English adventurers of the same times
were men of a different stamp.

Without holding any very strict notions of the
meaning of the words *mine* and *thine*, or being
actuated by any very unselfish motives in these
visions of discovery, they were yet, for the most
part, gallant English gentlemen, who, abhorring
Spanish cruelty and tyranny, were burning with the
desire for fame, and full of patriotic notions about
adding to the country's glory.

There were many such in Elizabeth's reign, and
more especially among the Devonshire gentry. We
could not find a better specimen of the class than
that which is furnished by our next adventurer, Sir
Humphrey Gilbert, a native of Compton in Devonshire, and half-brother to Sir Walter Raleigh.

Full of talent, as well as of romance, his writings
on the subject of north-west discovery are said to

have exercised great influence on the mind of Frobisher ; and it is stated that he first formed the plan of British colonisation in Americ. His brothers Adrian and Sir Walter Raleigh also deeply sympathised in his views—the former being, indeed, the head of a company called 'The Colleagues of the Fellowship for the discovery of the North-west Passage,' and the latter accompanying him on one of his voyages.

Sir Humphrey Gilbert obtained from Queen Elizabeth the gift for ever of all the heathen and barbarous countries which he might discover, with absolute authority therein, on the condition of doing homage to the sovereign—who assumed this power of disposing of other people's property—and of paying a fifth of the revenues to the crown. And thinking, no doubt, that he was going to do the benighted natives a great kindness by thus taking possession of their fatherland, Sir Humphrey set sail with four vessels, the 'Swallow,' the 'Delight,' his own ship the 'Golden Hind,' and the 'Squirrel.' But twice had he to turn back on account of bad weather and the faint-heartedness of his crew; and as soon as they reached Newfoundland the 'Swallow' had to be sent home, with some of the crew who had fallen sick, while the 'Delight,' a fine large vessel, struck on a rock and went to pieces.

So Sir Humphrey was left with the two smaller vessels, and on board the 'Squirrel' he hoisted his flag. After taking a formal possession of Newfoundland, and parcelling out the land (although, as we

know, he was by no means its discoverer), he started
on a voyage to the south, where he hoped to find
silver and gold.   However, having had great losses,
the crew soon saw that the choice lay between starvation and return ; so that poor Sir Humphrey, whose
own courage was equal to any emergency, was obliged
to yield and abandon the enterprise.

Leaving these coasts, on which the French and
Spaniards had long had extensive cod-fisheries, they
turned their helms homeward in bitter disappointment.   But very soon they were once more overtaken
by a violent storm ; and the little 'Squirrel' was noticed by its companion to be labouring fearfully
amidst the waves ; while its gallant commander stood
on the deck with a book in his hand, and cried to
the other vessel as she passed that 'they were as
near to heaven by sea as by land.'   Darkness soon
came on, and nothing more was seen for hours of the
tiny bark but one little light, which rose and fell
with the waves.   About midnight that disappeared ;
and the crippled 'Golden Hind' had to return alone
with its dismal tale.

And yet, only two years later, John Davis of
Landridge, another Devonshire man, was found willing, at the bidding of 'divers worshipful merchants
of London and the West country,' to take the
command of two vessels—the 'Sunshine' and the
'Moonshine'—and with them to sail again in
search of the passage to Cathay.

The ships left Dartmouth in June, 1585 ; and in
six weeks after found themselves among the ice of

Greenland, and enveloped in a dense fog. At first, therefore, they could not understand what it was that caused such a mighty roaring as that which met their ears, but soon ascertained that it was the grinding together of the huge masses of ice. They came in view of the land next day, which Davis called the most 'dreary that it is possible to conceive;' adding, that 'the lothsome view of the shore, and the irksome noyse of the yce, was such, that it bred strange conceits' among them: 'so that they supposed the place to be wast, and void of any sensible or vegitable creatures; whereupon he called the same " Desolation."'

However, after a little time they sailed westward, and soon got out of the ice, and among 'many greene and pleasant isles, bordering on the shore,' where they got into a very friendly intercourse with the natives, and began to barter for furs.

But a favourable wind soon caused him to abandon this, and sail north-west across the strait which still bears his name. In great spirits they rounded a cape, which he called 'the Cape of God's Mercy;' thinking that he had actually found the passage which he sought; and sailed on in water, which was of 'the very colour, nature, and quality of the main ocean,' for about eighty leagues, without meeting with any ice, until they came to a cluster of islands. Then, strange to say, when again fogs and storms came on, they quietly abandoned the enterprise; and thinking to prosecute it at some future day, they returned homewards very cheerily.

Twice again Davis sailed from Dartmouth, in 1586 and 1587, and each time he visited the same coasts, discovered something more, and got a little further northward—further, indeed, than any previous navigator had been; but the remonstrances of his crew and the constant fear of the ice prevented him from remaining out long at a time.

Men thought not then of waiting in these northern regions year after year until they had accomplished their purpose; but before we charge them with faintheartedness, we must remember that each one made the matter easier for him who came after, and that the arts of preserving food to keep for years, and of protecting vessels from those shocks of the icebergs, which might crush them at any moment, —were then unknown.

The naval spirit of England was growing then; and it has progressed even to the present times.

However, Davis had been three times out without accomplishing his task; and, like his predecessors, he had thereby lost credit. The talk of invasion by the Spanish Armada also stopped the design for a few years; but in 1602, the last year of our great Queen's reign, George Waymouth was sent out by a merchant company, and bound not to return under one year. Nothing particular was, however, added to the previous knowledge by his voyage, except that, as Fox, one of his successors, of whom we shall soon have to speak, says, ' He and Davis, probably, lighted Hudson into his Straits.'

Waymouth's crew mutinied, and turned the helm

homewards while he slept, declining to go further north than latitude 60°; and he does not himself appear to have been much of a seaman.

It was just at this time, when some of the principal nations of Europe were engaged in war, that the Danes took up the idea of the North-west Passage, which had so long been left to England. Yet the King of Denmark did not, in fitting out his expedition, professedly aim at that object. Ostensibly he sought to explore the coast of Greenland, where he still believed that not only gold, but silver also, was to be found. Singularly enough, the king employed in this service chiefly Englishmen; and although the chief command was given to Admiral Lindenau, yet the names of Hall and Knight, the pilot and one of his companions, became much more distinguished than that of their chief.

That of Henry Hudson, however, who, in 1607, was sent out by the Muscovy Company to endeavour to find a passage across the Pole itself, throws theirs completely into the shade.

He was a man remarkable, not only for his discovery of the straits and bay which bear his name, but for his great personal qualifications for the work which he had undertaken; so that, had he lived in modern times, he would, perhaps, have distinguished himself even among those who have recently gained their laurels in those seas. But his end was even more melancholy than those of some of his predecessors. Four times did he sail from our shores on the old errand; twice directly north, and twice nominally

in a north-easterly direction; though, as the bent
of his mind was for north-westerly discovery, a little
thing caused him to alter his course.

In his first voyage he reached even as far as 81°
north, and coasted along Spitzbergen. Then, his
provisions failing, he was obliged to return home.
In his second, the ice prevented his passage further
than Nova Zembla and latitude 75°. It was on
this occasion that he found the sea so full of seals,
morses, and whales, that he hoped he should by
means of them pay the expenses of his voyage. But
he was disappointed in every way, and, ' void of hope
of a north-east passage,' he made sail for England.

During this voyage some of the crew declared
that they had seen a mermaid; but, unfortunately,
she did not favour them with her company long
enough for their companions to confirm the statement.

After these two voyages Hudson took service in
the Dutch East India Company, and sailed in the
direction which he preferred.

A Moravian missionary to the Indians of Penn-
sylvania has left us an account of his visit to those
parts; received, as he tells us, from the Indians
themselves.

It was before the natives knew anything of white
men that some of them once saw a large object
floating in the sea, which some thought to be an
enormous house, and others, an enormous animal.

At length they concluded that it was Mannitto,
the Supreme Being, coming to visit them in a large

LARGE SEAL, OR SEA-BEAR.

canoe, and an assembly was held as to the manner
of receiving him.   Conjurers were set to work, a
feast prepared, and a dance arranged.

Soon the great canoe stopped, and a little one,
in which was, as they thought, the great Mannitto,
put off for the shore; where he was received by a
council of chiefs, who, terrified as they were, dared
not depart for fear of offending the deity.

His white skin and red dress astonished them
beyond description; and he spoke to them in a
strange language.

After a while a hockhack, or bottle, and a cup,
were brought to him by his men, and, after
drinking himself, he filled the glass again, and
handed it round to the chiefs.   Only one, however, dared to drink; and he, lest the Mannitto
should be offended, took it and drank, saying
that it was better for one man to die than that
the whole nation should be destroyed by the
angry god.   No sooner had he drank than he fell
down apparently dead, and was mourned as such,
until he jumped up and declared that he had never
in his life felt so comfortable and happy as when in
this state; on which all the company drank and
became intoxicated.   The whites afterwards brought
them from their vessel presents of beads, axes, hoes,
stockings, &c., and left, saying that they should
come back next year with more, and then ask for a
little land on which to raise herbs.   According to
promise they came back, and found the hoes hung
round the natives' necks as ornaments, and the

stockings used as tobacco-pouches: at which they laughed exceedingly, and the good-humoured people joined in the merriment.

Still taking Hudson for the Mannitto, and his companions for inferior deities, they treated them with all honour, and readily granted what they asked, namely, as much land as could be compassed by a bullock's hide, though they were rather astonished when they found the bullock's hide cut into strips and made into a thin rope, so that a good-sized piece of ground was encompassed by it.

The whites remained some time, and in like manner obtained so many grants that the Indians thought they would get the whole land; as, in fact, they eventually did.

Hudson returned home again; and in 1610 he took his fatal voyage from the Thames.

Two gentlemen, who were quite persuaded of the existence of a north-west passage, fitted out the ' Discovery,' and entrusted the command to him. It was then that he found the strait which bears his name; and in spite of icy barriers, and murmurings among his crew, he persisted in pushing on towards the west, until he saw that great bay before him which he concluded must be the Pacific Ocean.

But winter was coming on; and it was absolutely necessary to look for some milder spot in which to spend it. It is not known exactly where they settled down; but in a few days they were all frozen in, with little prospect before them but that of starvation.

Hudson, however, offered a reward to whosoever

should find any living thing; and, happily, at first they killed a great many white partridges. When these were gone their sufferings became terrible, and they only just held out until the ice again broke and let them out.

And all this time a horrid plot had been brewing among them, instigated by a young man named Green, whom Hudson had brought with him from England, in the hope of rescuing him from the bad courses into which he had fallen.

Hudson had on one occasion spoken sharply to this young man, for which he had vowed a deadly vengeance. Others, unfortunately, were ready to join him, and the mutiny broke out just as they were making preparations for their return.

As he was leaving his cabin one morning Hudson was seized from behind by some of the wretches, and forced, with eight sick men, on board a small boat, with provisions only for two days; and thus was he, who had allowed himself to be regarded as the Supreme Being, left to perish miserably.

Green meantime vowed never to land in England until he had received a promise of pardon ; but he never reached England, for on their arrival at Cape Digges he and some of the most guilty of his companions went ashore, and in a quarrel with the natives got killed.

The rest of the mutineers, after suffering dreadful privations, reached the coast of Ireland in safety ; and, strange to say, not only did they escape punishment, but two of them, Bylot and Prickett, were employed in the next expedition under Sir Thomas Button. Both, however, declared that they had acted under compulsion; and as it was difficult then to find men used to these northern latitudes, and Bylot was an excellent pilot, perhaps Sir Thomas Button was glad to make use of him.

The latter was a man of learning and ability; but he, too, was thwarted by the murmurs of his crew, and did not accomplish much. Sailing direct to Digges' Island, in Hudson's Straits, he encamped for the winter at the mouth of a river, which he named Port Nelson, and exerted himself to divert the minds of his men from their hardships by proposing to them questions in navigation and geography. In April, when the ice broke up, they proceeded northwards as far as Cape Comfort, then back to Mansell's Islands and home again, where he declared that he believed the passage to exist, though he had failed in finding it.

Nothing daunted by this, and one or two other similar discouragements, the Merchants' Company again fitted out the 'Discovery' for a new Arctic voyage; and here we are introduced to another of those great names which serve as land-marks in our course—that of William Baffin, the discoverer of one of the finest bays in the world.

In 1612 he had made a voyage with Hall, one of the men who had been employed in the Danish expedition; and that voyage is remarkable as the first on record in which, by an observation of the heavenly bodies, a method was adopted for taking the longitude at sea. Baffin had also made a voyage to Greenland previous to his employment by the Company.

It was in 1615 that the command of the 'Discovery' was given to Bylot, and Baffin appointed as his mate. Being far the better educated of the two, he seems to have really directed the course of the expedition; and some of his lunar observations on this occasion were made with so much accuracy that, two centuries later, they called forth the praise of Captain Parry, who always held Baffin in great respect.

No very particular discovery is recorded as the result of this voyage, though it added perhaps a good deal to the general knowledge of those parts. But next year the same ship and officers were again sent out, and with such confident anticipation of success that they were ordered to bring back a Japanese on their return!

They sailed direct for Davis's Strait, up which they continued in a northerly direction until they came to Cape Dudley Digges, Whale Sound, and Cary's Isles, in the very north of what has since been called Baffin's Bay, but which they supposed, and as it now proves truly, to be open sea. Under that idea they were constantly trying to make their way westward, though fruitlessly on account of the ice.

In July, however, this began to melt very fast, and they continued coasting along to the north till they came to an island to which they gave the name of Hackluyt, after Sir Richard Hackluyt, the first

compiler of a volume of voyages; then on to Smith's
Sound, at the extreme north of the bay; and next
round by the western side to Jones' Sound, to both
of which they gave the names.

At length they began to suspect that they were
in a great bay, and not in the open sea at all, and
their hope of a passage became daily less and less.
But in their southward course they passed another
great inlet, Sir James Lancaster's Sound, little
thinking that it led into an open strait, for it was
barred up by ice; nor was it until Parry's time that
this barrier was passed, and the passage to the open
ocean this way discovered. Coasting along as close
to the shore as they could, they now pursued their
way down the western side, until, arrived once again
in Davis's Strait, they came to Cumberland's Island,
where a consultation was held, in which it was
decided 'that, having come to an end of their discovery,' they should cross 'to the coast of Greenland,
to see if they could get some refreshment for their
men.'

Accordingly they anchored in Cockin Sound, so
named by that Hall who had accompanied the Danish
Admiral Lindenau, and thence, on the 1st of August,
they steered their way home.

Little more is known of the after-life of Baffin,
except that he joined in the British attempt to
expel the Portuguese from the Persian Gulf, and
that at the siege of a small fort near Ormuz he was
killed.

In a letter to one of the gentlemen who sent him

out, Baffin speaks of the 'worst being now known concerning the passage,' and declares that 'there is no passage or hope of a passage in the north of Davis's Strait;' but he dwells on the advantages of the discoveries which had been made thereabouts, and of the vast numbers of whales to be caught in those seas.

One effect of this expedition of Baffin's was naturally to damp the public expectation of this grand discovery; and it was fifteen years before any other attempt of importance was made by Englishmen. But the establishment of the Greenland Whale Fishery, and the formation of the Hudson's Bay Company, were two very substantial results for the commercial world; and these soon began to occupy the attention of the country.

Meantime, Denmark again began to take an interest in the subject; and in 1619 Christian IV. fitted out two ships, of which he gave the command to Jens Munk, a very experienced seaman; but it proved one of the most melancholy voyages on record.

They sailed first to Davis's Straits, but were prevented by the ice from proceeding northward, and therefore turned and passed into Hudson's Straits, Munk changing the names which had been given by former voyagers as he went along, though he has not succeeded in getting other people to adopt his alterations. They took up their winter quarters in Chesterfield's Inlet, which is in the north-west of Hudson's Bay, built themselves good

huts, and found plenty of game; so that they had a
good prospect of being very comfortable until spring
returned, and they were able to resume their voyage.
But the men were superstitious, and not being aware
of the extraordinary phenomena which they might
expect to witness in those northern seas, were
greatly alarmed when in November they saw three
distinct suns, and in December an eclipse of the
moon, which seemed to be surrounded by a transparent circle, with a cross in the centre dividing the
moon into quarters.   These things appeared to
them as bad omens of their future fate; and they
became utterly depressed.   Then the frost set in
with such severity that their beer and spirit-casks
burst; the scurvy appeared among them, and they
became so weak as to be unable to kill the game
which abounded around them; and famine stared
them in the face.   Munk remained in his hut four
days without food, and when at length he got
courage to crawl out, he found that of a crew of
sixty-four he and two companions were the sole
survivors.

In despair the three set to work to dig into the
hard snow, and then discovered some plants which
proved valuable remedies for their sickness; so they
soon recovered, and were able to fish and shoot,
until they grew strong enough to repair their smaller
vessel, in which these three men embarked, and
reached their native land in September, 1620.

Eleven years after this Captain Luke Fox, or
'North-west Fox,' as the clever but conceited York-

shireman chose to call himself, revived the subject in England, and obtained the loan of a vessel for the purpose of Arctic discovery from King Charles I.

Baffin's report had convinced him that the passage must be sought through Hudson's, and not through Davis's Straits; so, with a crew carefully selected, although, as he regretted, without one man who knew those seas, he sailed in that direction.

Passing several small islands, he came into Hudson's Bay; and coasting along the north of it, under Southampton Isles, he reached a strait on the west, in which was an island of which he boasted that he was the discoverer, and named it Sir Thomas Rowe's Welcome, now the name of the strait in which it lies, and through which he declared that he believed the passage would eventually be found.

However, he did not pursue this passage, but turned again towards the south, until at length he passed out of the bay again, and into the Channel which bears his name, as far as 66° north, until he came to a point of land which he called ' Foxe his farthest.' Then the season being rather advanced, he made the best of his way home, where he boasted considerably of his discoveries, though they really amounted to very little.

While in Hudson's Bay he had met with a rival explorer, who had been sent out by the Bristol merchants on the very day that he himself had sailed. The two commanders had entertained each other on board their respective vessels. Fox pronounced this Captain Thomas James to be ' a practitioner in the mathematicks,' but said that he found him to be no seaman. He certainly does not seem to have been quite the man for such a charge; as we may judge from his declining to take any seamen who had before ' us'd the northerly icy seas,' in order that there might be no disputing of his authority.

It would be a long story to tell of all the troubles which the crew of the 'Maria' encountered. They began early, and continued throughout the voyage. Even off Cape Farewell the men were engaged night and day in warding off the blows of the ice; but at length Resolution Island came in sight, and with much difficulty they made their way into Hudson's Strait, and so down into the bay. James's aim was to reach the bottom of the bay, and so find, if possible, a passage into 'the river of Canada;' or, 'failing that, to winter on the main.'

His journal is full of most dismal relations of sufferings, first from cold and then from heat; from plagues of insects and from scurvy : yet when, by the advice of his officers, he at length bore up the helm for England, he says that ' it was with a sorrowful heart that he did so.'

His name has been immortalised in James's Bay, as that of Fox has been in the channel to the north of it. Hudson's Bay was, in fact, growing to be the centre towards which the attention of all those whose eyes were directed to the New World was becoming attracted.

CHAPTER III.

EXPEDITIONS IN THE EIGHTEENTH CENTURY.

FOR some time past the French had been settling in considerable numbers in Canada; and now an enterprising man amongst these settlers, named Monsieur Grosseliez, seeing the advantages which would result from the formation of settlements along the coast, represented the matter to his government.

But the unfavourable report concerning the climate which the last traveller, Captain Thomas James, had given, entirely discouraged them from taking it up, and thus France missed the opportunity.

The English Minister at Paris, however, saw the proposition in another light, and sent Grosseliez over to Prince Rupert in England, who warmly entered into his scheme; and the result was the formation of the Hudson's Bay Company, and the grant to it of all that vast territory known as Prince Rupert's Land, under a charter, in which was included an express stipulation binding them to follow up the discoveries which had been already made.

Having once, however, obtained the monopoly, the subject of discovery and of the long-sought passage was for some time entirely forgotten. In fact, when in the beginning of the 18th century Mr. Knight, the governor of the factory on Nelson's River, having learned from the natives that at some distance to the north of Hudson's Bay there was to be found a rich mine of copper, asked for ships that he might discover the truth of the report, his application was entirely refused, until he threatened to call on the Government to enforce the terms of the charter.

Unfortunately for him, he then gained his point, and sailed with two ships which never returned. Nor was it until 1769 that any tidings of the fate of the expedition were gained. Then, in consequence of the continual reports about the copper-mine, the governor of Prince of Wales' Fort sent out Samuel Hearne to search further into the matter, and he heard from the Esquimaux the following particulars :—

'It was late in the year,' they said, 'when the vessels got into harbour near Marble Island, in the west of Hudson's Bay; and the larger one was much injured. The two crews numbered about fifty; and they immediately began to build their house. After that was finished they were always at work on the long boat; from which it appears that the ships were disabled. Next spring the Esquimaux paid them another visit, and found their numbers much reduced. In the following winter they found but twenty; and in 1721 their number was reduced to five. The Esquimaux had often supplied them with provisions; and on this occasion they were in such distress that they ate the blubber and seals' flesh raw, after which they all became ill: in a few days three had died, and the survivors seemed to have scarcely strength to bury them.

'These two,' they said, 'used often to go to the top of a rock and look out earnestly, as if for a vessel coming to their relief. Then they would sit down close together, and weep bitterly. At last one died,

An Esquimaux Dog.

and the other, in trying to dig him a grave, fell down and died, too.'

Hearne was sent out three times in search of the 'Neethasan-saw-Dazey,' or Far-off Metal River, accompanied by Indian guides; and he penetrated for hundreds of miles into the interior. But, though he added much to the geographical knowledge of the country, he never discovered more than one small piece of the copper ore.

On the third journey he reached the very river which was said to hold such treasures; and near its mouth he had the horror of witnessing an attack made by the Indians on some Esquimaux tents, pitched in the neighbourhood, and of seeing a young girl, who clung to him for protection, transfixed by the spears of two savages; who only laughed at his entreaties that she might be spared, and asked him if he wanted an Esquimaux wife?   This spot he named in consequence the Bloody Falls.   Then, continuing his course up this Coppermine River, he soon came in sight of the Frozen Ocean, the very existence of which was then still doubtful.   Hearne was, therefore, the first European to witness it; and his journey opened the way for future discoveries.

Thus we have brought our sketch to the reign of George III., and must hasten briefly to notice the various other efforts of the last century.

The Hon. Daines Barrington was one of the chief supporters of such movements; and having induced the Royal Society to take the matter up, a plan for attempting the passage across the Pole was laid before the king; and the ' Racehorse' and ' Carcass' sent out, under the command of Captain Phipps and Captain Lutwidge; with the latter of whom went as coxswain no less a person than Horatio Nelson himself, then a mere boy.

They did not, however, reach a higher latitude

than 81° north, and came back with the conviction that to proceed beyond that was utterly impossible.

Disappointment having attended every attempt to reach the Pacific by the Atlantic, it was next proposed to reverse the plan; and the great Captain Cook was sent on this, his last voyage, round the Cape of Good Hope, and directed to work his way up the western shore of America, and through Behring's Straits, across the ocean at the north of the Continent, in case such an ocean was found to exist: for we must remember that, as yet, it was uncertain whether in some parts the land did not reach to the very Pole itself.

Captain Cook sailed to a point which he named Icy Cape; and finding the ice beyond impregnable, he returned to winter at the Sandwich Isles, intending to make another attempt in the next summer: but in a quarrel with the natives, as is so well known, he was slain.

It was a long time before any vessel passed Icy Cape, although several navigators made attempts to pass this way; Vancouver leaving his name on an island discovered by him, and Kotzebue in the sound just north of Behring's Straits: while Captain Meares, who made several voyages in the employ of some merchants of Bengal, has given us a most curious and interesting account of the natives of the country round Nootka Sound and Prince William's Sound. He tells us that they live in immense dwellings, supported on the trunks of trees and large carved

images; that they are gentle and courteous in their
bearing, and are yet so fond of human flesh that
men's heads and limbs are sold in the markets; that
they are fond of water-processions, and of hunting
the whale; and that many of them sing beautifully;
whilst their extraordinary fondness for metals —
especially for copper — enabled him to carry on
with them a very profitable barter for furs. This
was the chief object of his voyage; and on one
occasion he obtained a large quantity of the
skins of the sea-otter in exchange for two copper-
kettles.

So profitable, indeed, was this kind of trade found
to be, that a great jealousy of the Hudson's Bay Company had long sprung up in the minds of many, not
fortunate enough to have a share in it, and in consequence an opposition, called the North-west Company, was started; and so violent a struggle between
the two companies ensued, that, as has been very
fairly remarked, 'the Indian must have smiled to
hear the white man call him SAVAGE.'

However, in connexion with this new company
we find one of our greatest North American travellers.
Hearne had declared that he had seen that ocean of
which the very existence was as yet a question; but
though recently entirely verified, his report was at
that time received with much distrust.

In 1789 Mackenzie followed in his wake, or,
rather, he resolved to cross the whole continent from
Fort Chipewyan to the extreme west; and accompanied by a party of Canadians, he in a few days

reached Slave Lake, and embarked on the river which now bears his name, down which he persisted in continuing his course, in spite of the opposition of the Indians, who tried by all sorts of horrid stories about monsters inhabiting its banks to turn him from his purpose.

He at length reached the mouth of this river: and, finding there an island which was surrounded by many whales, he called it 'Whale Island.' Then, ascending the highest ground which he could find, he saw both east and west, as far as the eye could reach, nothing but ice; and thus, therefore, Mackenzie also no doubt saw that same ocean which Hearne had discovered, and which the Indians call 'The Great Stinking Lake.'

He afterwards started on another journey from Athabaska Lake, ascending Peace River until he came to the Rocky Mountains, up which they had to cut a passage through the snow and haul their canoe, until they fell in with another little river, down which they were able to float it. And here their course led them through many settlements of beavers, which, in order to make their dwellings, had felled whole acres of trees. Their course would have been stopped here—for the Indian guide, tired of the dangers of the way, pretended to know of no river westward—had not Mackenzie overheard a man with whom the guide was talking speak of a large river flowing towards the midday sun, and insisted on resuming the journey. So at length they arrived at the Gulf of Georgia, and Mackenzie wrote his

name on the rock, and inscribed under it the date,
' July 22nd, 1793.'

It was where Mackenzie's journey ended that
Captain Vancouver, who had been a midshipman
under Cook, began his examination among the
archipelago of isles in the neighbourhood of this
gulf, to ascertain whether somewhere in the midst of
them the passage did not exist.

Thus have we slightly narrated the various attempts made to the north and to the west, noticing
a few to the eastward as we went along; but before
proceeding to relate at greater length those suc-
cessive and persevering expeditions in search of the
North-west Passage made in this century, which have
at last been crowned with success, we must notice
two other remarkable attempts in a north-easterly
direction, which have been purposely left until last,
namely, those of Barentsz the Dutchman, and of
Behring the Dane.

It was just after that fearful struggle for political
and religious liberty, in which the brave Hollanders
were so long engaged, that the merchants of the
United Provinces requested permission of the States
General to send an expedition round the north of
Europe and Asia, in order to ascertain if a passage
to the Indies existed in that direction. They eagerly took up the scheme, and fitted out three ships
and a small bark for the enterprise, giving the
command to a clever seaman named William
Barentsz.

At Kola, in Lapland, the little squadron sepa-

rated; and Barentsz soon reached the extreme north
of Nova Zembla, to which he gave the same name
as that afterwards conferred by Cook on one of the
north-west points of America, Icy Cape; but he could
advance no further. The other vessels reached
Waigatz Island during the brilliant Arctic summer,
and found it gay with flowers of every colour.
Leaving it, they sailed on till they came to the sea
of Kara, which, from its blue colour and the sudden
bend of the coast, they took for the open sea, and
imagined it to be that which washed the shores of
the Indies.

Under that impression they, with Barentsz, whom
they had rejoined, returned home in September, and
found the States so well satisfied that seven ships were
soon laden with merchandize, and Barentsz again
placed in command. A storm, however, arose, which
compelled them to diverge from their original course;
and this expedition proving a failure, the government declined further assistance, though they offered
a reward to any successful explorer.

Barentsz was, nevertheless, soon once more employed by some private adventurers, in conjunction
with Rijp; and on this voyage they discovered not
only Bear Island, but the larger one of Spitzbergen,
so named from its sharp-pointed mountains. At
this point the two commanders differed as to their
course, and at length separated; Rijp after a while
being unsuccessful returned home, while Barentsz
passed on to the north of Nova Zembla, and there
became involved in fogs and such masses of floating

ice that the ship was sometimes completely lifted out
of the water, almost in a perpendicular position ; and
on this dreary coast, finding it impossible to extricate
the vessels, these seventeen poor creatures were compelled to winter.   There seems, notwithstanding, to
have been neither mutiny nor murmuring among
them.   Bravely and cheerfully they built a hut, and
made themselves as comfortable as they could.

This was in October ; and every day it became
colder, until the beer froze and burst the casks, and
even the fire seemed to have lost all power of con-
veying heat, for clothes hung by it to dry would
freeze on the side furthest off; and stockings would
smell of burning before the feet felt any warmth.
The sun disappeared on the 4th of November, and
did not again show himself until the 24th January ;
and the cold continued unabated until April.

Yet, even amidst their sufferings, the brave old
Dutchmen intreated to be allowed to keep the ' Feast
of the Kings' on the 6th of January ; and no sooner
did the temperature become milder than they began
to form plans of escape.

What stock of food they possessed in the meantime we are not told ; but by the moonlight, even
in the depth of winter, they occupied themselves in
the capture of the little Arctic fox, which proved to
be very pleasant food.

As long as the sun remained above the horizon
the great white Polar bear had frequently alarmed
them by his visits ; but he disappeared, much to their
relief, when the long nights set in.

It was not till June that they were able to leave their dreary prison, and commit themselves to the ocean in the two boats; the ship being immovably fixed on the shore. But before they lost sight of that terrible coast their brave and worthy commander had expired. He had been failing for some time; but on the morning of his death he had desired to be lifted up in the boat, and, to the great grief of the crew, he breathed his last while apparently taking a farewell gaze of the island where they had for so long been imprisoned. Twelve of the seventeen reached Holland in safety; having first fallen in with some Russian vessels, and afterwards met with Rijp himself, who was out again on a trading voyage.

A century and a quarter after this Peter the Great determined to ascertain, if possible, whether or no any connexion between Asia and America existed; and though he did not live to carry out his plan, yet on his death-bed he drew up a scheme, which the Empress Catherine carefully carried out after his decease, giving the command to Captain Vitus Behring, an officer in the Russian army.

He and his company journeyed by land to Ochotzk, from whence they sailed from the river of Kamptschatka on their voyage.

It was unsuccessful, as was also another made the next year; yet, in 1741, Behring again sailed with two vessels, the 'St. Peter' and 'St. Paul,' which in a storm soon became separated, and never met again.

Tschirikow, the captain of the one vessel, soon

sighted the American Continent, and sent a boat ashore, properly armed, with instructions to make signals to the ship on landing ; but nothing was ever heard of this boat's crew again. Next day, two canoes coming off to the ship in a very threatening manner, Tschirikow could only cruise along the lonely coast for some days ; and at length he determined to turn the vessel homewards.

Commodore Behring's vessel, however, proceeded, and soon came in sight of the stupendous snowy mountains of the New World ; one of which he named Mount St. Elias.   Here they landed, and found some trace of human inhabitants.

Proceeding on their way round the coast, they soon found the navigation very difficult and dangerous, on account of the many small islets which studded the coast.   The scurvy also broke out among them, and Behring himself was attacked and confined to his bed ; so that Lieutenant Waxel had to take the command.

They were next involved in a heavy fog, lasting for days ; and then a tremendous gale sprung up and drove them before it : so that they were in constant fear of shipwreck among the islands.

Very few of the crew were fit for duty ; and as they had only brackish water, and the tough flesh of the sea-otter, many died.

At length land was seen, which proved to be a small island on the coast of Kamptschatka ; and here they were driven ashore : so, seeing no alternative but to winter there, they began to remove the sick to the land, and place them in hovels which they had prepared.   But many died from the exposure to the cold ; and on the 8th of December Behring himself expired.   It is, therefore, in a melancholy manner that the name of this worthy man is connected with these Straits.

Good food and water being now within their reach, the rest of the crew were soon restored to health; and in May they began to build a small vessel, their own being now useless.   In this, though a crazy affair, they, on the 14th of July, committed themselves to the ocean; and in a few days saw the coast of Kamptschatka, and landed shortly afterwards in Awatchka Bay, where, having long been given up as lost, they were warmly welcomed back.

CHAPTER IV.

SIR JOHN ROSS' FIRST EXPEDITION.

ALEXANDER MACKENZIE'S land journeys may be said to have been the concluding efforts of the last century in a north-westerly direction. They had thrown some light on the subject, as had every great previous attempt; and yet still, at the beginning of our present century, all beyond the Arctic Circle was a blank in our maps from Icy Cape to Fox Channel, with the exception of the two isolated points reached by Hearne and Mackenzie, while to the east of the Channel something like the bare outline of Baffin's Bay was all that could be traced.

After so many apparently fruitless efforts it almost seemed as if the question must be given up, and the problem remain for ever unsolved, when a communication made by Mr. William Scoresby, captain of a whaling-vessel, to Sir Joseph Banks, President of the Royal Society, reawakened the hopes of scientific men, and of the nation at large.

The name of Scoresby ought indeed to be ever prominently mentioned in connexion with the recent geographical discoveries; and well qualified would its owner have been to take the command of an expedition of discovery.

The son of the inventor of 'the round top-gallant crow's nest,' said to have been one of the greatest boons ever given to Arctic navigators, and of one of the most intelligent and successful whaling captains of his time, William Scoresby early distinguished himself in his profession.

In 1806 he, with his father, had reached a higher latitude than had been yet attained, and he was only in his twenty-first year when the elder Scoresby retired from active life and left to him the command of his vessel.

It was in the year 1817 that he noticed a remarkable change in the condition of the northern ice-fields, about 18,000 square miles of the Greenland seas, between the parallels of 74° and 80°, being perfectly free, and large quantities of ice being at the same time found in some parts of the Atlantic, where it was usually quite unknown ; and he at once conjectured that some great disruption of the vast fields of ice at the North Pole had taken place, and that the opportunity for undertaking further discoveries had at length arrived.

In the hope of being appointed to some such undertaking he seems to have written to Sir Joseph Banks, the President of the Royal Society, on the subject ; for who was so likely to enter into his feelings as the man who had made voyages to Iceland, Newfoundland, and the South Sea. Islands, solely for the purpose of making discoveries in natural history, and who in 1768 had accompanied Captain Cook on a voyage to the South Seas, simply that he might observe the transit of the planet Venus over the disc of the sun? Sir Joseph immediately memorialised the Government on the subject, and endeavoured to procure for Scoresby a commission to proceed on a voyage of discovery towards the North Pole.

The project was taken up, but not the man; for, in conformity with a rule of the service, the Lords of the Admiralty selected an officer of the Royal Navy to carry out the scheme. And Scoresby, after making several other voyages, and becoming the author of some remarkable works on the Arctic regions and the northern whale fisheries, and having been elected a Fellow of the Royal Societies of London and Edinburgh, eventually took holy orders, and became chaplain of the Mariners' Church at Liverpool. He died in 1857, just four years after the arrival of the despatches from Captain M'Clure announcing the actual accomplishment of that which had been the aim of three centuries.

In the late Secretary of the Admiralty every scheme like that of Scoresby's found a warm advocate. Sir John Barrow at once consulted with Sir Joseph Banks, and having in some measure matured their plan, laid it before Lord Melville, the First Lord of the Admiralty; and the sanction of Government being obtained, orders were soon issued for the preparation of four ships; two to proceed in search of the passage between the Atlantic and the Pacific, and two towards the North Pole, by way of Spitzbergen.

The three names thus joined in council came at no distant date to be those of the unknown lands and seas. But we must not anticipate: only, as Sir John Barrow had so much to do with these and succeeding expeditions, it may be well to say something of this distinguished man before we go further.

In early life he had himself 'paid a visit to the Spitzbergen seas, as high as Hakluyt's Headland, near the 80th parallel,' and no sooner did the intelligence reach him of the breaking up of the northern barrier than various learned articles from his pen appeared in the Quarterlies, pressing on the English nation the honour which now lay open to them of completing that work which their own navigators had first begun. He also wrote a 'Chronological History of Voyages in the Arctic Regions.' In fact, the great movements of this century in the way of Arctic discovery are generally ascribed to him.

The 'Isabella' and the 'Alexander,' of respectively 385 and 252 tons, were the two ships appointed to make their way into Baffin's Bay, for the purpose of discovering whether or not it were bounded by land, as the charts generally represented it, or whether in any part there were a communication with the main ocean. Baffin had, we know, sailed all round, and had declared that all hope of a passage that way was at an end; but information which had from time to time reached the Admiralty of a current running from the north towards the upper part of Davis's Straits had led them to suspect that the sagacious old navigator had fallen into a mistake.

The first thing, therefore, was to ascertain what hope lay in this quarter; nor were any pains spared in the preparation of the vessels, which were as strong as it was possible to make them, and no doubt very different affairs from the old 'Discovery,' in which Baffin had made his voyages.

Scoresby being set aside entirely as incapacitated, on account of not having served in the navy, it was necessary to look about for a suitable person to command the expedition; and on the recommendation of Sir George Hope, Commander Ross, now better known as Sir John Ross, was appointed.

He had served in the navy, the merchant service, the East India service, and again in the navy during the war, at the close of which he had had to settle down on half-pay, and without employment. As an active man, though not an adventurous one, he was only too glad to be again employed, and hesitated not to accept the command offered to him, notwithstanding that he was perfectly ignorant of that particular kind of service, and perhaps naturally disqualified for it.

Under him was to serve as commander of the 'Alexander,' Lieutenant Parry, the son of Dr. Parry of Bath, who thus began a career in which he afterwards became so famous.

Parry had served first in the 'Ville de Paris,'

which was employed in blockading the French coast round Brest and Ushant, just at the time when an invasion by Buonaparte was expected. He had also seen service in the Baltic, and afterwards in the protection of the whale fishery; while still later he had crossed the Atlantic, and arrived at Halifax the day following the action between the 'Shannon' and the 'Chesapeake;' so that he had already made some way towards accomplishing the wish expressed in his childhood, when found astride of a globe,— 'How nice it would be to go round it!'

And yet it is a noticeable circumstance in the history of this remarkable man, that he did not enter the naval service of his own accord, nor by his own desire. In fact, until within a few days of his first voyage, Parry seems never to have had any other idea than that of following his father's profession.

But a lady friend of Dr. Parry's family, who felt sure that he was formed for an active life, and had often advised that he should be sent to sea, at that moment gained her point. Admiral Cornwallis, her near relation, being then in command of the Channel fleet, Edward was allowed to make trial of a sea life by one cruise; and thus his future destiny was fixed.

In 1817, having been recalled to England from the Bermudas in consequence of his father's severe illness, he had, after some months of inaction, written to a friend on the subject of further employment; but before posting his letter, a paragraph in a newspaper, relating to the proposed Polar expedition, attracted his notice; and, though he had been speaking of African discovery, he seized his pen again and added, that 'hot or cold was all one to him—Africa or the Pole.'

This letter was shown by his friend to Sir John Barrow, who saw at once that he was the right man; and accordingly he was appointed second in command.

It was on the 18th of April, 1818, that the 'Isabella' and 'Alexander' sailed from Deptford, bearing with them many valuable instruments for the purpose of making observations in astronomy, navigation, magnetism, and other sciences.

These things were specially intended for the use of Captain Sabine of the Royal Artillery, who, on account of his great scientific attainments, and his skill in the use of such mathematical and astronomical instruments, had been particularly requested to join the expedition.

Another very different, but most valuable person, had also expressed a wish, and had obtained leave to join.

This was a young Esquimaux of the name of Sackhouse, who was then on his second visit to Scotland.   This young man, who belonged to a tribe which had been under the instruction of the Danish missionaries, had first come over to the British isles in a whaling-ship, having a great desire to make acquaintance with the English, and to acquire the art of drawing.   His attractive appearance and manners at once gained him friends. He was kindly treated, instructed in English, and sent back to his own country the next year, either to stay there or return as he pleased. On his arrival he found that a sister, his only relation, had died during his absence, and he therefore decided on the latter course.

Mr. Nasmyth, the artist, then took him in hand, and soon after Captain Basil Hall recommended him as interpreter for this first Arctic voyage. We call it the first, because Ross's was the first of this century. We shall soon see how invaluable the Esquimaux proved: he was to have been sent out again with Lieutenant Parry, but in the meantime, while on a visit to his friends in Edinburgh, he was seized with an inflammatory complaint and speedily sank.

It has long been the fashion to speak of the countrymen of this sociable, intelligent, and kind-hearted young man, as below the standard of ordinary savages, but Sackhouse was the first to prove that an Esquimaux may be a very fine fellow in every sense of the word. His kindness to children had been remarked at Leith, where, meeting two little ones on a snowy day shivering with cold, he took off some of his own clothes, and wrapping them carefully round them, brought them safely home. He soon became a favourite on board the ' Isabella,' on account of his self-denying good-nature; and he is also described as ' unaffectedly pious.' He died with an Icelandic Catechism in his hand, thanking his friends for their kindness; but telling them that it was of no use, for his sister had appeared to him and called him away.

The instructions given to Captain Ross at starting were very clear and explicit. Before leaving Shetland, where he was to meet the vessels 'Dorothea' and 'Trent,' which were to attempt the passage by the Pole, he was to fix on a rendezvous in the Pacific. If there, or elsewhere, he should meet with them, he was to take them under his command; and despatches were to be prepared and sent home by every possible opportunity. He was to sail direct to Baffin's Bay, and, if fortunate enough to find a passage, he was then to endeavour to make his way along the north of America to Behring's Straits, and through them to the rendezvous in the Pacific, returning home next year, if possible, by the same way. But if not able to do that, he was to edge down to the north coast of the American Continent, and winter there as comfortably as he could. Particular directions were also given that, should he meet with either Indians or Esquimaux, he was to cultivate a friendship with them; and for that purpose he was supplied with all kinds of articles likely to be agreeable to them; so that thus they were to be induced to carry an account of the situation of the crew to any settlements of the Hudson's Bay or North-west Companies, with an urgent request that it should instantly be transmitted to England.

It was also said that, although the first object of the voyage was to discover a passage from Davis's

Strait along the north coast of America; yet, so far as could be done without hindrance to the expedition, every facility was to be given to the officers, and especially to Captain Sabine, for adding to the geographical knowledge of those regions, and for contributing to the advance of science in general : besides which, he was to cause views of bays and headlands to be taken, and charts to be made; in which work Lieutenant Hoppner, a very skilful draughtsman, was to be employed.

Great stress was laid on the ships keeping together. And we must not omit to mention that both vessels were supplied with printed papers, which were to be filled up with date and position each day, enclosed in bottles, and thrown overboard. These papers contained a request in several languages, that the captain of any vessel that picked them up would forward them to England as soon as possible.

On the 30th of April the four ships met at Lerwick, in Shetland, and started on their respective expeditions; nor is it surprising that after such elaborate preparations the highest hopes prevailed generally as to their success.

They soon began their Arctic life; for when only half way to Greenland they met with their first iceberg, which appeared to be about 40 feet high and 1000 long. The magnificence of such an object as it comes riding through the ocean, and assuming an endless number of fantastic forms, can hardly be conceived. A white lion, some of the sailors called it; others, a horse rampant; and others, the omen of all good luck, namely, the lion and unicorn on the British arms. Another seen shortly after formed a kind of crystal tunnel.

On the 1st of June the vessels had passed Cape Farewell, the most southerly point of Greenland, and were in sight of Coquin's Sound, where old Baffin went to refresh his men on his return from his last voyage; and now they were in the midst of icebergs and floating fields of ice.

Let us stop here and try to picture to ourselves their position, and the strange kind of scenery through which they were about to pass. The west coast of Greenland is, like that of Norway, beset with many rocky islands, and cut up by numerous deep inlets of the sea, of a singular shape, which sometimes wind like rivers for 80 or 100 miles into the interior. These are called, like those of Norway, *fiords*. Danish names also are found in all maps of Greenland, although of late we have given a few English ones to certain points. For, after Frobisher had re-discovered the country, and Davis had explored its coasts, the Danes and Norwegians again visited and colonized it; so that we sometimes find it called Danish America.

These deep inlets often have a wildly romantic appearance. They are hemmed in by rocky mountain barriers, whose tops are hidden in the clouds, and which generally terminate in glaciers; which are gradually pushed forwards by the plains of ice behind, until they roof in the fiord, or stretch out, like bold headlands, into the sea. Underneath the

ICEBERG SEEN BY THE CREWS OF THE 'ISABELLA' AND 'ALEXANDER.'

surge is gradually undermining them; and at last they fall with the noise of thunder into the sea, which is thus set boiling for many miles around.

These falling masses—of which one traveller saw twenty-three descending at once—form the icebergs, which are then either carried away by currents, or stranded on the Arctic coasts; and as the ice is very transparent, they are often seen glittering in the sunlight in blue, green, and orange tints, which contrast beautifully with the gloomy rocks, or with the whiteness of the vast plains of snow.

There are, however, comparatively warm and sheltered spots even in Greenland; and along the banks of the southern fiords there are meadows, in which stunted beech and willow-trees may be seen, and where the service-tree bears fruit. For there it is that Danish colonists and missionaries have formed their settlements; but the Esquimaux are found up to the very north of Baffin's Bay.

We have spoken of the Danish missions more than once; and though it may interrupt our narrative for a few minutes, yet this will be the most suitable place in which to speak of their origin and history.

Little enough did the two Venetian brothers—Anthony and Nicolas Zeno—ever dream that their voyage and shipwreck would be connected with anything of the kind; but so it was.

> 'God moves in a mysterious way
> His wonders to perform;
> He plants His footsteps in the sea,
> And rides upon the storm.'

Strange and wonderful legends are connected with the countries of the Scandinavian race; and children love such tales.

So the Norwegian boy, Hans Egede, listened and wondered to the legends of his fatherland; and among them was one which he could never forget. It was the traditions of the Zenos; and it told how they not only were cast away on the shores of Greenland, but found there whole villages peopled by Christians.

True it was that no confirmation was added by seamen and merchants who had visited those shores: yet, for all that, as Hans Egede grew, the tale took stronger and stronger possession of his mind.

He entered the ministry, married, had four children, and became parish-priest of Vogen, in the north of Norway; but still thoughts of Greenland, and its deep need, haunted him day and night.

Every one laughed at the scheme; for missions were then no recognised work of the Church: his friends, and even his own wife, opposed it. But those words of his Saviour overbore everything else, —'Whosoever loveth father or mother more than Me, is not worthy of Me.' And he had no rest.

At last his wife gave way. She saw his earnest desire, and declared that she would renounce everything for his sake. By his advice she spread the matter before God in prayer, and soon became more eager to go than she had been to stay.

Then he applied to the Mission College; but they advised patience. He, however, had already waited long; and now even the tale of a ship's crew, wrecked

and murdered on the Greenland shores, did not deter
him from going himself to the king, and pressing his
project. Difficulties now vanished one after another.
The king gave him a favourable hearing; 2000*l.* were
raised; the 'Hope' vessel bought; and on 3rd July,
1710, the Norwegian family landed on the island of
Kangek.

But this brave missionary was to be only a sower:
others entered in and reaped the fruits. In sorrow
and bitterness of soul he laboured on for fifteen long
years; nor was he ever permitted to see a single con-
vert. At first the natives feared him, and called their
sorcerers to drive him from their land: but their opposition soon passed away; and when he could speak
the language he began to prepare the ground, by
telling them of the Creation, the Fall, and other
Bible stories.

The story of a Saviour's love he seems, from a
mistaken notion, to have kept until the minds of the
people were prepared for it; and thus their hearts
remained untouched: for what else could melt
them? At length Christian IV., who had always
stood his friend, died, and his successor resolved
to abandon the colony; and though permission
was given to Egede to remain if he would, he
was told that no further help would be given to
the mission. Yet he and his wife still decided to
stay, while their eldest son was sent to Europe to be
educated for the same work. Their faith never
failed, though it was sorely tried. It was when in
the decline of life that Hans Egede received a

request from the king that he would return to his
native land.   Then, looking on it as an intimation
of God's will, he went, leaving his son to carry on
his labours.

His farewell sermon was from the words, 'I have
laboured in vain and spent my strength for nought :
yet surely my judgment is with the Lord, and my
work with my God;' and he went back to teach the
language of the Esquimaux to future labourers : for
ere this others had presented themselves, and the
Moravian Church had stepped in to continue the
work, and to carry across the waters that story of
peace which soon bowed the heart of many a
Greenlander.

The settlement of Hernhutt had been formed
about this time, by many of that persecuted Church
who had found a refuge on the estates of the good
Count Zinzendorf. And to this praying people he and
one of their chief leaders sent word that the Danish
mission was abandoned by the Government; on
which several of them gladly offered themselves, and
soon joined the 'Apostle of Greenland.'   Nor was
it long after his departure that, after hearing the
history of the Crucifixion, one of the natives rose and
earnestly cried, 'Tell me that again, for I would fain
be saved too;' and soon similar results followed the
preaching all along the coast, and around the market
of Disco the very rocks resounded to the song of
praise.   It is interesting to know that not only
Egede's son, but also his grandson, laboured in the
same field.

But to return to our narrative. It was sometimes quite impossible for the vessels to proceed on account of the obstruction of the ice; and when this was the case the plan was to make the ship fast to an iceberg, on to which most of the ship's crew generally turned out, and which for the time being became an observatory.

Lieutenant Parry speaks of one such scene as ' magnificent beyond all description.' ' One half of the horizon,' he says, ' that to the eastward, was occupied by the bleak hills of Greenland, and some of its islands not more than two miles from us. Within a few miles all around us the water was clear; but the whole of the western horizon, from land round to land, was covered with innumerable masses of ice packed together. Here and there a tremendous berg appeared—each assuming some peculiar fantastic shape.' ' If the scene around were grand,' he goes on, ' that *upon* the iceberg was not less interesting. In one part was to be seen a group attentively employed in making the requisite observations. In another, a party of sportsmen firing at the numerous loons, mallemukes, kittewakes, &c. Below were the boats taking ice on board for water. Here and there a sailor or two amusing themselves in sliding down from the top of the ice to the valley below. The whole scene was extremely interesting and novel. We were employed in executing some of the most important objects of our mission, and this alone would have made it delightful.'

On one occasion, when the scientific proceedings

were interrupted by the non-appearance of the sun, both officers and men engaged in a mock fight; those who had gained the summit of the berg pelting those below with snow-balls — 'a pleasing proof,' Parry remarks, 'of the good understanding and good humour that existed among the crews. The two commanders were, therefore, evidently free from the great difficulty which had balked so many of their brave predecessors, namely, murmurs among their men.

.Slowly, and with difficulty, they made their way up to Waygatt Strait, which separates the island of Disco from Greenland; and here they fell in with a fleet of between twenty and thirty English whalers, who were waiting for the ice to open. It was a proud sight for an Englishman, as Parry observed, and gave that frozen region the appearance of a flourishing sea-port.

Here they endeavoured to gain information from the young Danish governor respecting the state of the ice; but his report was discouraging: for the last two winters the Danes had not been able to communicate with their northern settlements, and had been obliged to kill their dogs for food because they could not procure seals; and this year the bay and harbours, which were generally open in March, still continued shut. Yet, though they were surrounded with ice, the weather continued hot and sultry.

At Waygatt Island a party of Esquimaux came on board; and now the powers of their interpreter, John Sackhouse, were brought into play. He was charmed to introduce his countrymen and country-

AN ESQUIMAUX COOKING.

women, and as these had been under the instructions of the Danish missionary he had no cause to be ashamed of them.

Captain Ross asked of them a sledge and dog, offering them a rifle in exchange. They immediately went to fetch them, but refused to accept the payment until they had produced the sledge; which was soon brought in a boat, managed by five women dressed in seal-skins. Their canoes are, probably, the old kajaks seen by Frobisher; but this boat was of a different kind, and was called an ' oomiack,' or women's boat. Two of the women who rowed it were daughters of a Danish resident and an Esquimaux mother. The visitors were all invited on board, where they were charmed by having their portraits taken; after which they danced Scotch reels on the deck with the sailors, to the excessive delight of Sackhouse, who acted the part of master of the ceremonies, paying particular attention to one of the half-Danish young ladies, a girl of about eighteen, and, without question, the *belle* of the party.

One of the officers, noticing his preference, gave him a lady's shawl, ornamented with spangles, as a present for her; which the young man immediately offered in a graceful and respectful manner, and which was received with a bashful but eloquent smile, the fair one taking a pewter ring from her finger and presenting it in return.

Sackhouse accompanied his country-folk on shore, but next day, nothing having been heard of him, messengers were sent to search for him; when he was found in a hut with his collar-bone broken. Having gone to look for specimens of natural history, he thought 'plenty powder, plenty kill;' and so caused a recoil of his gun by overloading it. It was some time before this was quite cured.

Sixteen days after reaching Disco Island the ships passed the second barrier of ice, and found themselves off Sanderson's Hope. And here a very curious instance of unequal refraction was noticed: some of those whaling-vessels, which were only two or three miles off, appearing to be drawn up to an enormous height; while those more distant seemed flattened to the surface of the water.

The little group of islands to which, because some native women were seen hiding behind the rocks, Baffin had given the name of Women's Islands, were now in sight: but why they worked up this eastern side of Baffin's Bay at all it is not easy to understand; as, of course, the passage could not possibly be discovered there: but Ross had utterly misunderstood his instructions, as we see by his calling the account, which he drew up afterwards, a voyage made 'for the purpose of exploring Baffin's Bay.'

Under this delusion he continued coasting along northward, taking advantage of every passage through the ice; and when the ships were unable to sail, having them towed along by the boats. Sometimes all the crew would turn out, and, led by the Scotch fiddler, would haul the ships along. But the ice was moving rapidly, and breaking up; so that, from time to time, they came to a weak place, and one and another would fall in. However, as they never let go the rope, they were soon hauled out again : and these little incidents furnished considerable amusement for the sailors.

All this time they were still in the company of whalers; yet even before they left the fishing-ground they were placed in great danger by the ships being dashed one against another, with such violence that, but for their immense strength, they must have been broken to pieces. This concussion was caused by the rapid movement of the ice ; and they were thankful to escape with only damaged rigging.

A greater peril soon succeeded. The ice was moving in large masses called 'floes.' These are much the same as 'fields,' except that the extent of the latter cannot be seen from the mast-head. To one of these 'floes,' supposed to be stationary, the vessels had been moored after the catastrophe just mentioned ; probably in order to undergo repairs. Suddenly this floe was found to be drifting straight on to some stranded icebergs, and all hands were set to cut a dock : that is, to saw a hole in the ice large enough to receive the ships.

This is done in order to prevent their being 'nipped' between two floes.

The dock was just ready, though happily the vessels had not entered it, when the very part in which it had been cut struck with such violence against the berg, that it was forced at least fifty feet up its side, and the pieces scattered in all directions

Ha l the ships been docked, they must instantly have been crushed to atoms.

Something of this kind, indeed, happened to a whaling-vessel in their sight, and the crew barely escaped with their lives.

At length, on the 8th of August, a point was reached which seems to have been hitherto unvisited by Europeans, and on a little island some of the crew landed, and found some of those piles of stones which indicate an Esquimaux burial-ground, but no natives.

Soon after they had returned to the ship, however, some sledges were seen rapidly coming over the ice; but when Sackhouse, on their approach, hailed them in a loud voice, they seemed not to understand him: nor could he at first comprehend their reply.

After looking at the ship for some time in silence they suddenly turned, and rapidly made their way back again: nor did any of them re-appear for many hours. Presents were carried ashore, and white flags hoisted, in token of peace; and at last a few were seen timidly approaching. Then Sackhouse, whose eagerness was only equalled by the tact which he displayed, obtained leave to go ashore.

After exchanging many shouts, he thought that he perceived that they were only using a very drawling dialect of his own language, and immediately called to them, '*Kahkeite* — Come on;' to which they answered, '*Naakrie naakrieai-plaite* — No; go away;' and one added, drawing a knife from his boot, 'I can kill you.'

INTERVIEW BETWEEN CAPTAIN ROSS AND LIEUTENANT PARRY AND THE
ESQUIMAUX OF THE NORTH OF GREENLAND.

But Sackhouse was not at all disheartened, and only threw them some beads, a shirt, and, lastly, an English knife; on seeing which latter they picked it up, shouting, '*Heigh yaw!*' and pulling their noses. He repeated the words and actions, and something like friendship was established, so that they began to ask questions.

Pointing to the ships, they asked, 'What those great creatures were, and whether they came from the sun or the moon?' His answer, however, was not credited; for, when he told them that they were houses made of wood, they replied,—'No; they are alive: we have seen them move their wings.'

His account of himself, 'that he came from the south,' was also as little believed, for they said,—'That could not be; there was only ice there.'

At length, as they could not be induced to enter the ship, Captain Ross and Lieutenant Parry, who were both eager to communicate with these strange beings, took a number of presents, among which were some looking-glasses, and went ashore. This caused fresh alarm among them, and they were again about to retreat when Sackhouse called to the officers to pull their noses and shout, '*Heigh yaw!*' Then the Esquimaux came on, each receiving, as they did so, a knife and a looking-glass. It would be difficult to describe their utter astonishment on seeing their own faces in the glass. Shouts and laughter succeeded to the perfect silence which prevailed for the first minute or two; and the English officers, partly to express their good feeling, and partly because they could not help it, most gladly and heartily joined in the laugh.

As they proceeded, much interest was excited among the crew by the crimson appearance of the snow; and a few of them were sent on shore to procure some of it, when it was discovered to be of the same colour to the depth of ten or twelve feet. The discovery, however, was no new one, for crimson snow has been found on the Alps, and in Spitzbergen, while Pliny and other ancient writers have mentioned it; but scientific men differ as to its origin.

They continued to receive visits from their new friends, or from others who had heard of the English visitors through them, and they finally took leave of them, feeling that at least they had thoroughly impressed this new idea on their minds — that their tribe did not include the whole population of the world. Captain Ross bestowed the name of 'The Arctic Highlands' on the country.

Cape Dudley Digges was soon after passed, and Smith's Sound was now in sight; but instead of thoroughly examining this, and ascertaining whether it were in truth a sound or a strait, they passed it at a distance, and in the same way sailed by Jones' Sound on the west of the bay. Thus Captain Ross lost the merit of discovering that both of these are really straits.

On the 30th, the water to the westward being observed to be almost free from ice, the two vessels made direct for Lancaster Sound.

And here the accounts of the two commanders are completely at variance. Perhaps old Baffin's narrative had made a different impression on their minds; but as Parry's turned out to be the correct opinion, it will be best to follow his narrative of the proceedings.

The 'crow's nest' and 'mast-head' were at this point constantly crowded, he tells us; 'for the expectations of many were raised to the highest pitch. Here,' he continues, 'Baffin's hopes of a passage began to be less; here, on the contrary, mine begin to grow strong. I think there is something in his account which gives cause to suspect he did not see the bottom of Lancaster Sound, . . . nor have we yet seen the bottom of it.'

The 'Isabella,' under a press of sail, kept steadily on in advance of her consort. The 'Alexander' was a much slower sailer; and this had been a matter of great annoyance all through the voyage, and was particularly so at this moment, when the inlet looked more and more promising, and when there was a strong swell from the north-west, which they could but think was caused by its being an entrance into the ocean.

In a short account sent to a monthly journal by one of the officers on their return, we find it stated that here 'every officer and man, on the instant as it were, made up his mind that this must be the North-west Passage;' and the writer added,—'I firmly believe that every creature on board anticipated the pleasure of writing an overland despatch to his friends, either from the eastern or western shores of the Pacific.'

Yet at this very moment, and without any apparent reason, the ' Isabella' tacked and rejoined her consort, which she passed without a word of explanation.

The weather was said to have become somewhat hazy; and in his own account Captain Ross stated that to the westward it was thick and cloudy; and that on a report of some appearance of its clearing he went on deck, and ' distinctly saw the land round the bottom of the bay, forming a chain of mountains,' which he named Croker Mountains, but which will in vain be sought in any maps.

This was probably the first Arctic expedition in which both officers and men were obliged to return home against their will. In all former ones, as our readers will remember, it was the crews who hung back, and the commanders who were forced to give up. But this order of things was reversed in this case, and at a moment too when it was particularly vexatious to every one.

It is not surprising, therefore, that on their return many of them freely expressed their opinions, and that the disappointment of the public very speedily manifested itself. Lieutenant Parry at first made known his sentiments only to private friends; but when, in an interview with Lord Melville, his real opinion was communicated to that nobleman, as well as to Sir John (then Mr.) Barrow, the latter did not allow the matter to slumber.

Before the voyage we find, from Parry's own words, that he was not sanguine as to the existence of the passage; but on his return he told a friend that 'his sentiments had quite altered—that he knew it to exist, and that it was not very hard to find.'

CHAPTER V.

CAPTAIN BUCHAN'S POLAR EXPEDITION.

LET us now follow the other two vessels which we left at Lerwick, just starting on their northern course.

Their object was, as we shall remember, a still bolder one than that set before Captain Ross; for they were to endeavour to cross even the North Pole itself, and so to gain the Pacific. It was to be a repetition of the attempt made by Captain Phipps when Nelson was a boy; or, to go much further back, it was to be a following out of the scheme proposed to King Henry VIII. by the Bristol merchant, Mr. Robert Thorne. And with fully as much enthusiasm as his, though with far better vessels than his monarch could have provided, was the undertaking carried out. Yet 'that little way' just about the Pole, of which he spoke so slightingly, proved, in spite of 'its constant summer daylight,' a tougher piece of navigation than Mr. Robert Thorne had anticipated.

Captain Buchan was, however, well prepared for his task, having been much on the coast of Newfoundland; and by the 24th May they had already reached that little island which by Barentsz had first been named Bear Island, because bears were the only living things that he found there ; and afterwards by Captain Bennet (who knew not that it had been visited before), Cherie Isle, after the alderman who, in 1603, had sent him out.

Walruses.

The crews of the 'Dorothea' and 'Trent' met, however, with a different kind of living creatures amongst the ice, which detained them for a while in its neighbourhood. These were the walruses, which were so numerous that one ship's crew alone took between 900 and 1000 of them ; their character and habits are described by Lieutenant

Beechey, in his narrative of the voyage, as most curious.

Their affection for their young, and their compassion for any wounded comrade, whom they would never leave until they had carried him to a place of safety, were, he tells us, equally remarkable.

'When the weather was warm,' he says, 'animals of various kinds would crawl up out of the pools in the vast sheets of ice around the vessels to bask in the warmth of the sun.' A walrus rose in one of these pools close to the ship; and finding everything quiet, dived down and brought up its young, which it held by its breast by pressing it with its flipper. In this manner it moved about the pool, keeping in an erect posture, and always directing the face of its young toward the vessel. On the slightest movement on board the mother released her flipper, and pushed the young one under water; but when everything was again quiet, she brought it up again as before, and for a length of time continued to play about in the pool, to the great amusement of the seamen, who gave her credit for abilities in tuition which, though possessed of considerable sagacity, she hardly merited. The instructions which Buchan had received directed him to make his way between the coasts of Spitzbergen and Greenland, without stopping at either; but this order it was found impossible altogether to carry out. Even before they reached the latitude of Spitzbergen the two vessels had become separated in a fog, and were obliged to take refuge in the rendezvous fixed on in case of such a catastrophe,

namely, Magdalena Bay, on the north-east of that island—or, rather, group of islands; for Spitzbergen
is not one, but several islets, amongst which are to be
found on all sides many curious and magnificent
bays. Here, as the barrier of ice beyond was then
impenetrable, Buchan determined to stay for a few
days.

Like its Dutch discoverer, Barentsz, they were
to see the island in its summer beauty; and, like
him, they soon discovered it to be the home of a considerable variety of birds and animals, the sea being
as much alive as the land.

Bears and foxes abound everywhere; and, in
some parts, the rein-deer also. The latter take
freely to the water, and swim from island to island.
They feed on moss, and were found in excellent condition. On the Isle of Vogelsang alone the crews
obtained forty fine carcases. 'They were then in
pairs, and showed such evident affection for one
another, that when one was shot the other would
hang over it, and occasionally lick it, apparently
bemoaning its fate; and if not immediately killed,
it would stand three or four shots rather than desert
its fallen companion.'

And 'this compassionate conduct of theirs,' continues Beechey, 'doubled our chance of success, although it was obtained at the expense of our better
feelings.'

The crews tried to preserve some alive, but
they were so wild that, in their attempts to get
free, they broke their slender limbs; so that, to put

them out of their sufferings, they were obliged to be shot.

On another island the king eider-ducks were found in such numbers, that it was difficult to walk without treading on their nests. Yet the parent birds have a way of preserving the eggs against the attacks of wild animals; for when any appear, and they are obliged to fly, they first glue the down of the nest over the eggs with a yellow fluid, which has such an abominable smell that not even a fox will touch them.

Then the rocks reverberated with the cries of the merry little auks, of willocks, divers, cormorants, gulls, and other aquatic birds. In fact, these little auks, or rotges, came in such multitudes, that about four millions were supposed to be on the wing at one time. They darkened the air, and their chorus might be heard at the distance of four miles.

And at the same time might be seen 'groups of walruses basking in the sun, and mingling their playful roar with the husky bark of the seal;' 'while amphibious animals of all sorts, and fish, from the huge whale to the minute clio on which it feeds, swallowing, perhaps, a million at a mouthful, enlivened both the ice and the water.'

It is the comparative mildness of the climate which no doubt causes it to be, though destitute of human inhabitants, the resort of so many of the animal creation.

On the western side, even with the thermometer only a little above freezing, there was but little sen-

SPITZBERGEN.

sation of cold. Sometimes the sun had great power; and once at midnight, beneath his rays, the quicksilver rose to 73°. Grasses and lichens flourish in the more southern aspects; and, even to the height of 15,000 feet above the sea, Alpine plants were found.

It was summer time, however—the 3rd of June—when they anchored in Magdalena Bay; yet the ice in the harbour was not then melted, though by the beginning of August, when they returned, it had quite disappeared.

Four immense glaciers, of which one called the 'Hanging Iceberg,' which rested on the slope of a mountain 200 feet above the sea, distinguish this bay.

The islands derived their name Spilberg, Spitbergen, or Spitzbergen, from the sharp-pointed mountains which characterise the group. It was given by its Dutch discoverers.

But amidst these mountains, icebergs and glaciers, of course, abound. Of their appearance in the rays of an Arctic sun, and under an expanse of azure of which not even an Italian sky will give a just conception, we leave our readers to form an idea. It is better imagined than described.

It was shortly after their arrival that the crews had the opportunity of witnessing the extraordinary spectacle of the formation of a sea-iceberg. The report of a musket sufficed to bring down an enormous block of ice, which, by its fall, caused the sea to boil violently, even to the distance of four miles, at which the 'Dorothea' was riding. For a few moments the mighty mass entirely disappeared; then reared its head again above the water, and travelled on ; making a continual popping noise, like the cracking of a carter's whip — caused, no doubt, by the escape of fixed air — while a stream of water was seen pouring down its sides.

One of the boats was out, and its crew, supposing themselves quite beyond its reach, were quietly enjoying the scene, when they found themselves lifted on the crest of an enormous wave, and carried a distance, which they afterwards ascertained to be ninety-six feet, on to the shore : the boat was found to require much repairs before she could regain the ship.

It was summer time, as we have said, and yet did our crews vainly attempt to pass the barrier which lay between themselves and the Pole. It was impenetrable ; and resolutely did it hold them back, and keep them from crossing that 'little way,' and so gaining the laurels which they coveted.

After four days, however, they left Magdalena Bay, but immediately got amongst what is called 'brash ice,' i.e. small fragments of ice. This seemed to get thicker and more compact as they went on ; but soon a breeze springing up, opened a passage for them into clear water ; and they turned westward. Then they fell in with some whalers, who told them that it was useless to proceed in that direction, for that fifteen vessels were beset a little further on. So they turned once more towards the north, and passed Cloven Cliff at the north-west point of the island.

Almost immediately afterwards the ice once more

closed in; and it was only after great exertions that they got again into the floe, in which they were enclosed for thirteen days.

A movement then took place in the ice towards the south, and the ships got again into an open sea, and proceeded for a little while, but were soon forced back to take refuge in Fair Haven. Once more a channel opened, and Captain Buchan, spreading all sail, pushed into one of the openings, closely followed by the 'Trent.'

They had reached 80° 34' N., and soon they were 'closely pressed again by the packed ice;' and, after dragging the ships along with ropes for two days, it was decided at once to stand across for the coast of Greenland, and try their chance there. Suddenly, however, a violent gale sprang up; the ice was seen rapidly bearing down upon them, so that to avoid immediate destruction the 'Dorothea' was compelled to take refuge in the midst of it, by 'dashing at once into the furious line of breakers, in which immense pieces of ice were heaving and subsiding with the waves, and dashing together with a violence which nothing, apparently, but a solid body could withstand, occasioning such a noise that it was with the greatest difficulty we could make our orders heard by the crew.'

At that moment it seemed as if the collision between the ice and the little vessel must have proved fatal to her; and yet, with perfect calmness and decision, were the orders of the commander given and obeyed by the men.

Lieutenant, afterwards Captain, Beechey, is here speaking of the 'Trent,' and of his immediate commander, Lieutenant Franklin:—

'Each person,' he tells us, 'instinctively secured his own hold, and with his eyes fixed on the masts, awaited in breathless anxiety the moment of concussion. It soon arrived. The brig, cutting her way through the light ice, came in violent contact with the main body. In an instant we all lost our footing, the masts bent with the impetus, and the cracking timbers from below bespoke a pressure which was calculated to awaken our serious apprehensions. The ship's bell, also, which had never in any storm sounded of itself, began to toll so continually that it was ordered to be muffled.'

After this gale had subsided the 'Dorothea' was found to be in a foundering condition, and it was with difficulty that she was got back into Fair Haven for repairs.

But the 'Trent' being less damaged, its young and ardent commander requested leave to proceed alone; a request which, however, both his instructions and his own judgment forbade his chief to grant. So both vessels reluctantly turned homewards, and arrived at Deptford on the 22nd October.

CHAPTER VI.

SIR EDWARD PARRY'S FIRST EXPEDITION.

VERY truly had Lieutenant Parry observed, on his return from his voyage in the 'Alexander,' that 'all previous attempts had been relinquished just at a time when there was the greatest chance of success;' and that this had been the case in Ross's expedition, very soon became the opinion of the Lords of the Admiralty, and of Mr. (afterwards Sir John) Barrow, their energetic secretary, who was not the man to let the matter rest where it was.

The 'Isabella' and 'Alexander' had reached Shetland on the 30th October, and before two months had elapsed two other vessels, the 'Hecla' and 'Griper,' were selected under the advice of Parry, and sent into dock, to be prepared to encounter next spring the ice and storms of the north.

He felt sure, as he said, that 'he would have some finger in this new pie,' and that satisfied him: but who was to command the expedition was a matter for after-consideration. It was not long, however, before it was decided in his favour; and if anything could have added to his gratification in thus obtaining the object of his highest wishes, it must have been that this decision was arrived at after a very careful examination of all the officers' journals; the Board being determined this time to choose, if possible, the right person.

The perfect confidence reposed in him was likewise shown by his being allowed the entire control of the equipment of the ships, as well as the choice of all the officers.

To the command of the 'Griper' Lieutenant Liddon was appointed; but he was the only officer who had not served in one or other of the last two expeditions. There was no difficulty in finding seamen, for crowds of volunteers offered themselves; and the vessels were amply supplied with provisions for two years: so both officers and men started in the highest spirits.

Mr. Barrow observes, that the most singular feature in this expedition was, that Parry was again suff-red to go out as Lieutenant; while Commander Ross, for what he calls 'an unprofitable voyage of seven summer months, was at once advanced to the rank of Captain.' But Parry's own remark on the subject was, 'When I look at the "Hecla," and at the chart of Lancaster Sound, oh, what is promotion to this!"

The 'Hecla,' indeed, was a great pet of his, and he declared it all but perfect: but with the 'Griper' he was by no means so well satisfied; and its slow sailing proved a source of as much vexation as that of the 'Alexander' had been the last year.

They started a fortnight later than on that

occasion, but arrived at the mouth of Lancaster Sound a month earlier, as they sailed direct for it, and not round Baffin's Bay; their instructions being thoroughly to examine that opening, and, in the event of failure there, to pass on to Jones' and Smith's Sounds, as neither had been thoroughly examined by Ross.

Failure, however, did not await them; for this voyage was to accomplish what so many previous ones had failed in—it was to open the entrance to the North-west Passage! This, therefore, our readers may possibly think its great characteristic.

On first approaching the western side of the bay, they were considerably disconcerted to find there a vast sheet of ice, amongst which were many bergs; and once they had a narrow escape of being 'nipped,' between a floe and an iceberg, which was fast driving on to it. The boats had to be got out, and the ships were only just towed out of the way in time. But Parry was so sure that he should find clear water on the other side that he was determined to force a passage; and 'after a whole week's laborious sailing, tracking, and towing,' this was at length accomplished.

It was on the 1st of August that they had thus passed all these icy barriers, and stood at the entrance of what was then known as Sir James Lancaster's Sound, which Parry soon transformed into Barrow's Strait. 'It is more easy to imagine than to describe,' he writes, 'the almost breathless anxiety which was now visible in every countenance,

while, as the breeze increased to a fresh gale, we
ran quickly up the Sound. The mast-heads were
crowded by the officers and men during the whole
afternoon ; and an unconcerned observer, if any could
have been unconcerned on such an occasion, would
have been amused by the eagerness with which
the various reports from the crow's nest were
received; all, however, hitherto favourable to our
most sanguine hopes.'

On and on they sailed, and no ' Croker Mountains' came in sight ; so the name was given to the
first large inlet in the northern shore. Still they
dreaded lest the land should trend round, and join
the south coast ; and once the cry of ' land' from
the mast-head scared every one. But it turned out
to be only a little island, which they attempted to
pass on the south side. This passage proving impracticable, Parry gave it the name of Prince Regent's
Inlet, as it happened to be the Prince's birthday,
and returned up the strait, along which they were
now able to coast on the north side.

One very curious phenomenon we must not omit
here to relate. It was, that by the time they had
reached 100° west longitude from Greenwich the
compasses had entirely lost their directing power.
They had become very sluggish from the moment
they entered the strait, but when attempting to sail
up Prince Regent's Inlet they altogether failed, and
were put away as useless lumber; so the vessels had
to proceed without their friendly guidance.

Now it was one of their great objects to obtain

further light on the subject of magnetism ; and every opportunity was therefore, throughout the voyage, given to Captain Sabine and the other scientific men for making observations on this and other important subjects.

Had not the time been too precious, Parry would gladly have stayed here to ascertain exactly the position of the magnetic north pole, which he felt sure they were very near, and which he correctly surmised, from the above-mentioned circumstance, to be situated nearly where Sir James Ross afterwards found it, *i. e.* about two or three degrees from the meridian, 100° W. from Greenwich. But the season was passing, and they must push on.

At length, to the great relief of every one, they came out into a fine broad channel, on which Parry bestowed the name of Wellington, and now they soon reached the point at which the ship's crew became entitled to the reward of 5000*l.* offered by Government to the first of his Majesty's subjects who should sail thus far west. This point was meridian, 110° W., within the Arctic circle ; and the name of Bounty Cape was given by the men to the point at which the observation had been taken.

This was a promontory of Melville Island, just beyond which the ships anchored for the first time in the bay of the 'Hecla' and 'Griper.' Here, however, they did not remain, for they had not a day to lose, as the weather by this time was rapidly becoming colder, and the nights dark ; so that, without the aid of their compasses, they were obliged to sail slowly and cautiously, especially as navigation here was very dangerous, and each vessel more than once narrowly escaped destruction. Lieutenant Liddon was already suffering from an attack of rheumatism, caused by exposure to the cold, and whilst still ill his ship was violently driven ashore, and with difficulty got off again. Nothing could, however, induce him to leave his ship, even for an hour, while it was in danger. He determined to remain in her like a true seaman.

The month of September is usually the most favourable one in the whole year for sailing in these seas, because they are then the freest from ice; but in 1819 the season came to an end earlier than usual. By the 12th the ships were completely beset, and could not be moved; so, as coal had been observed on shore, a party was sent out to collect it. Another little company having also landed, lost their way in a snow storm, and four different parties were sent to search for them; but several anxious days passed before they all returned, most of them completely exhausted, and some considerably frost-bitten. It was evidently high time to look out for winter quarters; but after a spot had been selected, the terribly laborious work remained of cutting a passage through the ice, for the ships were still set fast.

This occupied three whole days, but, headed by their commander, officers and men alike worked on steadily, and though often up to their knees in water, not one complaint was heard. At length, amidst the heartiest cheers that British seamen

CUTTING A DOCK FOR THE 'HECLA' AND 'GRIPER'

could give, the 'Hecla' and 'Griper' were drawn
into Winter Harbour, Melville Island.

There had been no pause as yet, either as to
work or excitement ; but when both vessels had been
enveloped in thick coverings, and the berths warmed
by a stream of heated air from the stove, nothing
then remained but just to make themselves as com-

'Hecla' and 'Griper' in Winter Harbour

fortable as they could for a long dreary period of
some seven or eight months to come. And truly
this was a prospect sufficient to try the courage of
the bravest crews, still more so of their commander.

Now, indeed, was the time to dread lest murmurs,
or even mutiny, might break out among the men,
unaccustomed as they were to an inactive life, and

I

without those resources of education which were
sure to lessen the trial to their officers. But Parry's
own resources were unfailing. He had just the
natural tact and variety of talents which enabled
him to meet this emergency; and his contented disposition, and peculiarly bright and cheerful tempera-
ment, gained for him the affection and esteem of
his whole company. ' My attention,' he wrote in
his journal at this period, 'was immediately and
imperiously called to various important duties,
many of them of a singular nature, such as had for
the first time devolved on any officer of his Majesty's
navy, and might, indeed, be considered of rare
occurrence in the whole history of navigation.'

These various duties consisted in attending to the
security of the ships, as well as to the health and
comfort, the employment and amusement, of those
under his command; and in attempting to estimate
the difficulties attending these latter in their present
condition, we must remember that in the matter of
their own health sailors are very like children, and
have to be dealt with accordingly.

For a few weeks after their encampment at
Winter Harbour it was found possible to secure
fresh meat, exercise, and amusement by means of
hunting-parties; and the deer and grouse thus taken
were shared by officers and men, certain rules being
laid down, which were called ' the game laws,' pro-
hibiting any prize thus caught from being considered
as private property. But by the end of October all
animals had left the island and migrated towards

the south. Deprived of this resource, it was necessary to provide some exercise which should be obli-
gatory when the weather was too severe for the
men to leave the ships. The decks were therefore
cleared, that the men might be made to run round
them to the tune of a hand-organ or a song. They
were also obliged each day, under the eye of an
officer, to drink a certain amount of lime-juice and
water; the dread of the sailors' scourge, scurvy,
being, of course, ever before Parry's eyes.

Dreary in the extreme was still, as he says, the
view before them; not an object to be seen in any
direction except their own fires, or a sound, except
that of their own voices, to break the deathlike still-
ness: though even then the hope of spending a part
of the next winter in the sunny isles of the south did
much towards keeping up their spirits. But it was
now absolutely necessary to provide some amusements for both officers and men; and for this purpose two ideas were struck out by Parry: first,
that they should, from time to time, get up a play
among themselves; and, secondly, that they should
set up a weekly newspaper, of which Capt. Sabine
should be editor, and which should be called ' The
North Georgian Gazette and Winter Chronicle.'

The sun took its leave of them for the winter on
the 5th of November, and on that day they had their
first performance.

Parry took the liveliest interest in these amusements, and himself contributed both to their stock
of plays and to the journal. They were considered

very important matters by him, 'for he dreaded,' to use his own words, 'the want of employment, as one of the worst evils that was likely to befal them.'

They had as a Christmas piece 'The North-west Passage,' the product of his pen; and on the same day the officers dined off a piece of English roast beef, preserved since the preceding May, without salt, and simply by the cold.

It was not until the 3rd of February that a glimpse of the sun was again caught from the main-top of the 'Hecla.' His orb was not, in fact, fully visible for four days more; for it was the refractive power of the atmosphere which caused them to see this welcome sight before he really rose above the horizon; and notwithstanding his presence, the cold was then more severe than previously. During this month the thermometer was down to 55° below zero! and yet so cheered were they by the sun's return, that they now began to make preparations for the coming summer, though they had to wait until the end of April before the temperature rose to freezing point; which, by contrast, appeared to them so hot, that the men had to be restrained from leaving off their winter clothes. By the end of May the ice was, with much labour, cut through, so as once more to get the ships afloat; but it was not until the 1st of August that it was sufficiently melted to allow of the escape from their ten months' imprisonment.

Meanwhile, to pass away the time, Parry made

an exploratory tour into the interior of the island:
and the tracks of his cart were found thirty years
afterwards, as fresh as ever, by Lieutenant M'Clintock.

A large block of sandstone, on which they engraved a record of their stay here, became a still
more enduring record of their visit. Even when
they had got out of the bay, the free channel west-

Sir Edward Parry's Stone.

ward was so small, and the floes of ice so many and
so large, that the ships were in constant danger of
being crushed to atoms. After attempting, therefore, for many days to force a passage westward,
Parry and his officers were compelled to confess to
themselves that, at least for that season, the enterprise must be abandoned.

After a consultation, therefore, the two vessels were turned homewards on the 26th August; and they found the sea in that direction so clear that, in six days, they had passed through Lancaster Sound, and soon afterwards fell in with some whaling-ships, from which they heard the tidings of the death of the old King George III., and of his son, the Duke of Kent.

They reached England two months afterwards; and Parry then immediately obtained his promotion to the rank of commander, as an expression of the satisfaction with which his conduct of the expedition was received by the Lords of the Admiralty. Soon after, the corporation of Bath did him the honour of conferring on him the freedom of that his native city, which was presented in a box made of a piece of the wood of the 'Hecla.' Norwich followed the example. He was made a Fellow of the Royal Society; and, in fact, all sorts of honours were heaped upon him. But Parry's own first act on the arrival of his two vessels in the Thames was to go, at the head of all his men, to return their public thanks, at St. Mary's in the Strand, to Him who had so graciously watched over and kept them during all the dangers to which they had been exposed, and who had blessed them with so unusual a measure of health, that, notwithstanding all they had gone through, the whole of the two crews, officers and men, had returned as well and strong as when they left the shores of England; with the exception of one man, who had died at Melville Island of an old complaint. This act was quite in keeping with his general character, as we shall see more and more as we follow his course for a little while. He was, and he made no secret of it, even then, a religious man, though a considerable change in his views took place during his later years.

CHAPTER VII.

SIR JOHN FRANKLIN'S FIRST LAND EXPEDITION.

WE must now change the scene; and instead of continuing here our narrative of Commander Parry's adventures, proceed to give some account of the Arctic land expedition under the command of his intimate friend, Commander (afterwards Captain) Sir John Franklin, to whose name so melancholy and so lasting an interest is now attached.

For it seems better to keep to the chronological order in our history; and besides, this land expedition of Franklin's was intended to supplement, and, if possible, assist that of Parry by sea.

It was, therefore, in the same month (May) of the year 1819 that both of them set out; Franklin, and his little party of four, embarking on board the Hudson's Bay Company's ship, 'Prince of Wales,' for York Factory, on the east of Hudson's Bay, where they were to commence their journey. These four companions were picked men, and all distinguished themselves, more or less, by the zeal and ability with which they discharged their respective offices.

Dr. Richardson, a naval surgeon, 'deserves,' says

Franklin, 'all the credit for any collections or discoveries that were made in natural history.' Mr. George Back and Mr. Robert Hood, who were Admiralty midshipmen, were especially directed to make drawings of the land, natives, and natural objects: the former became afterwards Captain Sir George Back; while John Hepburn, their only and most invaluable attendant, made the fourth person.

In the mouth of Hudson's Strait the 'Prince of Wales' narrowly escaped shipwreck, just off the dreaded rocky shores of Resolution Island; nor was it until the 30th of August that they landed at York Factory: for few voyages of an equal length are so tedious or so dangerous as that across Hudson's Bay.

Not until June does that great sea, as it should really be called, open, and in September it closes again; while even during this short interval it is so encumbered with ice, and so disturbed by currents, that navigation is very dangerous.

At York Factory, which is one of the Hudson's Bay Company's stations, they were at once furnished with a very large and suitable boat, provisions and ammunition for their inland voyage, as well as with letters from the governor to the up-country agents. At the same place also they happily met with some of the North-west Company's agents, from whom they received further information, as well as an assurance of a welcome at any of their stations through which they might pass.

The service appointed for Commander Franklin required him to examine and map out the whole line of coast, from the Coppermine River eastward.   It was therefore his business in the first place to reach the mouth of that river, and in doing so to travel over the country traversed in the preceding century by Hearne.

He must, consequently, pass over territory occupied by those two rival companies to which we have referred; and as the feud between them was then so violent, that wherever the one party was the stronger it made a point of oppressing the other, to the extent of imprisonment, and even death, it required the exercise of all Franklin's natural prudence to keep on good terms with both, and thus to obtain the assistance that he needed.

As soon, therefore, as he entered the country he gave orders to his officers, and to all whom they employed, that they were on no account to mix themselves up with any of the quarrels which must come under their observation : and the wisdom of this order was most happily fully appreciated by them.

As has been already stated, the little band received all that they stood in need of from the officials of the older company at York Factory. They then immediately made the best of their way on to Cumberland House, on Pine-island Lake, in order to get into that chain of lakes by which they might reach the Coppermine River.   They arrived at Cumberland on October 22nd, after having travelled about 700 miles by means of ten rivers and nine lakes, and passed over many rocks, rapids, and portages, Messrs. Hood and Back making sketches as they went along.

Now York Factory is situated in about 57° N. lat., and is therefore only a degree or two more northerly than the north of England; and in going to Cumberland House they had first to pass, for a little while, even more to the south: nor was it for some months to come that they reached a really high latitude.

But Arctic weather and an Arctic climate are not, in the New World, confined within the boundaries of the Arctic circle; *i.e.* 23° south of the Pole. They, in fact, reign even down to about, on an average, 50° N. lat.: that is, fully to the south of James' Bay, which our readers will remember is the very southern part of Hudson's Bay.

The Arctic lands thus alone—to say nothing of the seas beyond—embrace about 30° of latitude, and the most part of these lands are denominated by the Canadians '*landes stériles.*'

It was, however, through their more southerly part that Franklin was for some months passing; and yet, when speaking even of that part during the winter's journey, he says that the mercury of the thermometer actually froze in the bulb, so that they could not ascertain the state of the atmosphere. The rapid changes in the temperature are on another occasion recorded by his young companion, Hood, who tells us in his journal that on one day the thermometer was down to 15° below zero, and that the next it had risen to 60° above it. This was in the end of March, and in April it went up to 77°

in the shade, when the various water-fowl began to return, and the whole country was deluged by the sudden thaw. Then, he continues, 'the noise made by the frogs was almost incredible.' These reptiles seem to outlive even a hard winter, and after being frozen hard for a long time may be thawed and revived by warmth. This was an assertion, which had previously been doubted, but various experiments have fully proved its truth, not only in the case of frogs but also in regard to some other animals.

This is, indeed, just the region in which to study nature in its primitive state. The very crust of the earth seems to remain much the same as at the moment in which the globe assumed its present form : on its shores there appear, amid the blocks of ice, the rough peaks of huge primeval rocks, which have been undermined by the force of the elements, intermingled here and there with the entire skeletons of whales and other enormous creatures ; while scattered over the land there are numerous specimens of the animal creation, often peculiar to itself; and in the air are seen vast swarms of tiny creatures, whose stings in summer-time are said to constitute a plague to which every other kind of hardship, even those of cold and hunger, must be allowed to yield the palm.

But to proceed with our story.

The little party met with the greatest kindness at Fort Cumberland ; and as the first idea was to make this their winter quarters, the governor began at once to enlarge his premises, in order to accommodate them the better.

These European forts are all very much alike,
and consist generally of a little group of dwellings,
enclosed in a palisade, in the midst of a desolate
wilderness of ice, or of forests, or of desert lands.

They contain each about a dozen men, some of
whom have families; and their business is to carry
on the traffic in furs with the surrounding natives.

But Franklin soon became convinced, by the information which he collected, that some of his party
ought to proceed at once to one of the stations on
the Athabaska Lake, and even, if possible, to the
northward of the Great Slave Lake beyond, as it
was found that only there could guides, hunters, and
interpreters, be obtained. Ever ready to take the
hardest work himself, he arranged to proceed on this
journey with Mr. Back and Hepburn, while Dr.
Richardson and Mr. Hood remained where they
were until the spring, collecting specimens and
making drawings and scientific observations.

It was on the 19th of January that they set out
from Cumberland Fort for Chipewyan, a station on
the north-western extremity of Athabaska Lake,
having been provided by Governor Williams with two
sledges and provisions for fifteen days. The distance
to be traversed was 857 miles: and the snow at this
season was so deep that, even in their snow-shoes,
they were obliged to keep to the frozen surface of
rivers and lakes whenever it was necessary to go on
foot.

These snow-shoes, although necessary, cause
all travellers much suffering, and more especially

those who are unaccustomed to them. The framework is formed of two parallel bars of wood, joined together by transverse bars, those over the instep being curved to admit the foot; each shoe or *raquette* weighs two or three pounds, and they vary in length from four to six feet. To use them at first without falling is, therefore, very difficult; and once down, it is no easy matter to get up again without help.

Mr. Hood, after once trying them, described the misery which they produce as so great that ' no object will divert' the mind of the wearer ' from his own agonizing sensations.' He says that ' he feels his frame crushed by unaccountable pressure, he drags a galling and stubborn weight at his feet, and his track is marked by blood.'

The travellers' other clothing was, however, more comfortable. A large cape, furnished with a hood to protect the head and neck from the snow, covered their shoulders; leathern trousers and mocassins of elk-skin the legs; and over all came a large fur mantle, confined round the waist by a belt, to which was attached a bottle, a knife, and a hatchet.

Thus equipped they travelled on by day, and at night thought themselves happy if they could meet with a patch of fir-trees, in the centre of which they could encamp.

On their way they met from time to time with various parties of Indians—the Chipewyan, the Cree, and the Stone Indians: the latter being the most prepossessing in appearance, but ' addicted to stealing whatever they can,' especially horses, which they declare to have been intended as common property.

It was the end of March when they reached Fort Chipewyan, one of the most ancient and important of these isolated posts: and here, in July, they were joined by Dr. Richardson and Mr. Hood. Meantime Franklin had been holding communication with other stations, and had arranged to receive two interpreters on their arrival at Great Slave Lake. Sixteen Canadian voyageurs and one Chipewyan woman were at once engaged, and with their provisions stowed away in three canoes they set off up the Peace River, paddling merrily along to a lively boat-song, sung by the three crews, until out of sight of the fort.

On arriving at Moose-deer Island, one of the North-west Company's stations, they secured Pierre St. Germain as an interpreter for the Copper Indians. and further supplies; and at Fort Providence the second interpreter, Jean Baptiste Adam. A Mr. Wentzel also joined them as superintendent of the Canadians, and to manage the Indians and get supplies; to which kind of work he had been accustomed for twenty years.

A very celebrated chief, named Akaitcho, also here paid them a visit, and made a speech, in which he declared himself the white man's friend, and said that his tribe, who had received kindnesses from white men, would gladly attend them to their journey's end.

Provisions had been running short at Chipewyan, and Franklin had gladly left that station with supplies for one day only, lest he should bring famine on the household, whose expected supplies had not yet arrived. He had been able to add to his small stock, as we have seen; but, as all through their journey, they knew that they must depend greatly on hunting and fishing, no offer of assistance was to be despised, and Akaitcho therefore received a welcome and hearty thanks.

He had heard of Captain Parry, and inquired with interest after his ships, while he took pains to inform himself of the object of this land expedition; and paid particular compliments to each of the officers, especially to 'the great medicine chief,' Dr. Richardson.

Franklin was now, therefore, in a condition to proceed at once towards the valley of the Copper-mine, and on the 2d of August, after engaging another Canadian and three women, the wives of some of the voyageurs, to make clothes and shoes for the men at their winter quarters, the journey was commenced; and they began travelling due north, but with only food sufficient for ten days' consumption.

In this journey they endured many privations; and before it came to an end, the Canadians became so discontented that they declared that they would not proceed further unless more food were given to them. Franklin was obliged to speak to them in the strongest terms, of his determination to inflict the severest punishment on any one who rebelled; while

he felt all the while that few could bear such sufferings without murmuring. Just at this critical
point, however, some hunters arrived, bringing carcases of rein-deer,—a welcome sight to the travellers.

'The counted length of the portages we had
crossed since leaving Fort Providence,' wrote Franklin, 'is twenty-one statute miles and a half; and as
our men had to traverse each portage four times,
with a load of 180 lbs., and return three times light,
they walked in the whole upwards of 150 miles. The
total length of our voyage from Chipewyan is 553
miles. In the afternoon we read Divine Service, and
offered our thanksgiving to the Almighty for His
goodness in having brought us thus far on our journey;
a duty which we never neglected when stationary on
the Sabbath.'

At length they reached the spot where it soon
appeared that they must be content to winter; and
the voyageurs set to work with alacrity to build a
house, which they named Fort Enterprise.

Franklin, however, was so anxious to proceed,
that it was some time before he could settle down
patiently; but the old chief, Akaitcho, refused to let
his Indians go further that season, and at length,
when Franklin had been remonstrating and warmly
urging the matter, Akaitcho replied,—

'Well, I have said everything I can urge to dis-
suade you from going on this service, on which it
seems you wish to sacrifice your own lives, as well as
the Indians who might attend you : however, if after
all I have said you are determined to go, some of

my young men shall join the party, because it shall not be said that we permitted you to die alone, after having brought you hither : but, from the moment they embark in the canoes, I and their relatives shall lament them as dead.'

The two young men, Hood and Back, were therefore sent on in a light canoe, with a few Canadians and an Indian, to find out the distance from Coppermine River, and its size; while Franklin himself, with Dr. Richardson, set off on a pedestrian expedition to the same point.

After much suffering from cold and hunger both parties got back on the same day, and were glad to reach Fort Enterprise safely; but they very soon discovered that they had not, and were not likely to obtain, a sufficient quantity of food to carry them on to the sea.

On hearing this, the ardent young Back instantly volunteered to return to Fort Providence, and, if necessary, even to Chipewyan, to hasten forward the supplies which were expected from Cumberland House; and on the 18th October he set off with Mr. Wentzel, two Canadians, two Indians, and their wives. Wentzel, on reaching Fort Providence, found there two Esquimaux guides, with whom he returned in December to the fort, and whose long names were changed into Augustus and Francis.

But Back went on to Chipewyan, and did not reach his party again until the 17th of March, after travelling on foot and in snow-shoes more than 1100 miles, with only a slight covering at

night, and often spending days together without
food.

The Indians who accompanied him were happily
his very good friends, and most generously refused
at times to taste the fish or birds which they caught;
saying, 'We are accustomed to starvation, and you
are not.'

'One of our men,' he relates, 'caught a fish, which,
with the addition of some weed scraped from the
rocks, called *tripe des roches,* made us a very tolerable
supper . . . While we were eating it, I perceived
one of the women busily scraping an old skin, with
the contents of which her husband presented us.
This consisted chiefly of pounded meat, fat, and a
greater proportion of Indian's and deer's hair, than
either; and though such a mixture may not appear
very alluring to an English stomach, it was thought
a great luxury, after three days' privation in these
cheerless regions.'

On one occasion, when the Indians and their
wives complained of illness and want of rest, Back
served out to them a flagon of mixed spirits, and
enjoyed the spectacle of their happiness; for they
had won his esteem, not only by their generous
kindness towards himself, but by the affection
which they manifested towards their wives and
children.

During this journey Back had many narrow
escapes: falling once through the ice, and another
time feeling it bend under him so much that he had
to run at his full speed to get off before it gave way.

On the whole, indeed, this journey is one of the most remarkable on record.

Meantime, at Fort Enterprise the anxieties and sufferings of his companions had been by no means inconsiderable.

A good quantity of fish had been taken in the season, but by the 5th of November the fishing had quite failed, and was given up.

The house, however, had been finished some days before; but on the same day, unfortunately, Akaitcho and his hunters came in, forty souls in all, who expected to be provided for.

One of the voyageurs who started with Back was the first to cheer them by his return. He came in crusted over with ice, but brought letters from England, and some news of the provisions; which had, however, it appeared, by some mistake, gone astray: so that another party had to be sent out to assist in bringing them in.

At length Akaitcho and his people were induced to leave the camp once more, as there was no possibility of feeding them; but he insisted on leaving behind his wife and daughter, and some other women, to be taken care of. The daughter was looked upon as the *belle* of the tribe, and was named Green Stockings. Though only sixteen, she had had two husbands; and her mother, who wanted her as a nurse, did not altogether approve of her portrait being taken by Mr. Hood, fearing that the 'Great Chief' in England might send for her.

The party lived chiefly on *pemmican*; that is,

the flesh of the rein-deer kneaded up into a kind of paste with fat: they had no vegetables, and but little flour.

Each day they drank twice of tea without sugar, and on Sunday had a cup of chocolate. For ten whole months were the party shut up here; but the officers, we are told, generally found plenty of employment in writing their journals, calculating their observations, and finishing their drawings.

The aurora shone out frequently with great brilliancy, and they took particular pains in studying this remarkable phenomenon. Its influence on the magnet they established to be a fact, but could never assure themselves of the truth of the report that it is accompanied by strange noises. In the evening they joined the men in the hall, and took part in their games.

Sunday was always kept in the best way that was possible, and the woodmen had to provide on Saturday for all that would be required, while Divine service was regularly performed; at which the Canadians, though Romanists, and not well acquainted with English, always attended.

Franklin regretted that he had not with him a French Prayer-book; but he says that the Creed and the Lord's Prayer were always read to them in their own language.

During their stay here, Hepburn became an experienced soap and candle maker; and when this operation was going on no woman was allowed to come near the kettle, as it is considered a very mysterious operation by the Canadians, and always supposed to fail if a woman is present.

On the 1st day of the new year, 1821, an attempt was made at something like festivities; but the provisions were very low, and they had no spirits to give the people. A fortnight after, however, a large supply of food came down from Fort Providence; but by the end of March they were again so low that sometimes they had but one meal a-day.

Neither hunting nor fishing produced anything at this season; and the sufferings of the Indians, who crowded round the house, were terrible. Franklin says that he had often tried to persuade them to move to Akaitcho's lodge, but that the most part of them were sick or infirm, and did not like to lose the daily medicines which Dr. Richardson gave them. They would clear away the snow to look for bones, deers' feet, bits of leather, and other offal; and little did the English think when they saw them boiling these down that they would one day be reduced even to collect the very same bones from the dunghill.

Things improved, however, when spring came and the rein-deer returned; and now they began to think of the long journey down the Coppermine River to the coast, and eastward.

Before they left, the Indian chief faithfully promised that provisions should be brought to Fort Enterprise before next September, in case they should return that way; and on the 4th June the first party, under Dr. Richardson, set off, Captain Franklin following on the 14th, with three canoes, each dragged by four men and two dogs.

They all set out on foot, and with a very scanty store of provisions. The men who had to carry the canoes over the portages had dreadfully fatiguing work, and many of them became lame; so that at Point Lake one canoe was left behind. Franklin and two others fell through the ice in crossing a lake, but escaped unhurt; and by the end of the month they were all able to embark on the Coppermine.

Very soon now they expected to meet no longer Indians, but Esquimaux; and knowing the deadly hatred that seems always to have existed between the two races, Franklin earnestly endeavoured to persuade Akaitcho and his Indians to come to terms with them.

This they promised to do, but it was evident that they greatly dreaded the meeting; and when he further proposed that, until he had himself come to a good understanding with them, they should remain in the background, they altogether declined, saying that they were not strong enough alone to encounter a surprise, and that they would travel with the English, or return as quickly as possible to their own more southerly country. On the other hand, they soon observed equal tokens of fear among the parties of Esquimaux, who all retired into their own solitudes at their approach, and on the 18th the Indians beat a retreat, promising to meet them at Fort Enterprise. Mr. Wentzel and four Canadians

were also sent back next day to Slave Lake, in order
to reduce their numbers; and that he might forward
despatches to England, and see that the Indians fulfilled their promise regarding the provisions.

Before this date, however, they had got a distinct view of the sea, and had had good success in
killing several musk oxen.

These creatures abound in this part of the coun-

Musk Ox.

try, and it is said that, on being attacked, they herd
closer together; so that several are easily killed.
According to their instructions, they searched carefully for copper all along the course of the river, but
only found a few pieces.

On their arrival at the rapid named by Hearne
'the Bloody Falls,' from the dreadful conflict which
he had there witnessed between the two native races,

they found that it abounded with excellent salmon, of which they caught forty in one net.

The cascade is bounded on each side by walls of red sandstone, having lofty green hills on either side.

On their arrival at the sea-coast some of the Canadian voyageurs, who had never seen the sea before, were at first amused, especially at sight of the seals swimming about; but they soon began to tremble at the idea of a long polar voyage in two birch-bark canoes; and Hepburn had to exert his powers of rhetoric to make them ashamed of their fears.

The whole remaining party, amounting to but twenty, however, at length embarked. They had travelled from their winter quarters a distance of 334 miles, of which the canoes and baggage had been dragged over snow and ice 117; and now they had food but for fifteen days.

On the 21st July the embarkation took place; and they paddled all day amidst a number of rocky islands, the water being little encumbered with ice, but very full of drift-wood.

After proceeding thirty-seven miles, they encamped just where the coast was covered with vegetation, and found here some mussel-shells. Three groups of islands were named by them 'Berens,' 'Sir Graham Moore,' and 'Lawford.' Beyond, the coast was barren and dreary; but they came to the conclusion that all ice is there melted in the summer.

Provisions were again running short, especially as two bags of pemmican had turned mouldy, and the beef was scarcely eatable; and hitherto only one deer had been killed and three salmon-trout taken: so, after passing the entrances of two bays, the hunters were sent ashore, and soon returned with two small deer and a brown bear.

Of all the inlets and sounds which they passed as good charts as possible were made during their progress. One was named Arctic Sound; another, Bathurst; and another, Melville; and the whole large gulf, in which all these inlets were, was called Coronation Gulf; and its extreme point, Cape Turn-again, because they were now tolerably certain that this would prove the end of their voyage, as the season was far advanced, and the provisions were rapidly failing, while they were at a great distance from any trading stations.

A violent storm came on soon afterwards, and the canoes having become all but useless, it was therefore determined to abandon further discovery, and to return by way of a river in Arctic Sound, which had been named Hood's River. This way was chosen because game had there been found more plentiful than elsewhere, and because their canoes would hardly carry them further. They proposed, when once in this river, to make smaller canoes out of their damaged ones, which could also be more easily carried across the barren grounds to Fort Enterprise.

It was a great falling short of what they had proposed at starting, which was to go as far as that bay named Repulse Bay by Captain Middleton in 1741, and which is situated only just to the west of

ROCKY SHORE ON THE ARCTIC OCEAN.

Fox's Channel: but there was no help for it, nor any time to be lost.

The Canadians were delighted to turn their backs on the sea, and eagerly anticipated the pleasure of exchanging their one scanty meal of pemmican for the *eight pounds of meat* daily allowed them by the Company. Little, indeed, they dreamed of the miseries that awaited them.

It was on the 26th of August that the party encamped at the first rapid on Hood's River; and some days before this the thermometer had been down to freezing-point, and snow lay on the ground. They had already once been reduced to sup on berries and a little country tea; but a couple of deer were killed soon after, which helped them on again.

A few miles up Hood's River they came to a magnificent cascade, 200 feet high, which Franklin named Wilberforce Falls.*

About this point they were detained by the necessity of making new canoes; and on 3rd September the last piece of pemmican, and a little arrowroot, were served out for supper.

A terrible storm lasted for some days, during which, having no fire or food, they remained whole days in bed.

On the 7th, when about to proceed, Franklin was seized with a fainting fit, but recovered on taking a little portable soup at the urgent request of some of the men.

* See Frontispiece.

The canoe-bearers, weak from fasting, were often blown down; and one canoe being broken to pieces was used to make a fire, by which the remnants of portable soup and arrowroot were warmed to serve as a scanty meal after three days' fast. A few partridges, and the lichen called *tripe des roches*, for some days saved them from starvation; yet the latter proved to many very injurious, especially to poor Hood.

On the 10th a musk ox was killed, to skin and eat up which was but the work of a few minutes; and the intestines, which were eaten raw, were pronounced delicious. But no other good meal was tasted by them for many days.

At length many of the Canadians became utterly wearied out, and reckless; so that, though it may scarcely be credited, the nets were thrown away, and the floats burnt.

Both the canoes also were abandoned; and thus they were left without any means of water transport. It was only now and then that they obtained a partridge. They lived on the *tripe des roches*, mosses, pieces of skin, deers' horns, burnt and boiled down, to which sometimes their own old shoes were added.

Once, however, they found a putrid deer's carcase, which made them an unexpected meal, as did also the putrid marrow found in the spine of another which had been devoured by wolves.

The health of the whole party was now rapidly giving way: Franklin was fearfully weak, and Hood was reduced to a perfect shadow, while Back could

only walk with a stick, and Dr. Richardson had, in
addition to his weakness, fallen lame.

On the 24th September, however, five young
deer were killed, and this in some measure restored
the spirits of the party.   They asked for a day's
rest, that they might quietly enjoy two substantial
meals after an eight-days' fast, and so be able to
proceed more vigorously.

On the 26th they reached a lake on a branch of the
Coppermine River, and then began bitterly to lament
their folly in destroying the canoes and floats; and
Back, being still the most active and vigorous, was
sent round with some of the hunters to the fort before
the rest, who lost several days in trying to make
a raft; which, when at last finished, they had great
difficulty in launching, and which, when launched,
they could not get to move for want of paddles, and
because it was made of green wood.   Yet they
knew that they had no strength to go round the
lake; and Dr. Richardson, therefore, feeling that
the lives of the party depended on the thing being
done, nobly volunteered to swim across the stream
with a line, by which the raft might be hauled over.

But the devoted man was too weak to bear either
the exertion or the cold, and after many brave efforts,
the party on shore, to their horror, saw him sink
just as he had nearly gained the other side.   They
instantly hauled him back, and, though in an all but
lifeless state, he revived on being wrapped up in
blankets and placed before a good fire; but having
been exposed to too great heat, the whole left

side was found to have lost sensation: and this did not entirely return until the next summer.

There was nothing for it now but to construct a canoe; and they were reduced to the last extremity of starvation before this was accomplished. The Canadians became utterly desponding, refused even to exert themselves to collect *tripe des roches*, and at several stages of this fearful journey one and another either refused to proceed, or went out to hunt and never returned; so that their party became greatly diminished.

But of the four English officers, and their brave, kind servant, it is impossible to speak too highly. One and all seemed simply determined to do their duty and leave the result to God. Their lives they knew were in His hands; and in their deepest distress they were persuaded that He would never forsake them. Nor would it be possible to say who was the most ready to run any risks, or bear any amount of suffering, for the sake of the rest.

At length the strength of young Mr. Hood and two or three of the voyageurs entirely gave way; and as it was impossible for them to proceed, the generous Dr. Richardson volunteered to remain with them while the others pushed on towards the fort.

Franklin and four others at length reached the spot on the 11th of October, three of the Canadians and one Italian having broken down, and requested leave to return to Dr. Richardson. These three were Michel, Belanger, Perrault, and Fontano, though Michel alone reached the camp.

At the fort they had fondly hoped to find the supplies which Akaitcho had promised by September: but what their feelings were we must leave our readers to imagine, when they found the place wholly deserted and no sign of any kind of food.

At length a note from Back was found, stating that he had gone in search of the Indians; and as this was very unsatisfactory, Franklin instantly decided to go himself in a few days with Benoit, and Augustus, who seems to have followed them to the fort, straight on even to Fort Providence.

He made the attempt, but so utterly broke down that he was obliged to let his two companions go on alone and return to the others. Eighteen miserable days passed, during which they had to subsist on *tripe des roches,* and any old bones and skins which they could find; and then one evening, when they were seated round the fire conversing on the probability of the speedy termination of their lives by death, one of the Canadians suddenly and joyfully exclaimed, '*Ah, le monde!*' but instead of the Indians, who he thought were approaching, Dr. Richardson and Hepburn alone entered, looking fearfully emaciated. Their fears for the others were instantly confirmed, by his communication that Hood and Michel were dead, and that nothing had been heard of the other Canadians; but the gloom which immediately overspread the party prevented him from at once entering into the shocking details.

A partridge which Hepburn had shot was held to the fire, divided into six portions, and ravenously devoured, being the first animal food which they had tasted for thirty-one days.

The circumstances attending poor Hood's death were then privately communicated to Franklin.

Hepburn, it seems, had found cause to suspect the Iroquois, Michel; and on his return to the Doctor and Hood this man soon became sulky, and refused to do anything. One day, having been out hunting, he returned, pretending to have had no success, except that he had found a dead wolf, of which he had brought them a part. They believed this at first; but many things afterwards led them to fear that it was really a part of the body of one of his unfortunate companions whom he had probably sacrificed.

They had before suspected that he had some private store of food; and now, with this idea on their minds, and so weak as to be almost unfit for any exertion, and certainly unable to resist any attack, their situation was by no means an enviable one.

It was on the 20th that Dr. Richardson, having gone out to collect *tripe des roches*, leaving Mr. Hood sitting by the fire arguing with Michel, whose surly behaviour seemed almost to show a diabolical state of mind, heard the report of a gun, and soon after the voice of Hepburn, calling him in great alarm.

On his arrival poor Hood was found lying lifeless, a bullet having passed through his head; and the first thought was that, in a fit of despondency, he had destroyed himself. But, on examination, it was quite clear that the ball had entered from behind, and could not have been discharged by himself.

Hepburn had seen Michel rising from just behind the poor young man immediately after the report; and, in fact, his whole demeanour pointed him out as the assassin. For the three next days he kept always on his guard, used threatening language, and never left his companions together. He was always armed, and still powerful; and they felt that they would be his next victims. The first time, therefore, that the wretched man went out, and Hepburn was able to give the Doctor a full account of the affair, they came to the conclusion that there was 'no safety for them but in his death;' and Hepburn proposed to be the instrument of it. 'But,' says Richardson, 'I determined to take the whole responsibility on myself, and immediately on Michel's coming up I put an end to his life by shooting him through the head with a pistol. Had my own life alone been threatened, I would not have purchased it by such an act; but I considered myself as entrusted also with the protection of Hepburn, a man who, by his humane attention and devotedness, had so endeared himself to me, that I felt more anxiety for his life than my own.'

After the arrival of these two survivors out of a party of seven or eight, two of the most faithful Canadians expired of utter exhaustion; and Franklin, Richardson, Hepburn, and one Canadian, remained alone for another whole week, hoping almost against hope for the supplies of which Back had gone in search.

They were now so thin that to lie on the floor — for they had no beds — produced soreness of the body; and so weak, that it was quite a toil to turn over. They seldom, however, spoke of their sufferings or of the prospect of relief: for their minds were too much weakened to dwell on such things. Sometimes they would read to each other, as they lay in bed, portions of some religious books, with which a lady had provided them before leaving London, one of which, Bickersteth's 'Scripture Help,' poor Hood had had lying open before him at the moment of his death; and the morning and evening services were never omitted. Sometimes, also, they would converse on religious subjects; but in the daytime they commonly spoke only of ordinary matters, as though nothing were amiss. In fact, each one thought the intellect of the other weakened, and that they had need of forbearance and advice, although it was only in a measure that they perceived this in themselves. They were fretful and pettish, too, in spite of themselves; and so conscious was Hepburn of this, that he once exclaimed, — 'Dear me, if we are spared to return to England, I wonder if we shall recover our understandings!'

At length, on the 7th of November, the long-expected relief arrived from Back, forwarded by three Indians, whose after-care for them, in cooking for them, and tending them, would, says Franklin, 'have done honour to the most civilized people.'

With the greatest caution against repletion, they now gradually recovered; and on receiving a note from Back on the 12th, that he was about to proceed to Fort Providence, they hastened to follow him; but Dr. Richardson was so reduced that they were only able to proceed slowly. At Moose-deer Lake the two companies met again, and obtaining now the requisite means of travelling, they passed from station to station, and at length reached York Factory in safety, having travelled in all 5559 miles; and endured, with almost unparalleled bravery, an amount of hardship and suffering which very few have had to encounter.

On their arrival in England they found that during their absence Franklin had been raised to the rank of Captain; Back and Hood to that of Lieutenant; and that Hepburn had been appointed to a comfortable position in one of the dockyards.

CHAPTER VIII.

SIR EDWARD PARRY'S SECOND VOYAGE.

WHEN Commander Parry returned home from Melville Island in 1820, he was certainly not aware that he had discovered the most important part of the North-west Passage; and that, had he been able to persevere in his course, he would have enjoyed all the honour, in which Captain M'Clure afterwards so justly claimed a share. He was, however, still fully persuaded that such a passage did exist; but thought that it must be sought by way of Hudson's, instead of Baffin's Bay; and the parts which he indicated were the channel on the west of Southampton Island, called Sir Thomas Rowe's Welcome, on the bay just west of that known as Repulse Bay, where, a few years before Hearne's land journey, Middleton's attempt had been defeated. And as his opinion had now great weight at the Admiralty, he was almost immediately appointed to explore those seas, being made commander of the ' Fury' bomb; while Lieutenant Lyon, who had recently distinguished himself in Africa, was appointed to his old favourite, the ' Hecla,' and promoted to the rank of commander.

His former able companion, Captain Sabine, did not accompany him; but was soon after despatched with Commander Clavering on a voyage to Spitzbergen, in the slow-sailing 'Griper;' on board of which he made a 'series of experiments to determine the figure of the earth, by means of the pendulum vibrating seconds in different latitudes:' to which observations he had eagerly devoted himself on his return from North Georgia. And though Parry, no doubt, regretted the loss of so scientific an assistant, he must have gladly changed the vessel which carried him for the 'gallant bomb' 'Fury.'

The 'Griper' was also again employed, in 1824, on much the same service as that on which Parry was now to be engaged. It was then commanded by Captain Lyon; but we shall not find space for an account of either of these two voyages.

The 'Fury' and 'Hecla' were found, to Parry's great satisfaction, to be of very equal powers: and many of his old officers and men again gladly accompanied him.

The voyage across the Atlantic was an ordinary one, with the exception of one melancholy incident, which happened as the ships were sailing down the Thames.

In manning the 'Fury,' Parry had gladly welcomed back John Gordon, one of his old seamen; a fine, tall, powerful man, and one always called for in any case requiring unusual strength and activity. This man had, during the long winter spent at Melville Isle, received such benefit from the instruction given on board, that from a reckless, swearing fellow, he had become an entirely altered man, and great benefit was now anticipated from his example.

' It was just off Gravesend,' says Parry, ' that Gordon was sent in a boat one morning to lay a kedge-anchor. In throwing the anchor out of the boat, one of the flukes caught the gunwale, bringing it to the water's edge. The tide running strong, Gordon saw that the boat must be swamped, and the crew greatly endangered, if the anchor were not instantly released. He flew from the stern-sheets past the other men, and, by the utmost effort of his own muscular power, lifted the anchor clear ; just in time to save the boat. But, in so doing, he neglected his own personal safety. As the anchor ran round, the bight of the hawser got round his body, and dragged him out of the boat : and we have never seen John Gordon from that moment to this. I cannot describe the sensation this melancholy catastrophe occasioned in the ship ; for Gordon was respected and beloved by all.'

No wonder that the ardent commander should soon after write to his parents: —' I can safely say I never felt so strongly the vanity, uncertainty, and comparative unimportance of everything this world can give, and the paramount necessity of preparation for another and better life than this.'

But we must hasten on.

Near the mouth of Hudson's Straits the icebergs began to beset their course : and here the ' Nautilus' transport, which had accompanied them with provisions, took her leave, and returned home with the last despatches.

The passage through the strait was slow and difficult; but as soon as they neared the land they met with some of a tribe of Esquimaux, who for about a century had held yearly intercourse with the English ships, and so learnt European vices, without gaining any knowledge, either of our civilization or of Christianity. The habits of these people were so extremely filthy and disgusting that the men gave them no encouragement.

On approaching Southampton Island, it was an anxious point to settle whether to make their way to Repulse Bay by the north or south of it. To go round the south was a ·long business; and yet between the island and the bay, on the north, there lay a passage which Middleton had called Frozen Strait; and supposing that this were found as he described it, much time might be lost in making a fruitless attempt.

This, however, was the course at last decided on; and though much hindered by the floating masses of ice, by rocks and islands, the strait was at length passed, and the bay 'unconsciously entered,' and as no ice was found there they were able thoroughly to investigate the shores, and so to arrive at the decided conclusion that no passage existed there.

To proceed with the examination of the north coast of the continent according to his instructions was, therefore, Parry's next care; and most diligently was every little inlet surveyed. Beyond Repulse

Bay another was found, which was named after Commander Lyon.

But multitudes of small islands obstructed their course; and the examination of this piece of coast was so tedious as to occupy a month.

The season for navigation was rapidly drawing to a close, and the sea so quickly becoming covered with young ice, that it was evident that no time must be lost in seeking winter quarters. On the southern coast of a small island, at the entrance of Lyon's inlet, these were found; and no sooner was a canal sawed through the ice, and the ships moved into their proper places, than they were fast frozen in.

It is unnecessary again to recount the various measures adopted for the health and comfort of the men. We need only say, that all that was tried on the last occasion was repeated on this, with many additions and improvements.

A large quantity of antiscorbutics had been brought from England, and were freely used; and besides mustard and cress being grown in considerable quantities in boxes on board ship, the crews were not wholly destitute of vegetables; while the ships were kept much warmer than on the former voyage by means of Sylvester's stoves.

A very large and excellent magic-lantern, which had been presented to them by a lady, afforded the men much entertainment; and in addition to their other amusements they were often treated to a concert, got up by the officers, several of whom,

including Parry himself, were very respectable per-
formers on various musical instruments.

But, besides these, regular employment was
provided for several evenings in the week, by the
establishment on the lower decks of each ship of
a school for teaching reading and writing; and this
was so highly valued, and so diligently used by
them, that when they returned home 'there was
not a man on board who could not read his Bible.'

Their position here was, however, really not so
isolated as it had been at Winter Harbour; for
during a part of the time they had constant intercourse with some Esquimaux, and those of a very
superior class, more simple and more interesting
than those they had met on their voyage. They
were perfectly orderly and quiet, and at their first
visit approached the ships only with a few blades of
whalebone, which were intended as a peace offering.

The women were well-dressed in clothes made of
the skin of deer; and, to the great surprise of the
officers, they immediately began to strip, although
the temperature was then at 23° below zero. But
it was soon discovered that they had other garments
underneath, and that the upper ones had been
brought for sale.

A village of five huts was now perceived at a
little distance; and it was a matter of wonder how
this could possibly have escaped the 'look-out' that
had constantly been kept; until, at Parry's request,
the process of building a hut was gone through
before them. These were not composed of skins,

like those made in summer by other tribes, but of snow cut out in solid blocks, and built up, strange to say, in the form of a dome; so that the arch and dome, about the origin of which there has been so much dispute, are found even among these wild inhabitants of the north.

They are made, and made correctly and well, in the space of a few hours, although they consist of several apartments.

With much curiosity the visitors entered one of these huts, and found inside snow beaten into bedsteads covered with skins, and fireplaces constructed in the same way, as well as various other articles of furniture; while the whole was lighted by windows of ice. A large bone was fixed across the ceiling, to which was suspended a stone lamp: and this the captain desired to purchase. So the good housewife took it down and emptied out the oil, as that was not included in the purchase; but as a little was left round the sides, and she had no mind to lose any, she wiped it round several times with her apron, and finished by giving it a final lick with her tongue.

An almost daily intercourse with these poor people proved a most agreeable interruption to the dreary solitude of both parties; and the many good qualities of the savages gained them great favour with their visitors. They were not only perfectly orderly and honest in their dealing with the crews, but also amiable and good-humoured in a remarkable degree.

Everything seemed to please and amuse them;

BUILDING A SNOW-HUT.

and the sound of the organ and fiddle sent them almost wild with delight. Many of the women possessed excellent voices, and were fond of singing; and one in particular, of whom Parry had requested a song, displayed not only a soft voice, but also a fine ear for music.

This woman, whose name was Iligliuk, was, however, a remarkable person altogether, and would have distinguished herself in any society, with a very small amount of instruction. She was an excellent sempstress, and particularly neat and clean in all her work: and instead of staring stupidly at whatever was new to her in English inventions, like the rest of her companions, she always appeared anxious to find out how and why things were done.

In fact, she soon became a general favourite on board the vessels, where with her husband, Okotook, she was a frequent visitor, and where she was regarded with even a certain degree of respect.

It was remarked in the dealings with this tribe that they were scrupulously honest, and that they would neither steal nor beg any of the many articles that must have been a great temptation to them.

On one occasion two dogs, which had been purchased by some of the 'Hecla's' officers, made their escape; but the next day when the Esquimaux had left the ship the same animals were found tied up carefully on board. Iligliuk was also very careful not only to keep her word, but indignant if she were supposed to have failed in her promise. Parry relates that she once promised to cover for him a little model of a canoe, but that through some mistake he supposed that she had not done so, and charged her with the failure. He could not understand her vehement protestations; so she waited until the bearer of her present entered the room, when she laid her hand on his arm, and looking steadfastly in his face, charged him with not having executed her commission.

The mistake was then cleared up; and Parry says ' it was impossible for him to describe the quiet yet proud satisfaction displayed in her countenance, at having thus cleared herself from a breach of promise.'

Noticing the extraordinary intelligence of Iligliuk, it suddenly struck Parry that from her some information respecting the direction of the coast might be obtained; so he placed before her several sheets of paper, and describing to her the direction in which they wished to sail, put a pencil into her hand, and requested her to trace the coast as far as she knew it. She soon understood his meaning and set to work on a large scale, naming the principal places as she went along, and one sheet after another had to be tacked on until a dozen were filled, the bystanders looking on with intense anxiety, and greatly relieved to see her bring the coast short round to the west and afterwards to the southwest.

This chart of the north-east corner of America, made by Iligliuk, was afterwards verified: and to her, therefore, in a great measure, is due, as Barrow says, the merit of the discovery of this line of coast.

Her son, Toolooak, seems to have inherited his mother's talents, and would sit in the cabin of the 'Fury' for an hour or two at a time, quietly drawing animals. Parry invited him to return to England with him; but he repeated, '*Nao*,'—No —a dozen times over with great emphasis, saying besides, that 'if he went away his father would cry.'

In these strong natural feelings he also resembled his mother, who had shown the greatest concern on one occasion when her husband was ill, sitting by him for hours with her hair dishevelled, and never taking her eyes off him.

Okotook then, for the first time in his life, took a dose of medicine. He drank it in fear and trembling, 'holding on to his wife by his other hand, and she on to him with both of hers, as if they expected an explosion.' Poor Iligliuk's head, however, got turned with the attention that she received, and by April she was a very different person from what she had been in February.

The lot of these poor outcasts of the human race is, at best, a very hard one. They depend for subsistence, during the months of March, April, and May, on the capture of the seal and walrus, and are frequently in a state of starvation. The hunts for these animals are attended by many dangers, and in particular the bears are found to be very formidable rivals, as they love seals' flesh quite as well as do the Esquimaux.

M

A poor fellow was once most unpleasantly disturbed while endeavouring to secure a seal which had been entangled in his net. He received a violent slap on the back, which he supposed to have been given by his companion, until, on its being repeated, he turned and beheld, to his extreme horror, a grim old bear, which instantly took possession of the prize, while the man decamped as quickly as he could.

Esquimaux Seal-hunter disturbed by a Bear.

Many of the poor creatures would have perished but for the supplies which they received from the ships; yet, even in this state, they were marvellously good-humoured.

Curious, indeed, are their tastes regarding food. We are told that, on one occasion, when the commander wished for a portrait of the prettiest woman

in the tribe, he could find no present so acceptable
for herself and her husband as a packet of candles,
which they ate with avidity; though he had the po-
liteness to draw the wicks out of the lady's mouth
whilst she swallowed the tallow.

An intelligent young man, named Ayonkitt, had
been invited by Lyon to dine with him, shown how
to use his knife and fork, and taught to wipe his
mouth before drinking. Afterwards he was conducted to wash his face and hands; and so anxious
did he appear afterwards to possess the cake of
Windsor soap, that Lyon presented it to him: when,
to his utter amazement, Ayonkitt swallowed it, as if
it had been a sugar-plum.

They are generally very improvident; but a few
of the most careful make a little pemmican.

Early in April they began to migrate westward,
and by the end of May the whole tribe were ready to
depart. They then received from the commander
such presents as produced in them the liveliest gratitude, which the women evinced by 'immoderate,
and even hysterical, fits of laughter;' and then they
took their leave by giving three hearty cheers.

After a residence of nine months in what they
had named Winter Island, sickness began to visit
the crews of the 'Fury' and 'Hecla,' and three
deaths occurred among the men. It was not until
July that the vessels were able to put to sea: and
both had very narrow escapes soon after starting
from the pressure of heavy floods of ice, borne down
upon them from the north.

On the 12th of July, however, they came to the mouth of a beautiful freshwater river, named by them Barrow River; and here they anchored for a while, that parties might be sent off in boats to enjoy the luxury of a visit to its banks. These, which were sloping by the water's side, rose afterwards to a considerable height. A splendid mountain cataract added greatly to the scenery, which was most sublime, and the vegetation rich and luxuriant; while, to heighten all, the sun was shining brightly in a cloudless sky, and several rein-deer were grazing peacefully beside the stream.

A pleasant run of fifty miles succeeded to this visit ashore, and the number of walruses which they observed pointed to this as the ordinary dwelling-place of their old friends, while information was brought to them by fresh Esquimaux visitors that they had now reached the strait which was to bring them to the Polar Sea, according to Iligliuk's chart.

But an impenetrable barrier of ice opposed their progress; and, after waiting a whole month, Parry's impatience to satisfy his mind on this point could not be restrained, and he therefore determined on a journey across the ice.

By August 17th he reached the extreme point of a peninsula, from which he was able to overlook the narrowest part of the strait; and having sent one of the party on for some of the water, which they found to be salt, he felt no doubt that he had discovered the Polar Sea, and named the strait after the 'Fury' and 'Hecla.'

A week after, however, the ships were, by the aid of a light breeze, carried a considerable distance through this channel; and being there stopped again by a barrier of what seemed fixed ice, three exploring parties were sent out to complete the investigation as to the termination of the strait, and to return to the ship in four days.

The matter was in this way pretty fairly settled; but it also became clear that not only the quantity of ice, but also the strong, perpetual current setting down it, would for ever prevent the strait from being used by ships. And as it was now the 24th September, Parry saw that winter quarters must for a second time be sought.

The ships were soon safely docked on the coast of Igloolik, the country of Iligliuk and her tribe. Their success had not hitherto been equal to their anticipations; and it appeared to the commander that, in order to complete the discovery, he must in some way make the provisions last for a year longer than at first proposed. The only expedient which he could think of was a bold one, namely, that as soon as the ice thawed again the greater part of the 'Hecla's' provisions should be transferred to the 'Fury,' and the former sent home alone with despatches, while the latter continued the investigation. Of this proposal, however, he only spoke to Commander Lyon, and for the present said nothing to the men.

The two ships were separated this winter by such large masses of ice that the crews could not meet for their old evening amusements; but it is pleasant to know that the schools were established, as before, on board each ship. Frequent visits from their old friends again enlivened the dreary months, and among them frequent mention is made of Toolooak, the son of Iligliuk, whose marriage took place during their stay; the ceremony consisting in his coming and seating himself outside the tent with his young bride, after which they departed laden with presents.

The summer and winter dwellings of these people were both here visited, and the former were found to be made of skins perfectly water-tight, and supported by a pillar of bones. Quantities of the flesh of various animals were kept inside these dwellings, and the smell inside was often intolerable; while on the outside were found heaps of carcases, as well as bones of seals, whales, bears, &c., mingled with human skeletons: of the latter of which they were very generous, bestowing several skeletons on Parry and his companions.

Parry confidently anticipated a successful termination to this expedition, and wrote in a despatch, which the ' Hecla' was to have taken home, that he trusted his next might go *viâ* Kamptschatka. His determination to remain out with the ' Fury,' when made known, was well received, and all the men were willing to do just as he should require of them. But his plans were at the last moment entirely altered by the appearance of the scurvy, hitherto almost a stranger amongst them.

The surgeon, whose opinion was then taken, having pronounced against a third winter in the ice, and the ice itself, even in August, remaining as fixed as ever, he seemed to have no choice, but was obliged to give up his cherished scheme: and therefore took his voyage home in company with the 'Hecla;' feeling once more that he was relinquishing a fair prospect of honour, to which he had seemed very close.

Franklin was by this time home to welcome him; and very heartily did the two friends exchange congratulations on what the other had achieved.

Each was now advanced to the rank of Captain; as was also Parry's late companion, Commander Lyon. And every one of the three, so far from being daunted by what they had undergone, was quite ready to go out again and renew the search.

Captain Lyon was, therefore, appointed to the command of the strong, but sluggish 'Griper,' and sent to complete the survey of the north-east part of America, and, if possible, either by sea or land, to reach the point at which Franklin had stopped, namely, Cape Turnagain; his instructions being to sail direct either for Repulse Bay or Wager River: and he started on this expedition in July 1824; but, after bravely encountering the most fearful perils, he was able to get no further than Sir Thomas Roe's Welcome.

In fact, his voyage only tended to confirm the impression of the peculiarly uninteresting and dangerous nature of this coast.

CHAPTER IX.

SIR EDWARD PARRY'S THIRD EXPEDITION, AND HIS POLAR VOYAGE.

CAPTAIN PARRY had a dangerous illness almost immediately on arriving at home, yet by the spring of the same year, 1824, he was eager for another voyage; and his own impression being that the wisest way now would be to make a further attempt on Regent's Inlet, the Admiralty, who had the fullest confidence in his judgment and experience, again placed the two vessels—'Fury' and 'Hecla'—at his service.

He chose the latter as his own ship; while Commander Hoppner, who had served with him as Lieutenant in the 'Alexander,' as well as in his last two voyages, was placed in command of the 'Fury.'

They sailed from the Nore on the 19th of May, 1824, and in a month's time fell in with the ice in Davis's Strait, where an instance of Parry's presence of mind and coolness in danger occurred.

It was on a Sunday morning, and, as usual, all the ship's company were mustered for Divine Service, which he was conducting; when near the conclusion of the sermon which he was reading, the quartermaster came hastily from the hatchway, and whispered a few hurried words in his ear. Parry, without exhibiting any signs of emotion, asked some questions in a low tone, and bade him return to his post. He then re-opened his book and continued his sermon, as though nothing had occurred; concluding with the blessing. Then raising his hand he said,—'Now my lads, all hands on deck—but mind, no bustle.'

A mist, which had been hanging over them, had suddenly cleared, and land was seen just ahead; and the Captain, who, from the quartermaster's report, had judged the danger not immediate, now took his post, and issued the needful orders for altering the ship's course.

'We *knew* we could trust him,' said one of his own seamen.

It will be unnecessary to describe again all the difficulties of this, the first part of the voyage. Suffice it to say, that not until the 27th of September had they fairly rounded the north-east corner of Prince Regent's Inlet.

Here, our readers will remember, they were stopped by a barrier of ice in 1819; and here also they had, for the first time, found their compasses perfectly useless.

Had they, on this second occasion, arrived some weeks earlier, they might probably have sailed southwards, down the inlet, and wintered on the American Continent; but the delays in that tedious passage across Baffin's Bay and through Lancaster Sound are unavoidable; and as the season was now past, they had at once to look out for winter quarters.

These they found at 'Port Bowen, a convenient harbour on the east coast of the inlet.'

One long period of isolation at Winter Harbour, Melville Island, another at Winter Island, off Lyon's Inlet, and a third at Igloolik, had given them a pretty good idea of what to do and what to expect. But this fourth winter was the most trying of all; for, being on old ground, they had neither the novelty of place or of situation to help them on.

Here, too, were no Esquimaux, and no animals; so that all resources must come from within themselves; and every conceivable device had to be resorted to in order to amuse the men. Rational occupation, however, was even more necessary than amusement; and was felt by all to be so.

The schools were, therefore, again re-commenced, and were so thoroughly appreciated that all the ships' company took part in them; 'making the whole,' says Parry, 'such a scene of quiet occupation as I never before witnessed on board a ship. These schools were placed under the superintendence of Mr. Hooper, purser of the 'Hecla,' in whose own words we have an account of the good effects of that held on Sunday evenings.

He writes in his journal as follows: — 'I have been, this evening, gratified beyond measure by the conduct of my school. We assembled as usual, and Captain Parry read to us an excellent sermon. We then read over three or four times the second lesson for the day; and I expounded it to the best of my ability. After this we went to prayers, and having closed, I wished them good night as usual, when my friend John Darke (one of the 'Hecla's' seamen) said he wished to say a few words. He then went back to his knees, and in a few simple but affecting words returned thanks for the blessing enjoyed by himself and shipmates in a Christian captain and a Christian teacher, imploring the blessing of God in behalf of both Captain Parry and myself. After this he desired, for himself and shipmates, to thank me for the trouble I had taken, and the countenance of every one spoke the same thing, and showed that they had deputed him to do this.'

Pleasant, indeed, it is to think of the work that was really going on whilst the brave captains and their crews seemed to be wasting their time for so many months on that barren coast. And a great work it was that Captain Parry was thus permitted to carry out, while so often allowed to suffer disappointment in the work which he had set himself — great not only in itself, but because of the effect which his example produced on the conduct of subsequent expeditions.

For the officers, however, there was no need to make employment. They were fully occupied in various scientific researches, especially on the subjects of magnetism, refraction, and the aurora borealis.

Of the latter they witnessed but few very brilliant displays, but one is worth relating.

The captain, with two of his lieutenants, were admiring its beauty from the observatory on one occasion, when suddenly all three ' uttered an exclamation of surprise at seeing a bright ray of the aurora shoot suddenly downward from the general mass of light, and *between them and the land*, which was there distant only three thousand yards.'

Parry observes, that had he been alone at this time he should have attributed the phenomenon to fancy; but as three persons saw it, he had no doubt that a ray of light did pass within that distance of them. Something of the same kind was observed by poor Hood during Franklin's journey. The variation of the magnetic needle was found to have increased since their first visit, and a regular system of hourly experiments on the magnetic intensity was instituted.

Lunar observations for the longitude, and observations for the latitude by the sun and stars, were constantly going on; and these things fully occupied their time.

The re-appearance of the sun was also an event anxiously looked forward to as soon as January had passed away; but it was not until February 22nd that he was seen at the ships, though a glimpse of him had been obtained many days earlier from the top of high ground. But even then, for a long time, he was only seen, and not felt; nor was it until the 11th of April that the thermometer rose above zero.

To occupy the time that must yet intervene before the ships were released, parties were sent out in several directions to explore; and as soon as the ice

began to crack, plenty of active employment was
found for the men in the work of enlarging these
splits, until, by the 18th of July, they were able to
begin coasting along the land on the western side
of the strait which Parry had called North Somerset,
feeling as they did so that the voyage had but now
commenced.

They started in high spirits, but were again
doomed to disappointment; for both ships soon got
among large floes of ice drifting in towards the shore.
The 'Fury' was swept irresistibly past the 'Hecla,'
almost running the latter down, and both stuck
fast. At high water both ships were got off; but
the poor 'Fury' was so damaged that four pumps
were constantly at work to keep her afloat. They
got her into a dock that she might undergo repairs;
but instantly the wind destroyed this basin, and the
'Hecla' was obliged to tow her out to sea. Sails
were passed under her keel to stop the worst leaks;
but on the 21st of August she was hopelessly stranded
on an open and stony beach, with her hold full of
water; and both crews, officers and men alike, were so
completely worn out, that 'some of them fell into a
kind of stupor, which rendered the individuals so
affected incapable of comprehending an order.'

There was clearly nothing for it but to abandon
the poor vessel and return home; which, as the sea
southward was then very open, was extremely dis-
appointing. However, as every corner of the 'Hecla'
was occupied by the reception of the other crew, and
the 'Fury's' stores could not be received, there was no

possible alternative; and thus ended Captain Parry's third and last attempt in search of a north-west passage.

He had discovered many northern lands, had found out that many things could not be done, and so spared his successors much fruitless labour, and left them but to find out the one connecting link; but he was not suffered to achieve the whole.

We have seen, however, how to some of those under his care the time spent had been far from lost; and the same thing may be not less truly said of himself.

Parry's home-ties had been very strong ones; and one of these he had found broken on his return from Igloolik, where the news of his father's death had been communicated to him. This had made a deep impression, and had caused him to look more deeply into the grounds of his own faith. Alone, comparatively, at Port Bowen, or at least shut out from the outer world, and forced into a long retirement, the thought of that eternity on which his father had now entered, and to which every passing day was bringing himself nearer, pressed deeply upon his mind; and the question, of 'How a sinful man *can* be just with God?' presented itself as one that could not be satisfactorily answered by any general statement about the mercy of God.

From his youth up he may be said to have been ' a devout man.' To do God's will, and to suffer it also patiently, seems to have been his great aim; but the knowledge of that will had been hitherto but very imperfectly comprehended by him. He had read his Bible, and thought of Christ's love only in that general way that too many do; but now that his mind was thus exercised, he, as well as his men, found a good friend in Mr. Hooper. A close friendship was formed between them, and many were the conversations held between them on these all-important topics.

Mr. Hooper himself, in his private journal, notices the change which was taking place in the views of his 'esteemed friend,' and the delightful hours passed in his company, but does not appear aware how helpful his own counsels had proved. A regular study of the New Testament seems, however, to have been the means to which Parry himself attributed this change, more than to anything else. 'The entrance of Thy words giveth light,' he wrote, in allusion to his own state of mind; and this light showed him one great mistake into which he had hitherto fallen, namely, that of applying the promises of God indiscriminately, and without considering that they are given only to those who have put on Christ, and entered on the narrow way by the 'strait gate,' and that alone.

Naturally, therefore, his zeal for the spiritual welfare of his men assumed henceforth a deeper character than it had borne before; nor were his efforts suffered to be in vain. Of this one interesting proof, among many others, was given in a letter received by Mr. Hooper from one of the seamen, John Darke, in which he spoke of him and the Captain as

' the means of saving his soul,' and begged to know
how he might send them 10*l.*, to be appropriated to
any good object of which they might approve, as a
thank-offering for the good he had received on
board the ' Hecla.'

Although once more unsuccessful in this his
third Arctic voyage, Parry, on his return home, received fresh honours in testimony of his brave and
indefatigable efforts, and in acknowledgment of the
services really rendered to his country by the extensive geographical discoveries which he had made.
But he went home also to begin that manly career
as a Christian philanthropist which has rendered
his name familiar to many who might scarcely have
heard of it in connexion with naval enterprise.

This did not, perhaps, gain him any additional
favour among some of his old patrons; indeed he
himself tells us that it brought on him many a
sneer. But he would have been the last man to
shrink from ' nailing his colours to the mast ;' and
although some share of ridicule was to be expected,
yet Parry's professional character stood too high to
allow of any man of sense being easily prejudiced
against him.

Nor was his own professional enthusiasm one
whit less than it had ever been. He longed to be
out again on some other service, and if unsuccessful
in the north-west, he would try the North Pole
itself: not, indeed, with the same view, for to find
a passage that way does not seem to have been his
object. But the magnetic experiments which he

had witnessed, and in which he had himself assisted, interested him deeply, and he now strongly desired to follow these out at the Pole itself.

True, Captain Phipps had failed, and so had Buchan and Franklin. But then, in the accounts of both voyages, mention had been made of large 'fields of ice, free from either fissure or hummock,' which a coach might have driven over many leagues in a direct line, without obstruction or danger; and in sledge-borne boats Captain Parry now proposed to proceed beyond the point where a large vessel could sail.

A most daring proposition it was, without doubt; yet Parry was not the man rashly and uselessly to risk the lives of those under his command; and some time before the plan had been started by his friend Franklin, now absent on another Arctic expedition. Both thought the experiment worth trying; and, in accordance with the opinions of both, Parry was once more appointed to his favourite 'Hecla,' with instructions to proceed in her as far as Spitzbergen, there to leave her in some safe harbour in charge of one of the officers, while he and his men proceeded, according to his plan, in two boats, the 'Enterprise' and the 'Endeavour,' which had been specially prepared for the purpose, and each of which was twenty feet long and seven broad, flat-bottomed, and very strong.

Between his return from Regent's Inlet and his setting out on this his last Polar voyage, he had married the fourth daughter of Sir John Stanley, a

lady who had long taken great interest in the
subject of Arctic enterprise, and she it was who went
through the form of commissioning the ship by
hoisting the pendant, to the great delight of the
seamen.   Parry was determined to take none but
first-rate hands; but, notwithstanding this, the
‘ Hecla ’ was manned in three days.

And this voyage may be said to have begun in
the ice ; for at Deptford, where the vessel lay while
preparing, the river was frozen over, and Mrs.
Parry, who was on board with her husband for a
month, had an opportunity of hearing something
of the grating of the ice against the ship's sides, and
afterwards, when it became harder and firmer, of
seeing how the boats cut their way through, in order
to communicate with the shore.

‘ Mr. Ross and the officers seemed to delight in
it,’ she observed ; and her own and her family's enthusiasm, happily for them, appears to have been
almost equal to that of the Captain himself.

The Mr. Ross of whom she speaks was Lieutenant James Ross, nephew to Captain Ross, who
commanded the second boat.

The ‘ Hecla ’ sailed direct to Hammerfest, in
Norway, where they stopped to take in eight rein-
deer with a supply of moss, their ordinary provender,
and also to learn how to manage these beautiful
creatures, on which they depended to draw their
sledge-boats when they got on the ice.

These intelligent and docile animals are most
wonderfully adapted to this kind of labour.   They

eat about four pounds of moss a-day, but can go even five or six days fasting without injury : snow serves them for water and ice for a bed. A collar of skin round the neck, one trace and one rein, form the whole of their trappings, and under a skilful driver they will thus make extraordinary journeys, even in soft snow. A shake of the rein is all the urging that they need; and perhaps no animals are so easily managed. Our party soon became quite attached to them, so that the possibility of being obliged to feed on these very rein-deer was anything but agreeable.

After being beset in the ice for four-and-twenty days the vessel was at length brought to anchor in Treurenberg Bay, on the north of Spitzbergen, where so many Dutch graves were found, that Parry rightly surmised the name of the place to be taken from '*treuren*,' to lament. .

At length the two boats left the ship, taking with them only seventy-one days' provisions, as the season was far advanced, and his strict instructions were to return before winter—in time, indeed, for the ' Hecla ' to get away before she became frozen in. But the appearance of the ice telling them plainly that it would be long before either rein-deer, snow-shoes, or wheels could be of any use, Parry left the poor animals behind, after all ; and what became of them we do not know. Of the snow-shoes, which our readers will remember to be very large affairs, they made little sledges to carry some of their luggage, these were found very useful.

The rest of the voyage was perfectly unique in its character, and Parry's own words will best describe the plan of travelling :—

' It was my intention,' he says, ' to travel wholly at night, and to rest by day; there being, of course, constant daylight in these regions during the summer season. The advantages of this plan, which was occasionally deranged by circumstances, consisted, first, in our avoiding the intense and oppressive glare from the snow during the time of the sun's greatest altitude; so as to prevent, in some degree, the painful inflammation in the eyes, called ' snow-blindness,' which is common in all snowy countries. We also thus enjoyed greater warmth during the hours of rest, and had a better chance of changing our clothes; besides which, no small advantage was derived from the snow being harder at night for travelling. The only disadvantage of this plan was, that the fogs were somewhat more frequent, and more thick by night than by day. Even in this respect there was less difference than might have been supposed; the temperature during the twenty-four hours undergoing but little variation. . . . When we rose in the morning, we commenced our day by prayers ; after which we took off our fur sleeping-dresses, and put on those for travelling . . . We made a point of always putting on the same stockings and boots for travelling in, whether they had dried during the day or not; and I believe it was only in five or six instances that they were not either still wet, or hard frozen. This was, indeed, of no consequence; as they were sure to be

PARRY'S SLEDGE-BOATS.

thoroughly wet in a quarter of an hour after commencing our journey; while, on the other hand, it was of vital importance to keep dry things to sleep in.'

He then goes on to tell how, after breakfasting on biscuit and warm cocoa, they set off; and usually, after travelling four or five hours, came to a halt for dinner; after which they went on again for some hours.

When they hauled up the boats for the night it was always on the largest floe of ice in sight; and then, by putting these boats alongside each other, with their sterns to the wind, and placing the sails over them, supported by the masts for an awning, they got a more comfortable sleeping-place than might have been imagined. Before lying down both officers and men smoked their pipes; and the latter told long yarns: and this was often the only comfortable part of their waking hours.

Their only fuel was spirits of wine; and their only use for it to boil their cocoa.

But the state of the ice disappointed them much. Here was no smooth level, but quantities of loose rugged masses, over which they travelled slowly; having to go backwards and forwards to fetch their provisions and luggage; so that sometimes their progress was but very slow. Once it was only half a mile in four hours; and, indeed, from the 25th of June, when they started, to the 30th, they had only reached to 82° 40′ 23″; or 'eight miles of direct northing.'

With no objects but ice and sky for the eye to rest on, they had travelled until the 27th, when it appeared that, instead of advancing, they were really going backward. On the 23rd the highest point ever reached was attained, viz. 82° 45′; just 172 miles from the 'Hecla;' and now it seemed useless to proceed. Parry had long before given up all hope of gaining the Pole; and for some days had only urged on the men to attempt to reach lat. 83° N.: at which point, if they could have gained it, they would have been entitled to the reward of 1000*l.* This fact, however, he had kept from them; but had they known it, they could not have made more vehement efforts. It was the officers alone who could take the observations, who were aware that no perceptible progress was being made. On the 27th they dined with flags flying in both boats, and drank the king's health in a higher latitude than it had ever been drunk before; and after a day's rest they began their journey southward, with less satisfaction than they had ever turned homeward before.

They had a little amusement in hunting bears on their return; and as their provisions were getting low, they were now and then glad to feast on one. Not until the 4th of August did they hear the swell of the open sea; and on arriving at Table Island, where they had deposited some provisions, they found that, as one of the men said, 'the bears had been square with them;' having eaten all the bread. Their welcome at the 'Hecla' was a very warm one; and on the 28th of August she weighed anchor for

BEAR-HUNT ON POLAR SEA.

England; and by the end of September Parry was able to present himself at the Admiralty, where he had the joy of meeting his old friend, Captain Franklin, who had exactly at the same time returned from a second Polar land expedition; of which we have now to speak.

CHAPTER X.

SIR JOHN FRANKLIN'S SECOND EXPEDITION.

Sir John Barrow remarks, that a thorough-bred English seaman will scarcely ever succumb under any amount of danger or suffering, and that, instead of being disheartened, he will only grow more and more anxious to persevere in his career, in the hope of meeting with ultimate success; and he justly holds up Captain Franklin as an example of this kind of undaunted spirit. To any ordinary person it must be, indeed, inconceivable how, after enduring such almost unheard-of sufferings, he should have been not only willing, but eager, to pursue his researches in the very same regions: nevertheless, such is the fact. And what is more extraordinary still, his enthusiasm was not confined to his own breast, but was so fully and warmly shared by his wife, that although she was lying on what she knew must be her death-bed, when the preparations were complete she would not keep him a single day beyond that fixed for departure, but entreated him, 'as he valued her peace of mind and his own glory, not to delay a moment on her account;' adding, 'that it could be but to close her eyes.'

It was a heroism worthy of the highest cause—too high, perhaps, most persons will think, for a matter of mere discovery: but such men as Franklin, and such women as Franklin's wife, are apt to regard the interests and glory of their profession, and still more of their country, as far beyond any considerations of private interest or feeling. We must remember that, after all, had not our countrymen possessed this spirit of devotion to her honour, England had never risen to her present place among the nations. And it is cheering to think that both our own and other lands can furnish a few examples of as high a courage in a still higher cause—witness the names of Hans Egede, of Captain Allan Gardiner, John Williams, Adoniram Judson, and others.

Captain Franklin's wife, however, was not the only one who participated in his ardour; for no sooner had Government given consent, and directed him to prepare for his new enterprise, than many distinguished officers volunteered their services, and amongst others Lieutenant Back and Dr. Richardson. They, too, had forgotten their sufferings, and were as eager as their captain to complete the geography and natural history of the shores of the Polar sea; and probably also they were equally sanguine as to their escape from a repetition of those sufferings on the present occasion. Dr. Richardson even left a wife and family, and a comfortable position at home, to accompany his old friend.

They were now to go direct to the Mackenzie River—the 'Great River,' as it has been called by the settlers — and thence to proceed to its mouth, to examine the coasts westward as far as Icy Cape, and eastward to the mouth of the Coppermine River; and as Parry was then out on his third voyage it was once more hoped that they might meet with and assist him.

Profiting by experience, they did not trust to such canoes as might be obtained at the Company's stations, but sent out by way of Hudson's Bay large boats constructed for the purpose, and a little one called the 'Walnut-Shell,' to be used on certain occasions. Supplied with all kinds of comforts in the way of tents, bedding, clothing, waterproof dresses, and eatables of all possible descriptions, and with abundance of ammunition, as well as of scientific instruments, they had no fear of encountering their former difficulties.

On the 16th of February, 1825, Captain Franklin, Lieut. Back, Dr. Richardson, Mr. Kendall, the draughtsman of the party, and Mr. Drummond, the assistant-naturalist, embarked at Liverpool for New York with four marines, and on the 15th of July they arrived safely at Fort Chipewyan, on the north of the Athabaska Lake. As on the former occasion, they took every opportunity of engaging the necessary assistants — Canadian voyageurs, and Indian hunters from various tribes — while the services of their former excellent Esquimaux guide and interpreter, Augustus, were also secured; and Mr. Dease, one of the chief traders of the Hudson's Bay Company, was, happily, found willing to join them. The name of this latter gentleman is now to be met with in our maps of North America in several places.

Travelling steadily on, the whole party soon mustered in force on the Great Bear Lake river, which falls into the Mackenzie; and while Dr.

View on the Mackenzie River.

Richardson crossed the lake to that point which is nearest to the river Coppermine, and Lieutenant Back was left to superintend the preparation of winter quarters, afterwards named Fort Franklin, the Captain himself, with another party, embarked on the Mackenzie, and sailed towards the ocean.

As Mackenzie has mentioned in his account, they found along the banks of this river a quantity of wood-coal, which was on fire, and gave out a very disagreeable smell, but little heat. There was also a kind of unctuous mud, which the Indians now and then use for food, or even chew as an amusement. It has a milky taste, and is not unpleasant. They noticed, too, a dark bituminous fluid oozing from the rocks, and two streams of sulphureous water pouring into the river. At a place called the Ramparts, where it is rapid and obstructed by limestone-rocks, they met with some of the Hare Indians, laden with fish, berries, and meat. Both men and women were dressed in leathern clothes, and wore as ornaments beads and porcupine quills. They were entertained at midnight by Mr. Dease at Fort Good Hope, and by means of a half-caste young man, named Baptiste, they endeavoured to open a communication with these people: but it was unsuccessful, until Augustus presented himself. But no sooner had they perceived him than they welcomed him with the liveliest demonstrations of affection, which appears somewhat singular when we remember the hatred that exists between the two races. The river was so very broad at its mouth that it was some time before Franklin could ascertain that he had really reached the sea.

They landed as soon as they had done so ; and when the tent was pitched on shore he caused the silk Union flag, which his wife had made and presented to him as a parting gift, to be hoisted and unfurled, forcing himself, against his natural feelings, to join in the cheers with which the men saluted the British flag.

In fact, he was now compelled to keep up the

spirits of the party, for some of the Canadians were losing heart at this their first sight of the ocean; and, besides, an attack was hourly expected from the Esquimaux, whose territory they had now entered.

Unfortunately, however, the water which had been mixed with the brandy, with which they were to drink the King's health, turned out to be salt water; and they were obliged to pour the whole on the ground as a libation, instead of enjoying the then unusual draught.

Franklin would have rejoiced at once to proceed westward, which was to be his share of the exploration, but the season was too advanced, and the weather too rough: so they returned to the fort, where they found all the others assembled, and where very comfortable buildings had been prepared for their winter imprisonment of eight or nine months. There all soon settled down to their various employments.

As before, the officers naturally found work enough; but for the men it had to be made. In the establishment of schools, which proved very successful, and in which the officers taught, Franklin seems to have taken a lesson from his friend Parry; and the Sundays were kept as days of rest, when the whole party, except two or three of the Canadians, attended Divine service twice.

On other evenings a sort of hall was given up to the men for any games that they chose, and in these the officers invariably joined. So an excellent feeling was preserved between all parties; while the great admiration and esteem which were felt for their captain proved, moreover, a strong bond of union between them.

They got through the winter comfortably; though for a short time they were without both fresh and dried meats, and but little fish was caught: so that they were obliged to resort to their pemmican, arrowroot, and portable soup, which were to have been wholly reserved for the sea voyages.

Dr. Richardson kept a regular record of the migrations and return of the various animals and birds: —

'September 11th. Mosquitoes cease to be troublesome.

October 2nd. Swans seen in flight.

October 5th. Last swans seen.

January 3rd. All animals gone southward, except the wolf and fox.

On the shortest day the sun seen above the horizon, 2^h 38^m.

(We must remember that this was only latitude $65°$ $11'$ $56''$ N.)

April 10th. A house-fly seen out of doors.

May 6th. The first swans seen.

„ 7th. The geese appeared.

„ 8th. The ducks return.

„ 9th. The gulls.

„ 11th. The first rain fell.

„ 17th. Various singing-birds appeared.

„ 27th. First laughing geese seen.

„ 31st. The goatsucker.'

And so on.

They were now preparing for their voyage; another boat had been made, and in June all the boats were got afloat.

Franklin and Back took possession of the ' Lion' and ' Reliance,' which were manned by fourteen men; and Augustus went with them. Dr. Richardson, who had secured another Esquimaux guide, named Ooligback, had the 'Dolphin' and 'Union;' and Mr. Kendall went with him, and nine men.

It was a hot day in the end of June when they embarked, and the thermometer stood at $71°$ in the shade. The ice was drifting down so rapidly that they were obliged to lie to until next morning; and in the evening they reached the Mackenzie.

On the 2nd of July they arrived at Fort Good Hope, on the border of the Esquimaux territory; and here, therefore, each man was armed with a gun and a dagger, and provided with ammunition.

Next day they came to that broad part of the river where it divides into two branches, and where they were to separate—Richardson taking the eastern, and Franklin the western branch; the aim of the latter being to reach Icy Cape, where he hoped to meet Captain Beechey in the ' Blossom;' and of the former to sail along the coast to the mouth of the Coppermine, and then proceed by land to the north-east point of the Great Bear Lake, where a boat was to meet him to convey him back to the fort.

By the 7th of July Franklin reached the mouth of the river, and, landing, he soon discovered a whole encampment of the Esquimaux on an adjoining island. Instantly he returned to the boats to prepare presents, and arrange how in the wisest way to open a communication with them. Strict orders were issued not to fire until the word was given either by himself or Back, and the boats immediately steered towards the tents, with their flags flying; but, unfortunately, they ran aground when about a mile from the shore, and, without waiting to get afloat again, they made signs to the natives to come off. As soon as this was understood, canoes were launched in such quick succession that the sea seemed to be full of them. Elderly men were in the first canoes, and seemed to have been sent on purpose to negociate about trading, for which they were most eager.

Augustus went forward to meet them with a present in his hand, and explained that the boats had come to look for a passage, and that probably if they were successful a large ship would soon come and begin a profitable commerce with them. On hearing this they set up a deafening shout of applause, and all seemed to be going on smoothly, until, unfortunately, one of the kajaks got upset by one of the 'Lion's' oars, and an Esquimaux thereby placed in danger of drowning, as his head was stuck in the mud. The crew, however, hastened to get him out, and took him into their boat, where Augustus wrapped him in his own great-coat, and he soon became pacified. But once in, he got a sight of the many treasures which were concealed

WINTER DWELLINGS OF THE ESQUIMAUX.

from the natives by coverings, and his account of these to his countrymen caused such a rush on the boats that for a time the position of the crews was by no means pleasant.

At length the natives seized Back's boat, the 'Reliance,' and began dragging it ashore. The 'Lion' attempted to follow, but being aground, it was unable to proceed until also taken in hand by the savages; and then they perceived that the Esquimaux who had been taken in had stolen a pistol from Lieutenant Back. Finding that his theft was discovered, the fellow jumped overboard and joined his companions, carrying off Augustus' great-coat. At the same moment two of the strongest men jumped on board, and seizing Franklin by the wrists, forced him to sit between them: a third soon followed as he attempted to shake them off, and all kept repeating '*Teyma*,' and beating gently on his left breast, while they pressed his hands against their breasts.

As soon as they reached the shore the three men leaped out and made their escape, while others stripping themselves to their waists, and drawing their knives, began a regular pillage of the 'Reliance,' all the articles being handed to the women as soon as secured, and they as quickly making off with them. It was a violent contest, and at length Lieutenant Back ordered his men to level their muskets, but not to fire until the word was given. Happily, it was not necessary, for the natives all took to their heels; but Franklin believed, that had a man of them fallen, a deadly revenge would have been taken by his countrymen.

The boats were then got afloat, and soon seven or eight of the natives returned, and held a conversation with Augustus, inviting him to a conference on shore. Perfectly fearless as to himself, the lion-hearted fellow begged so earnestly to go, that at last Franklin consented ; and as they watched the effect of his speech they could perceive that it was approved by his compatriots, by the loud shouts of applause with which it was received.

On his return he told the crews that he had reproved the natives for their bad conduct, that it had been different from that of any other Esquimaux ; and that he had further told them how much better off they would be were they in connexion with Europeans, like his own tribe; that they never could expect to see white men again unless they instantly brought back all the stolen articles; and that, further, it was not fear, but compassion that had withheld the English from firing that day.

This bold conduct had the desired effect, for the natives strove to excuse themselves on the ground of never having seen white men before, and not being able to resist so many fine articles. They brought back the stolen things, and thus by a wise management all bloodshed was avoided, and affairs placed on an amicable footing.

The Esquimaux are not generally a warlike people, but these perhaps had become so by their constant collisions with the Dog-rib Indians.

As they proceeded westward they found them
more and more like the Chinese Tartars, and with
small, oblique eyes. Their ornaments were of a singular character, and were so highly valued that they
would not sell them. These consisted in a piece of
bone, worn by every man through his nose, and a
circular piece of ivory, with a blue bead in the
centre, fixed into holes in the under-lip, so as to
keep the mouth open. Some of the women were
good-looking, and dressed their black hair in a
tasteful manner, turned up on the top with strings
of blue beads or white cord, and divided in front
into two long bands to the waist, ornamented with
beads.

Lieutenant Back took a likeness of one, who was
highly flattered by the compliment.

On the 13th they pursued their voyage; but not
till they came to Herschel Island did they find a safe
anchorage for a ship. Here Franklin visited Mount
Conybeare, and had a good view of the various ranges
of the Rocky Mountains.

On the boundary of the British dominion (for all
this land was considered ours; we suppose, in virtue
of the grant to Prince Rupert) they found a river,
which, in honour of the then Lord High Admiral,
afterwards William IV., they named Clarence. They
also, however, took the liberty of naming one further
on, which was in the Russian dominions: this they
called Canning.

On the 4th of August they fell in with a peaceable
tribe of Esquimaux, with whom they traded; but the

further westward they went, the more were they troubled by fogs, gales, rain, and drifts of ice. By the middle of this month winter had really set in; and the men having already suffered much from cold and fatigue, in dragging or carrying the boats, Franklin reluctantly decided to return; having reached no further than a point in long. 149° 37' W; which he named 'Return Reef:' little knowing that at that very time a boat's crew, sent by Captain Beechey from the 'Blossom,' which had rounded Icy Cape, were actually within 160 miles of them.

It had been a harassing voyage along the coast from Mackenzie River, and it was an equally trying one back again. Indeed, in a violent squall near Herschel Island they all had a narrow escape of their lives.

By the 21st September they reached Fort Franklin, where the other party had already arrived, after a most prosperous voyage and journey.

Starting from Point Separation, Dr. Richardson and his crews had passed along a low, flat coast, where they had the gratification of seeing many sand-martins thinning the ranks of their great foes, the mosquitoes.

Rein-deer Hills beyond were clothed with trees to their very tops. At one spot, where was an immense spruce-fir tree, seven feet in circumference at four feet from the ground, they encamped; and next day they came to a small island, which being evidently one of the Esquimaux burial-places, they named Sacred Island.

A little further on they met with some Esquimaux, who used threatening gestures, and whom, at Ooligback's recommendation, they avoided by instantly embarking. The Indians in the party spoke of a large lake just beyond, which they call Esquimaux Lake; and on the 15th they crossed an inlet, supposed to be connected with it, which they called Russell Inlet. Low coasts and shallow water lay beyond; and on the 18th, whilst sailing between the little islands, a party of Esquimaux rushed out upon them, brandishing knives, and forbidding them to land. But when the Doctor shouted 'barter,' they were instantly peaceable; and the presents they received soon rendered them almost frantic with delight.

A bundle of beads, caught by one old woman, sent her into transports; while another, who stood by, became the picture of despair. It was divided, however, on Richardson's recommendation, and a pleasing song was sung in token of gratitude; to which they kept time with their oars.

The women 'drew their children out of their wide boots, where they are accustomed to keep them,' in order to obtain beads also for them: but at length the crew succeeded in getting free, and again pursued their voyage. Having rounded Point Bathurst they came to a bay, which Richardson named Franklin Bay; and on the opposite side of it was a point, which they named Parry Cape. Passing through a channel, which was called, after their boats, the Dolphin and Union Straits, they reached a spot at which there was much ice: and the 'Dolphin' was so nearly crushed between two masses, that they had to stop until she was again rendered seaworthy. 'This strait would always be dangerous for ships,' says Richardson, 'from the number of sunken rocks which it contains.'

One more rocky point was named by him Cape Krusenstern, after the Russian hydrographer, and then they came to Cape Hearne; and their arrival at the mouth of the Coppermine was announced to the men, who were quite unprepared for so speedy a termination of the voyage.

All were in excellent health, and ready to commence their journey back. They soon reached the Bloody Falls of Hearne, and found the river here so full of rapids that, the boats being utterly useless, they left them stowed with a few such articles as Esquimaux would like; and, dividing their provisions, proceeded on foot to Dease's River, on the Bear Lake, where the expected boat soon arrived; and they speedily reached the fort of which Mr. Dease had been left in charge, and found him ready to receive them.

It was thought necessary to pass a part of the following winter at the fort; and so severe did it prove, that on the 7th of February the thermometer had gone down to 58° below zero. But even in December Dr. Richardson had gone on to join Mr. Drummond in his botanising explorations on the Saskatchewan River, in order that he might be ready earlier in the spring for making his collections.

In the end of February Franklin followed, while
Back was sent on with the English party and the
Canadians, whom he was to send to Montreal, proceeding himself with the others to York Factory, and
so to England.

The two Esquimaux guides were carefully sent
back to their families at Churchill; and the parting
with Augustus was quite affecting. Their pay was
to be handed over to the Directors of the Company,
to be paid annually as they required it.

As far as navigation went the result of this expedition was discouraging; for all that northern
coast appeared dangerous, and without any natural
harbours for large ships: but science had, on the
contrary, gained much; and to Dr. Richardson's
exertions, in a great measure, was this owing. He
was, as he well deserved, eventually rewarded with
the honour of knighthood.

CHAPTER XI.

SIR JOHN ROSS' SECOND VOYAGE.

ONE expedition had thus succeeded to another in quick succession during ten years; and although the great point had not yet been gained, yet every effort had produced some results, and had been a step towards the attainment of the desired end.

Captain Ross, meantime, had lain under a cloud in public estimation, and had long been fretting for an opportunity of retrieving his lost reputation by making another and bolder attempt in the same direction.

Government, however, was almost tired of the heavy expense, and seemed to feel that if Parry and Franklin did not succeed, no one else was likely to do so. At least, it would not listen to any proposition made by Captain Ross. His only resource was, therefore, to do the thing on his own account, simply as a matter of private speculation. But the difficulty was, how to find the funds; and this would have proved an insuperable obstacle had he not had a wealthy friend, who not only felt great sympathy for his own uncomfortable position, but also took considerable interest in all such discoveries.

The promised reward of 20,000*l*., offered by Government to the discoverer of the passage, deterred this friend from coming forward at first, for he feared lest any unworthy motive should be imputed to him; but when, in 1828, that offer was withdrawn, Mr. Felix Booth at once, to the Captain's great delight, laid down the sum of 17,000*l*., to which Ross added 3000*l*., and immediately set about making preparations.

Having looked at several vessels, he finally selected the 'Victory,' a Liverpool merchant-ship, which he bought and sent into dock at Limehouse, to be strengthened for the hard service to which it was destined, and, moreover, to be turned into a steam-vessel; for, though these were the early days of steam, yet Captain Ross was enthusiastic on the subject, and quite convinced that this newly-discovered power would prove very valuable on the icy seas.

It was on the 23rd of May that the 'Victory' left the docks and steamed down the river; but the engine soon proved faulty, and caused several delays, so that it was past the middle of June before they fairly left the British shores. At Douglas, in the Isle of Man, they had to put in for repairs; and again at Port Logan, in order to send Hardy, the stoker, ashore, the poor fellow having had one of his arms nearly torn off by one of the spur-wheels, whilst in the act of oiling the piston-rod.

Another vessel, named the 'John,' had been engaged to join them hereabouts, and to accompany the 'Victory' as far as to the wreck of the 'Fury,' carrying stores out, and returning with her cargo. But the season was now getting advanced; and a suspicion having entered the minds of the 'John's' crew that they would be required to winter in the ice, they demanded from Captain Ross some security that this should not be the case. He refused to give it; and the 'Victory' had, therefore, to proceed alone on her voyage.

Long before they reached Cape Farewell the whole crew were heartily tired of their engine, which was constantly out of order; so that sometimes the captain and engineers were up all night endeavouring to repair the leaks in it, while the men were kept constantly at the bellows to keep the steam up, or gathering ice for the purpose of feeding the boilers.

At length the ship was got into a fine harbour in South Greenland, and made fast to the rocks. The Danish governor and minister came on board; and they had some pleasant intercourse with a few of the Esquimaux of this settlement, who appeared particularly honest and well-behaved.

It was, however, a dangerous coast; and the wreck of a London vessel, the 'Rookwood,' lay in the same harbour.

A bargain was soon struck with the governor for her stores, among which were many things of which they stood greatly in need; and after purchasing some warm winter clothes and skins they pursued their course, passing Disco Island, and running across Davis's Straits into Lancaster Sound, and up Barrow's Straits with a fair wind, and little or no obstruction from the ice.

On the 10th of August, having turned southwards, land was seen on both sides, and it was found that they were actually in Prince Regent's Inlet. The next day they passed Port Bowen ; and, crossing over to the western side, they arrived on the 12th in sight of the very spot where the ' Fury' should have lain.   All the officers went ashore and made a careful search, but no 'Fury' being visible, it was concluded that the moving ice had carried her down, and that she had gone to the bottom.

From the appearance of the tents under which her provisions had been stowed away, it was evident that bears had visited the spot ; but the hermetically sealed casks had entirely prevented these creatures from getting the least notion of what they contained ; and the stores of meat, flour, sugar, cocoa, &c., were consequently as good as when left there by Parry some four years before.

This addition to their supplies, though not perhaps of much apparent value at the time, as the ' Victory' came out with provisions for 1000 days, turned out in the end a most providential one ; and without it the whole crew of twenty-three persons would most likely have perished.   But little did they then imagine how long it would be before they again reached their native shores ; and Ross had no mind to linger here; for just as Parry had succeeded where he failed, so was he now anxious to succeed where Parry had failed.

It was a remarkably favourable season, and the vessel continued her voyage all down the western side of this inlet, the northern part of which had been named by Parry, North Somerset.

They found that the strait led, as the Esquimaux lady, Iligliuk, had said it did, into a large gulf; and this gulf Ross now named after his friend, the Gulf of Boothia: though Sir John Barrow says that it should be the Gulf of Akkolee, because all its western shores are called by the Esquimaux the land of Akkolee. At the bottom of this gulf, on the western side, and just opposite to the Fury and Hecla Strait, was a convenient harbour, to which the captain gave the name of Felix, also after his friend, and there it was soon evident they would have to winter. In fact, by the 8th of October they were fast frozen in.

It was necessary, however, to get the vessel further in shore; as, where she lay, she was exposed to the violence of severe gales. It was a work of considerable difficulty to get a canal cut, through which she might be hauled up, and also to get many of her stores, and especially the powder, removed to a secure spot on the land. This done, it was next discovered that the heavy snow which fell was penetrating through the decks into the berths; and, to remedy this inconvenience, the crew were set to dig holes on shore in search of gravel, which at length they very fortunately found, and with that they covered the upper deck. Then they adopted the curious expedient of putting a thick layer of snow over the gravel; and thus the danger of the berths becoming damp from any drift penetrating into them was obviated.

They had now supplies left for thirty months; but not so large a stock of fuel as they could have wished, the engine having consumed no small portion of it.

The 'Victory' was very inferior to both the 'Hecla' and 'Fury' in point of comfort and convenience; so that the men suffered far more from cold than the crews of those vessels had done. But Captain Ross did his best with the means in his power, and imitated the examples that had been set by Parry and Franklin in the establishment of schools, and in the enforcement of exercise when no active work was required. He had not, however, the same genial nature which had rendered them so beloved by their men; could not descend from the captain to the friend; and though he attended to their welfare in the main, he does not seem to have understood that in this dreary spot they required all the little pleasures and indulgences that could be afforded them. It was well, therefore, perhaps, that so much labour was absolutely necessary in order to make themselves comfortable, and that thus they had less leisure on their hands.

A few bears and wolves now and then afforded them a little sport; and the men used at times to amuse themselves by setting traps for foxes and seals, the skins of which, as well as the oil of the latter, were very valuable to them. Commander James Ross, who had accompanied his uncle, was particularly successful with his seal-traps; and he also shot a few grouse, gulls, and ptarmigan; the two latter belonging to very beautiful species.

The male ptarmigan was perfectly white, with large scarlet eyebrows, and the legs and feet of both male and female were covered with long white feathers down to the claws. One of the gulls was a kittewake, the most elegant bird in the species. Its bill is lemon-colour, its plumage ash, black and white, and its legs a livid shade.

In November the aurora borealis began to appear in the heavens with uncommon splendour. It would be seen first in broad masses, and then suddenly break out into columns and streamers, which spread all over the sky; and, in the absence of the sun, it must have been a never-ending amusement to watch its varying forms and colours. The rays vary in colour, and are sometimes of a steel-grey, yellowish-grey, pea-green, golden, violet, or purple; at others every description of red, pink, or orange; sometimes the beams take the form of arches, and are tinged with black; sometimes it appears very high in the heavens, while at others it seems to flash across the earth like lightning.

Commander James Ross endeavoured to ascertain the truth regarding the noises which some persons speak of as accompanying this appearance,

but he could come to no conclusion.   Its influence
on the magnet had, however, been pretty well ascertained, and chiefly by observations made by Franklin,
Richardson, and Back, as we have before stated.
Early in January, however, they had a pleasanter
and more cheering interruption to their solitude,
for the report of one of their guns brought them
some human visitors.

Captain Ross was on shore when Allan M'Inniss,
the second engineer, shouted that he heard strange
voices, and a few minutes after a tribe of Esquimaux
were seen on the beach.   So the officers instantly
went off in search of the captain; and a friendly
intercourse was soon established with these people,
although at first they were rather shy.

An old man, who had to be drawn on a sledge,
was introduced first, together with his son Tullooachia,
who had but one leg.   They were found to have
come from the south, and to be well acquainted
with the surrounding country, and when introduced
into the cabin, and shown the various pictures and
charts, they were easily made to comprehend their
meaning and use.   Like those whom Parry had
met, they were soon ready enough to contribute
charts themselves; and in drawing them it was remarked that they always noted the places where
provisions were to be found, necessity having
sharpened their wits in this matter.   They described the land to the south as only a narrow strait
dividing two seas, the correctness of which statement it was determined to ascertain as soon as the
spring returned.

These poor people were very different from those whom Franklin had met in the north; they were good-humoured, peaceable, and evidently pleased with their visitors. They also gave token of possessing a virtue not common among savages, namely, gratitude; for in return for the presents bestowed on them they seemed anxious to perform any acts of kindness in their power. They were an ingenious people, too; and their clothes and various domestic implements, sledges, knives, and spears, showed considerable skill. The men and women dressed exactly alike, and in winter they wore a double suit of clothes, both sets being made of skins; the fur of one against the flesh, and of the other outside. These clothes were neatly made, being sewed firmly with bone needles and moss thread. The women carried their infants either in their hoods or in their enormous boots, the latter of which served as general store-rooms, even food being kept in them.

It was a curious sight to watch these Esquimaux when hunting for seals. The first thing they did was to build a semicircular snow-hut near to a seal's hole; and in this they would sit crouched down for hours, no matter how great the cold, watching for the appearance of the desired snout, like a cat watching for a mouse. When it came up the hunter would make no movement, but remain still and quiet, almost holding his breath, until the animal had got to some distance from its hole, when he suddenly rushed upon him and killed him with his spear.

Some persons may possibly be curious to know how savages amputate a broken leg; so it may be worth while to describe the manner in which the operation was performed on Tullooachia. In the first place, the upper part of the leg had been bound tightly with leathern thongs; then all the flesh stripped off the lower part with their rude knives, the bone placed in a hole in the ice and snapped asunder. The surgeon of the 'Victory,' however, thought that a new one might be made for the poor fellow; so he called the carpenter to come and take his measure. As soon as Tullooachia understood what was proposed he went into a rapturous fit of delight, and when it was finished and fitted on, his joy was still more extravagant, and he walked about with it in the proudest manner.

In April, Commander James Ross began his journeys across the land, of which he made five or six, discovering at different times the narrow isthmus of Boothia, its width—only about fifteen miles, with a lake in the centre—and the strait to the west, which bears his name. He seems to have been the only man on board at all acquainted with geology, natural history, and botany, and in each department he collected numerous specimens. In fact, most of the discoveries of every kind that were made during this voyage, if not all, were made by him. On his journeys some of the Esquimaux generally accompanied him as guides; but on the third occasion, when visiting their village before starting, for the purpose of securing some companions, a most extraordinary change seemed to have come over the people. Perfect silence reigned there, and instead of the usual welcome, a number of Esquimaux were soon perceived approaching, fully armed, and all the women and children set on one side behind them—a sure sign of war. All at once an old man sprang out of a hut, and began brandishing his knives in the air with the most furious gestures. He looked wild and furious, and would have rushed on his visitors had not his two sons pinioned his arms.

Commander Ross attempted in vain to obtain an explanation; but when others appeared ready to second the old man, and formed themselves into two lines, in order to cut off his retreat to the vessel, he and his companion, the surgeon, lowered their guns, and were about to fire. Happily, this motion was sufficient; for the whole company took to their heels and fled.

After some time one woman timidly approached; and from her they learnt that a young adopted son of the old man, having died in consequence of a stone falling on his head, the English were suspected of having caused the disaster by magic, in which the Esquimaux have a firm belief; and therefore they determined to have their revenge. After a considerable expenditure of eloquence, Commander Ross persuaded them, however, that it was all a dream of their own imagination; and then he started off with his three guides.

In the month of June the crew began to be em-

THE GOOD UNDERSTANDING BETWEEN THE ESQUIMAUX AND WHITES DISTURBED.

ployed in preparing the 'Victory' for her departure from Felix harbour, although it must be some time yet before the ice opened. But there was plenty of amusement as well as work at that season, when all kinds of animals and birds flock back to their usual haunts.

Both Captain Ross and his nephew made various expeditions into the country: and the latter was indefatigable in his endeavours to find out more of the geography of the country, in order that they might be prepared to sail in the most eligible direction as soon as the ice broke up.

He used to go out with sledges drawn by dogs, but on the 14th of this month he came back with only two out of nine of these animals : their provisions having fallen so short, that he had been obliged to kill the others. Thus the labour for the men had been greatly increased, and on their return they looked almost ghastly from want and fatigue.

The Commander was also disheartened, because he had failed to discover a passage out of the gulf; and he determined now to try in a more southerly direction for an opening.

It was not, however, until the 4th of September that the vessel was able to leave Felix harbour, although it had appeared probable that she might get out in July; and even when off, she had scarcely gone three times her own length before she grounded on a rock, slipped off, and grounded again on the bottom of the water.

As quickly as possible her stores were got out, and placed on shore, in order to lighten her; but the most intense anxiety was felt as to whether she would float next high tide. It was almost a question of life and death to the crew; and at any rate, should she remain fixed, their only alternative must be to proceed in their boats to Baffin's Bay, and there obtain a passage home in some whaler. But no whaler could be looked for that season; and so there would be no alternative but to winter once more on that dreary coast.

The tide, however, came rolling in; the ship began to heave; and intense was the relief experienced when the watch on the bows shouted, 'She floats! she floats!'

But September was getting on, and the young ice again forming; so that there was no time to be lost. On the 17th, however, a strong wind opened the ice; and the ship was got under sail, and proceeded about four miles. Then it was fastened to an iceberg, to wait until next morning.

This step seems to have been a false one; at least it was thought by some that the Captain might, by a bolder course, have been able to clear the narrow passage, and get out into the open sea.

No doubt the position was a difficult one; but the opportunity was certainly lost: and soon the pressure of the ice became so great, that there remained no alternative but to get the 'Victory' back into her old quarters; and how the hearts of the crew sank within them, may not be easily imagined.

The consequence, however, was the discovery of the Western Magnetic Pole; of which Parry had been in search during his several voyages.   He had, as we have related, observed the sluggishness of the magnet about long. 93° 30′, and lat. 70° N., and surmised that they were near that point; but in order to discover the exact spot it was necessary to have placed the needle where it should not move at all.

This Commander James Ross accomplished; and having done so, he writes that he 'leaves his readers to imagine his transports,' and how 'all his perils and fatigues were forgotten;' while he 'felt as if he had nothing to do but to go home and be happy for the rest of his days.'

That winter passed, and August came again, when they must try once more to get the 'Victory' out of its harbour.

Yet once more were they doomed to disappointment; for she came out only to be forced to enter another harbour, and pass a third winter there.

It was in the month of April, 1832, that they came at last to the sorrowful conclusion that, if saved at all, it must be by abandoning their poor vessel, and proceeding northward with their stores, partly in boats, carried overland, and partly in sledges.

This course was now decided on; but so terrible was the labour of the undertaking, and so often had they to return to the ship, that, by the end of the month, although they had traversed 110 miles, yet they were only eighteen from the spot whence they started.

On the 28th of May they drank a final glass of grog on board the ship, and sadly bid adieu to their old friend. It was the 1st of July when they reached Fury Point, where still some supplies remained, and anxiously did they watch the ice in the vain hope of getting into Davis's Strait before the whalers went home. A fourth winter had to be passed at Fury Point; and July came round again before they could make another effort. This time they got half way up the inlet to Batty's Gulf; but there, again, they had to stop awhile, watching the weather in agonies of hope and fear.

At length a clear passage opened one evening; and by four next morning all the crew were cutting a passage through the brush ice on the bank, and once more the boats were launched. It was truly a last attempt; for if again driven back to Port Fury they must all have perished by starvation, or by the jaws of wild beasts; but this time the channel continued to open and to widen. They went on and on, past Leopold Isle, and the east point of the strait.

Forced once by a hurricane to land at York Cape, they went on next day, and did not rest again until the 25th of August.

They then landed again, set up their tents, and were repairing their boats, when the joyful word, ' A sail!' was heard from the watch; and every one sprang to his feet, asking, ' Is it a sail, or only an iceberg?'

Quickly their boats were launched once more; but there was little wind, and their progress was but slow. But no disappointment awaited them this time: their doubts were soon at an end, for a ship was distinctly seen. More than that, a second at the same time appeared from the north, and the crew believed that they were seen.

But no; one vessel, at least, has not perceived them: for she is spreading her sails, and is soon out of sight.

It was a moment almost of despair; but the captain cheered his men by declaring, what he scarcely believed, that they were now nearing the other.

A calm, however, providentially saved them: they pushed on vigorously, and were perceived.

A boat was lowered from the vessel, and approached Ross's boat.

'You have lost your vessel?' said the officer in command.

'Yes,' replied Ross; 'and we entreat you to receive us on board. What is the name of your vessel?'

'The "Isabella," once commanded by Captain Ross,' answered the officer.

'I am that Captain Ross,' replied the latter; ' and these men were the crew of the "Victory."'

'Impossible!' returned the other; 'for Ross has been dead these two years!'

We need not enter on the means taken to convince him. Suffice it to say, that Ross was soon on board his old vessel, receiving the enthusiastic cheers of the whole crew, and that all the rescued men were treated by Captain Humphreys with the greatest kindness.

The scene that followed could only be described by an eye-witness; so we will not attempt it.

Every one had to talk, and every one had to listen. There was news, public and private, to be inquired into and communicated. The rescued crew, too, had to eat, wash, shave, and dress, at one and the same time. It was a scene of delightful confusion.

But in the 'Victory's' crew, which had already been diminished by some deaths, there were several sick men. These were overpowered with attention, for every one was anxious to serve them.

To those who had so long been used to hardships, and to sleeping on rocks and snow, the ordinary comforts of life had lost their charm.

They could not sleep in beds; and even the captain states that he was obliged to throw himself into an arm-chair, in order to get any sleep.

On the 19th of October they arrived in London, where the case of Ross was brought before a Committee of the House of Commons, who immediately voted him a sum of 5000l. to make up for his losses, while double pay was given to the men up to the time of their abandonment of the ship, and full pay after that time till their arrival in England. Good situations in the dockyards were also given to them.

BOATS OF THE 'VICTORY' SAVED BY THE 'ISABELLA.'

Commander Ross was appointed to the command of the 'Victory' for a year, that he might at the end of that time receive post-rank; while Mr. Booth, the patron of the expedition, was created a baronet.

Captain Ross afterwards obtained the honour of knighthood.

CHAPTER XII.

SIR GEORGE BACK'S JOURNEY, AND MESSRS. DEASE AND SIMPSON'S DISCOVERIES.

WE have seen Captain Ross and his party through all their difficulties, and once more safely at home, receiving the congratulations of their friends, as well as the rewards and honours which were freely lavished upon them. But we must remember, that from the time that they entered Regent's Inlet until the 'Isabella' returned with her double crew, the British public knew nothing either of their proceedings or their fate. Consequently, almost as general a state of excitement prevailed on the subject as has since been felt about Sir John Franklin.

Ross's was not, it is true, a Government expedition; but for all that, when the duty of sending an expedition to the rescue of so many brave Englishmen was pressed on the nation, first by Dr. Richardson, and then by numerous other persons of weight and standing, Government was by no means backward to lend its assistance. A committee of those most deeply interested was soon formed, and public meetings on the subject held. Captain Ross's friends were willing to put down a large sum towards the necessary expenses, and a considerable addition was raised by subscription; while the Hudson's Bay Company most readily offered supplies of provisions, and every assistance in their power.

But all this would have been very useless, had not a suitable leader early volunteered his own personal services; for, indeed, except under an able man, no one would then have dared to risk other lives in search of those which, for aught any one could tell, had been already sacrificed.

An able man, probably the ablest that could be found for this service, had, however, offered himself as soon as he heard of the anxiety that prevailed. This was no other than Captain Back, once the young and ardent companion of Captain Franklin, who, being in Italy at the time, immediately hastened home, and put himself into communication with the leading parties.

His offer was promptly and thankfully accepted, and a scheme rapidly proposed and matured for an Arctic land expedition to the shores of the Polar Sea, and primarily to those parts which it was known that Captain Ross intended to visit.

By the usual track of fur-dealers, and, it may be added, by the very route taken by Sir Alexander Mackenzie, the party were to proceed as rapidly as possible to Norway House, on Lake Winnipeg, from thence on to Great Slave Lake, somewhere in the neighbourhood of which it was known that there was a river called by the Indians Thlew-ee-choh-desseth, or Great Fish River—*desseth* meaning river; and this, it was supposed, emptied itself into the sea somewhere in the neighbourhood of Ross's proposed circuit of exploration.

Back had, as we have seen, accompanied Franklin, first on his visit to the Coppermine, and afterwards to the Mackenzie River; and although thirteen years older than when we first made his acquaintance, he had evidently lost nothing of his enthusiastic ardour, although he had added to it a large amount of knowledge and experience.

Mr. Richard King, a surgeon and naturalist, was appointed to accompany him, and three men only were to be taken from England; but those three had all been out with Franklin.

On the 9th of February, 1833, they started from Liverpool for New York, which they at length reached safely, though after an unusually tedious and boisterous passage. It will be remembered that New York was Franklin's starting-place on the last occasion, as Fort York, on Hudson's Bay, had been the first time.

Here Back was received with every demonstration of esteem, and of sympathy in his undertaking; yet he delayed not a moment, but at once proceeded by steamboat to Albany, and from thence to Montreal by coaches and waggons, every hour being precious.

It was not till the 9th of April, however, that they reached Montreal, where the Captain received a communication from Mr. Keith, the principal officer of the Hudson's Bay Company at La Chine, stating that 'all preparations were hurrying on, and that provisions were being hoarded for them at every station in their route;' but he added, that the best assistants would be obtained at the still distant Norway House, among the 'old winterers.' All was so far favourable; but, on the other hand, Back had the mortification of discovering, during this short delay at Montreal, that two of his three men had lost heart, under the impression that the sympathy which was everywhere manifested betokened coming danger; and it was with difficulty that their services could be retained,—only, in fact, by sending them on at once to begin their journey.

Meantime, four fine fellows in the Royal Artillery there had volunteered their services; and Back, who was now particularly glad to secure any checks on his own refractory men, procured their leave of absence; and thus reinforced, they embarked at La Chine in canoes, on the noble river St. Lawrence, down which they shot rapidly under the able conduct of Paul, an old Iroquois, whose knowledge of all the rapids in their route made him a valuable servant, in spite of his propensity for strong drink.

At a short distance down the St. Lawrence they turned off into the Ottawa, one of its branches; and after passing the rapid St. Anne, encamped on an island in the lake of the Two Mountains; beyond which, by permission, they paddled through the government canal, in order to escape the dangerous rapid, Long Sault.

At the next portage they were entertained by an old dealer, who so warmly entered into their undertaking that he said it was with difficulty that he could restrain himself from bearing them company.

Through Lake Nipising they passed into one of the five larger ones,—Lake Huron, and so into Lake Superior, whose deep, clear waters, and abundant fish, well justify its name. But the navigation on this lake is sometimes very dangerous, on account of the thick fogs which suddenly envelop the voyager; and in one of these they were entangled for a time: but after a good many narrow escapes, the guide, in some incomprehensible manner, and without the aid of the compass, contrived to steer them through. So, on the 20th of May, under a salute of guns, the party landed at Fort William; at which place, in anticipation of the many coming portages, they exchanged their larger canoes for others that could be more easily carried; and Captain Back made a regular distribution of crews and ' pieces.'

This was a point which it was by no means easy to settle to the satisfaction of the *voyageurs,* as they well knew, by painful experience, what a vast difference even a small addition to the weight of any package might make: accordingly, a great deal of balancing and disputing went on, as the Captain made it to be understood that nothing then settled could afterwards be altered.

Their next encampment was at a spot of extraordinary beauty in the neighbourhood of Mountain Falls, which are but little smaller than those of Wilberforce or Niagara, and even superior to them in respect of picturesque effect.

Just beyond this they received, at Savannah portage, letters from England.

On the river of the same name they obtained

from some Sautous Indians an abundance of large sturgeon. For a fish weighing fifty pounds, one of the men only paid a pint of peas; though it afterwards appeared that the Indians expected some payment beyond that which they named, for when Back's party were taking leave they were suddenly assailed by a volley of fishes' heads and pieces of turf.

These Indians dressed their hair in plaits, ornamented with feathers, and wore brass rings in their ears and on their fingers; but although they had evidently been in the habit of trading with white people, they went, during the summer, almost naked.

On the 6th of June they had reached the bottom of Lake Winnipeg; but as Governor Simpson, who was to meet him there, had not yet arrived, Captain Back was obliged to content himself with making observations for the dip of the horizon in the interval.

On the 10th Mr. Simpson came, and his report of the assistance to be provided for them was very encouraging. In particular,— in order to induce certain desirable persons to accompany them, they were promised early promotion, and an increase of salary at once.

But, notwithstanding all that could be done, it was evident that it must be a work of time to reach the sea; and, indeed, few of the party even hoped to do so before the summer of 1834. The Captain's impatience was, however, fully equalled by that of the poor *voyageurs*, who, in addition to their heavy work, had to bear, while on land, the dreadful torment caused by mosquitoes and sand-flies, which

came in such myriads that all defence was impossible: and sometimes caused the blood to stream
down their faces.   So all parties were anxious to get
afloat once more; and having embarked on the lake
they reached its opposite end on the 17th, and were
gladly received at Norway House, where they succeeded in hiring men, though at a very high rate
of wages.

Here the real journey was to begin; and here,
therefore, Captain Back entrusted the command of
the boats, containing the chief part of the heavy luggage, to Mr. King, and prepared to go on himself, as
soon as he had completed his crew, in search of the
Thlew-ee-Choh river.

On the 28th of June he was able to leave Norway
House, proceeding in a light canoe, and with a heart
' full of hope and joy.'   In his journal he called this
' a happy day for him;' ' for now,' he says, ' he was
in a fair way to verify the anticipations of his
friends:' and, he added, that his spirits were raised
to a more than ordinary pitch of excitement.

It was his first great object to push on to the
Athabaska and Slave Lakes, and on his way to ascertain, if possible, the direction of the Thlew-ee-Choh
river.

A strong gale, however, obliged him to land and
wait awhile; and as ' a moody fit was gathering,' he
took his gun and plunged into a thick wood, until the
weather became calm.   However, next day he overtook Mr. King's boats in Sturgeon River, which is
one continuous rapid, and beheld them ' sometimes,

unable to resist the impetuous force of the current, swept back ; at others, suspended on the arched back of a descending wave, struggling and labouring, until again in the shelter of a friendly eddy.' They were, however, working safely and steadily, as he saw at a glance : nevertheless, his own frail canoe, with its motley crew of English, Canadians, Métifs (half-breeds), and Indians, glided quickly past them, under the wonderful guidance of De Charloit, a Métif steersman.

On the 21st of July, after passing through some small lakes and portages, they arrived wearied, foot-sore, and nearly maddened by the attacks of their tiny persecutors, at Portage La Roche, a high ridge of ground, where, after labouring through thick woods, they came suddenly out on to a wondrous prospect — a large extent of country, all in its summer dress, lying spread out below them, at the distance of a thousand feet.

Even the most jaded of the party stood here a moment, lost in silent astonishment ; but Back had passed this romantic spot twice before, and all his desire now seemed to be to get on.

On the borders of Little Lake they were obliged, however, to encamp ; for the men were utterly ex-hausted. Disposing quickly of their burdens they threw themselves on their faces, and remained for an hour perfectly motionless. Then the canoe was re-gummed, and all embarked again.

At Pine Portage, on the other side, they obtained a welcome addition to their number in the person of

Mr. M'Leod, whom Governor Simpson had so much desired to join them; and his help was quickly found to be most valuable, as they soon met with some Indians, from whose old chief, 'the Camarade de Mandeville,' as he was called, they hoped to obtain intelligence respecting their route to the river; and Mr. M'Leod soon showed them that he knew the way to manage him.

A formal meeting, commenced 'by the Indians' beloved social puff, was convened; and patiently did Mr. M'Leod listen to his long stories, until at length the Camarade was induced to sketch the position of the Thlew-ee-Choh, and the river which he called the Teh-lon, or Little Fish River, which ran parallel to it, and by his account was far safer.

It was afterwards found all along the route that the Indians had everywhere the same abhorrence of this Thlew-ee-Choh; and the Camarade at length impatiently declared, that 'if the Great Chief persisted in going by it he must travel alone, as no Indians would accompany him.'

Afterwards the reports of other Indians were taken; and, much perplexed by their conflicting accounts, Back determined to go himself in search of it : so, leaving five men to escort Mr. M'Leod to the east part of Slave Lake, where he was to prepare them winter quarters, and saying that he might be expected in September, he embarked once more on the lake with four men, after having left written directions for Mr. King, to be delivered to him when he should come up with the boats.

It was now the 11th of August, and on the 19th, having passed under mountain heights of Alpine grandeur, they reached the entrance of the steep and rocky Hoarfrost River; and after a most fatiguing journey of a week, through several little

Portage on Hoarfrost River.

lakes and over many portages, they landed; and, on ascending a very high hill, Captain Back saw before him an immense expanse of water, in which were many small islands, and which he named Aylmer Lake, after the Governor-General of Canada.

Several parties of Indians had been passed in the latter part of the way, and some had been induced to accompany them; so from this lake Maufelley, the interpreter, with three other Indians, were sent on to look for the river, being victualled for three days; but meantime Back himself accidentally discovered its source; on which, throwing himself on the ground, he says he rapturously drank a hearty draught of its clear waters.

The men returned soon after laden with game, and having found the river; so this event was celebrated by a draught of grog divided amongst the crew.

The Thlew-ee-Choh has since received the name of Back's River, by which it is now known.

On the 31st of August they embarked on it, and continued to meet with many Indians as they proceeded up its course; among whom were two of those whom Captain Back had formerly known, and who belonged to his old friend Akaitcho's party.

They soon came to a series of such rapids as fully justified the Indians' dread, and which their canoe was too weak to run, in spite of all Charloît's skilful management; so they were, therefore, obliged to return to their encampment, having, indeed, been compelled to abandon the canoe, and finish their journey on foot.

They met Mr. M'Leod at the junction of a small river with Great Slave Lake, and found that their winter house, Fort Reliance, was almost complete; but that, unhappily, it was constantly surrounded, and the hall almost filled, with crowds of starving

Indians. Their own stock of provisions was by no means too large, and they had wished to reserve the pemmican and dried meats till they reached the sea; but Captain Back was not the man to turn a deaf ear to the entreaties of hungry people, and he could never resist the cry of a child for food.

The adults, it is true, rarely complained, though worn to mere skeletons; but, nevertheless, a strong feeling took possession of them that the various observations made with the scientific instruments were for the purpose of 'raising the Devil,' and that this was the real cause of the scarcity: so that it was almost essential to mollify them with gifts.

In the end of November Akaitcho himself very opportunely arrived, and brought with him a little meat. This curious old man, Indian-like, did not ask after either Captain Franklin or Dr. Richardson, though he seemed pleased to hear about them, and to receive little remembrances from them. He was a great assistance to the party, as his influence helped to maintain order; and with him some of the party were at last persuaded to leave the fort, while others went out to fish at a lake, of which one of his Indians had told them. De Charloît and some of the men were also now discharged, according to agreement; besides it being important to save the pemmican, they were glad to reduce the party.

It was a fearful winter; yet but for Akaitcho's firm friendship things would have been far worse. He regularly started every morning on a hunt, and, being an excellent huntsman, often procured supplies. Still, with every alleviation, it was a dreadful time. A deep melancholy fixed itself on the mind, even of Back himself, in spite of all his efforts to cheer others. This was especially the case when, early in April, he learnt that Augustus, his old and faithful Esquimaux interpreter, had been on his way to join him, but that it was apprehended that he had been starved to death on his road; for this intelligent young man had come to be regarded quite as a friend.

A sharp knock at the door on the 23rd of April, the anniversary of their departure from La Chine, terminated this moody state. The knock was instantly followed by the entrance of the man without, who, thrusting an English despatch into the Captain's hand, exclaimed,—

' He is returned, sir!'

' What! Augustus? Thank God!' answered Back.

' Captain Ross, sir! Captain Ross is returned!' replied the man.

They could scarcely believe the good news, but two extracts from English papers confirmed the despatch now hastily read; and, ' in the fulness of their hearts, they assembled together, and humbly offered up their thanks to God' for ' so wonderful a preservation.'

The whole day was passed in a state of feverish excitement, a treat given to the men, and the joyful occasion turned into a festival.

Free, therefore, from this great anxiety, Back

prepared, as early as possible, to pursue the other object of his journey; and on the 1st of June, the weather being then very sultry, they left Fort Reliance—not, however, in as good spirits as might be expected, for the news of the melancholy end of poor Augustus had just been confirmed, while there was reason to fear that Williamson, one of the artillerymen, had perished on his way home with the despatches with which he had been entrusted.

On the 28th their boat was launched on Back's River; and soon after they had to take leave of their excellent friends, Mr. M'Leod and the chief Akaitcho. The former, besides being a very good friend in other ways, was a first-rate hunter, and had been of the greatest service to the party, which he promised to rejoin in September.

The voyage down this river was, indeed, difficult. For a time the ice impeded their progress; but on its breaking up they entered on a course of rapids, lakes, and cascades, such as they had never seen before. A less determined man would, probably, never have reached the sea; but Back had resolved to do so, and nothing short of absolute impossibility could ever stop him.

He had imagined that the mouth of the river would be found in Bathurst's Inlet; and, therefore, its turnings and twistings, eastward and southward, rendered him almost frantic with impatience. The roar of the water of some of the cascades could be heard a mile off; and not a single tree adorned its course for more than five hundred miles.

R

Pelly, Garry, and Mac Dougal lakes being passed and named, they came lastly to Lake Franklin, where they met with some very friendly Esquimaux, who assisted the crew over the last and most difficult portage; and thus they reached Point Victoria, and

Esquimaux at the Portage.

found themselves on the sea-coast, no very great distance from the farthest points attained by Sir James Ross.

Naming the various points of the western peninsula of Adelaide, Back attempted, according to his instructions, to reach the Point Turnagain of Franklin; but the state of the ice rendered this impracticable, even to him. A land journey along the coast was next planned and attempted; but as they sank knee-deep at every step, and had scarcely any water to drink, this idea also had to be relinquished. After raising and saluting the British flag, they returned, therefore, by the former route; that is, up the same wild and turbulent river.

Faithful to his promise, Mr. M'Leod met him at Musk-Ox Lake; and during the ensuing winter Akaitcho proved himself, as of old, a most excellent ally.

An hour every other night was devoted to the instruction of the men, and Sunday was always a day of rest. They were not lonely, having again plenty of Indian society: nevertheless, the early arrival of the packet from England was a great treat, and with the first breaking up of the cold all were eager to get away.

Mr. King was directed to proceed with the Europeans to York Factory, at the proper season; and Captain Back himself, being obliged to return through Canada, left Fort Reliance on the 21st of March, and reached Norway House by the end of June.

As he proceeded exactly by the old route, nothing worthy of note occurred on this homeward journey, except a visit which he paid at one place to a mission station amongst the Indians, which appears to have excited great interest in his mind.

'Two hundred converts,' he writes, 'had been

gathered into the Church by the worthy missionary during the space of only two years;' and it is impossible to help regretting that this visit had not been paid on his journey out. For if all Christian men, and some of these Arctic officers we believe to have been really such — if all these, who were thus compelled to pass whole months in the company of Indians and Esquimaux, had but set themselves heartily to the work of preaching the Gospel among them, what grand results might not have been the fruit of the Arctic voyages!

Captain Back had been absent from England, as we have seen, for two years; yet his ardour was not abated, and he was quite ready for any other reasonable expedition that might be proposed.

One was suggested almost immediately by the Royal Geographical Society, and the idea adopted by the Admiralty.

Its object was to sail direct to Wager River or Repulse Bay, and from thence to proceed, by means of several land parties, to examine the bottom of Prince Regent's Inlet, the coast towards Fury and Hecla Strait, and that to the westward as far as Cape Turnagain.

And their Lordships of the Admiralty, in their instructions, gave it as their decided opinion, that all this might be done in one season; and 'that this Arctic expedition might be distinguished from all others, by the promptness of its execution, and by escaping the gloomy and unprofitable waste of eight months' detention.'

No doubt, if the thing could have been done, Back was just the man to do it: but it seems to be of very little use to make plans regarding time for people who are destined to work in these icy seas. The expedition was certainly distinguished from all others; but not in the way that these gentlemen expected.

It started in June, 1836, and returned not until the autumn of 1837; and then without having accomplished anything!

For nine whole months were they wedged up in the ice; not, however, in any chosen harbour, but on a floating mass of ice, driven about at the mercy of the elements, and without being able to control the ship in the slightest degree. Indeed, for four months of the time they were fixed in a sort of icy cradle. Yet no blame seems to have been attached to any one; while 'the tranquillity and constant good-humour of Captain Back, and the unremitting exertions of Lieutenant Smyth,' are spoken of by Sir J. Barrow as 'above all praise.'

Captain Back had been told that he might choose between Frozen Strait and the Welcome in proceeding to the point at which his first sea-voyage was to terminate; and he chose the former, because Parry had been so successful there: while from the Welcome Captain Lyon had escaped with difficulty and danger.

On entering Davis's Strait they saw an enormous iceberg, of 300 feet high; and shortly after beheld the fall and formation of another. This was near Savage Islands, in the neighbourhood of which they were

hailed by a fleet of kajaks and oomiaks, with the cry
of ' *Teyma*—Peace;' and a curious kind of barter
was opened. Some of the native articles proved,
however, more unsaleable than their owners expected: as, for instance, children offered in exchange
for a few needles, by their own mothers; and a
young woman's hair generously offered by its possessor
to a rather bald officer, at the low price of a curtain
ring !

Past Salisbury and Nottingham Isles they sailed
smoothly and easily; and now, keeping to his resolution, Captain Back steered to the north of the
large one, known as Southampton Island; to the
north of which was Middleton's Frozen Strait and
Repulse Bay, into which, like Parry, he hoped to
sail easily.

But Middleton's difficulties were small compared
with the troubles that awaited Captain Back; for,
by the 5th of September, they were firmly fixed in
the ice: the weather was foggy, and the compasses
not to be trusted.

Here, therefore, they were 'thumped about
amidst the hummocks of ice, and severely nipped,
apparently only about four miles from land; but
closely blocked in by packed ice, and not a pool of
water visible anywhere.'

' To the mercy of Providence alone,' Back says,
' could they look for rescue from their perilous situation;' and he adds, ' that none but they who have
experienced it can judge of the weariness of heart,
the blank of feeling, the sickliness of taste, which

get the better of the whole man, under circumstances such as these.'

All September were they thus whirled about in the vicinity of old Baffin's Cape Comfort, and by the end of it the captain and all the officers had come to the conclusion that nothing more could be attempted in that direction. Seeing, then, no prospect of escape for months to come, they were about to cut a dock for the ship, when suddenly a violent commotion took place in the ice; one large mass coming in contact with a smaller one, and crushing it to powder, while the ship was driven about in imminent danger.

'Thus,' says Back, 'ended a month of vexation, disappointment, and anxiety; to me personally, more distressing and intolerable than the worst pressure of the worst evils which had befallen me in any expedition.'

This was strong language for one who had been in the navy since he was twelve years old; who had seen much service in the Peninsular War; been taken prisoner; had accompanied Franklin on his two Arctic land journeys, and made one himself: but if we consider his position we shall, perhaps, agree with him.

In the first place, there was the hourly danger of wreck and destruction from the violent collision of the ship with the ice; then the crew themselves had little or no work, and were a constant source of anxiety. There were only a few 'men-of-war men' among them, he tells us: 'the rest were chiefly undisciplined whale-fishermen, or colliers; and instead of the hearty good-will, sociability, and above-board manner of regular tars, there prevailed a spirit of suspicion, which was anything but conducive to comfort and quiet.'

One man died, and sickness prevailed to some extent : while the cold was intense.

The officers, however, did their best both to amuse and instruct the crew; and their efforts seem to have been not altogether unavailing.

But still more alarming circumstances were yet to take place.

In February an opening in the floe was noticed; and soon the crack widened and lengthened until it passed directly through the centre on which the ship stood.

A hoarse, rushing sound was heard; the ship groaned and strained; and the crashing, grinding, and rushing noises underneath were appalling. At length all communication with the shore was cut off by the breaking up of the floes into masses; and though the ship was now in the water, she could not move.

The ice formed again, however, under the vessel, and other similar convulsions took place; so that it seemed often little short of a miracle that the ship could live.

Sometimes enormous waves of ice, like the side of a house, were dashed against the vessel; and still, even in June, it stuck to the ship in such a manner that she seemed in a mould.

Early in July the crew began to work at cutting this away, and making a trench; and on the 11th, when her deliverance was effected, Back was just in the act of descending to his cabin, when a 'loud rumbling noise announced that she had broken her icy bounds, and was sliding gently down into her own element.' 'It was a sight,' he says, 'not to be forgotten,' and hastily did he run on deck to join in the general cheers.

Still, there she lay for several days on her beamends, so that no one could walk on deck without holding on to the ropes. Quite suddenly, at last, she righted; and a scene followed which no one who saw it could ever forget.

Nothing remained then but to make the best of the way home with the poor battered vessel, which was in such a crazy condition that, had not a favourable wind blown them quickly to their native shores, the 'Terror' must have foundered before she reached them.

So ended this extraordinary voyage, and Captain Back soon after was rewarded for all his troubles by the honour of knighthood; which, notwithstanding that this voyage was an utterly fruitless one, no man ever more entirely merited.

He was not on this occasion able to contribute anything towards the completion of the survey of this northern coast; but that work was finished during the next two years by two gentlemen belonging to the Hudson's Bay Company, Mr. Dease and Mr. Simpson.

In 1837 they traced the whole space left between the utmost point westward attained by Franklin on his second journey, and that to which the boat sent round Icy Cape to meet him by Captain Beechey of the 'Blossom,' had attained, a distance of 160 miles.

Encouraged by this success, they started again next year from Fort Confidence on Great Bear Lake, and reaching the sea by Dease's River, encamped at the mouth of the Coppermine, whence, after being imprisoned by the ice for some days, they succeeded in pursuing their course westward past Cape Barrow, round Arctic Sound, for they could not cross its opening; past Barry Isles and Cape Flinders, just beyond Franklin's furthest encampment eastward, where, for twenty-two days, they were utterly blocked up by the ice.

Determined, however, not to go back, and, in fact, unable to do so, Mr. Simpson started off with an exploring party on foot, with a wooden-framed canvas canoe and tent, which they carried with them, in addition to their provisions.

Thus they quickly reached Cape Franklin; and, in three days after, on ascending some high ground, Mr. Simpson suddenly came in sight of the welcome view of an open ocean rolling beneath his feet. He had reached, in fact, to the further extremity of Dease's Strait, and stood on a headland, to which he gave the name of Cape Alexander; while he named the whole country northward Victoria Land.

But a short distance, comparatively speaking, now remained between that point and the late discoveries of Captain Back and Captain James Ross; but this line of coast had to be left for a future voyage, as the season was far advanced, and some of the men had fallen lame.

The next season happened to be a favourable one, so that they reached Cape Alexander a month earlier than in 1838, and by the 11th of August reached Simpson's Strait; and, passing Points Richardson and Ogle, came, on the 16th, to Montreal Island, where a *cache of pemmican*, left by Sir George Back five years before, was found.

Encouraged by this wonderful success, the two enterprising explorers determined to ascertain still more about the country beyond. So round the peninsula of Adelaide they sailed, past Victoria Headland, which they knew at once from Back's drawing, and so, crossing a fine bay, ran about forty miles to the north-east, till they came in sight of what was probably a part of Boothia.

The wind changed then, so they were forced to return. By the 24th of September they once more reached Fort Confidence, after a voyage along this northern coast, with which no previous one can be compared in length, having bravely battled with dangers, and successfully overcome difficulties, of which it is impossible for those who have not experienced similar ones to form any idea.

CHAPTER XIII.

SIR JOHN FRANKLIN'S LAST VOYAGE, AND SOME OF THE
EXPEDITIONS SENT IN SEARCH OF HIM.

CAPTAIN BACK'S melancholy voyage in 1836 seems
to have had the effect of somewhat damping the
courage of our countrymen; for it was not until
eight years later that another Arctic expedition was
proposed.

Meantime, however, the 'Terror' had been put
into thorough repair, and in company with the
'Erebus' had been again encountering ice and storms
in Antarctic regions, under the command of Sir
James Ross; while the successes of Messrs. Dease
and Simpson once more whetted men's appetites for
fame and distinction: so that Sir J. Barrow's new
proposition for one final attempt to find the passage
was pretty sure to meet with supporters.

It must be remembered, too, that although much
had been suffered in former attempts, and some of
these had been attended with little or no success, yet
in modern times no exploring party had been lost.

Nor was Sir John Barrow the only one who still

retained all his former eagerness about the complete settlement of the old puzzle. He was fully supported by Lieut.-Colonel Sabine, who thought that thereby great service would be rendered to those scientific subjects to which he had almost devoted his life; and the enthusiasm of Sir John Franklin himself was such, that when a doubt was raised about the propriety of sending out so old a man, his friend, Sir Edward Parry, said,—'If you do not let him go, the man will die of disappointment.'

Sir John Franklin was, however, spared that kind of death.

In May, 1845, he sailed as commander of the 'Erebus,' and of the expedition; Captain Crozier, who had accompanied Sir James Ross in his Antarctic voyage, being appointed captain of the 'Terror;' and the transport 'Barretto,' under the command of Lieutenant Griffiths, being ordered to accompany them.

This latter was laden with extra supplies, and was to be sent home as usual from Davis's Straits. The vessels were in every way fitted for the expedition, and each was provided with a steam-engine and screw-propeller, to be used only in case of pushing through ice with an adverse wind. They were provisioned for more than three years; and the two crews consisted of 138 men.

The instructions given to Sir John before sailing, directed him to take the course followed by Sir Edward Parry on his first voyage, namely, through Barrow's Straits, Melville Sound, Banks' Straits, and so onward towards Behring's Straits.　This course, after many experiments, seeming to promise the most fairly.

He would thus, after passing Barrow's Straits, have on his north the Parry Isles; of which the three principal are North Devon, Cornwallis, and Melville Isles: and as the shores of these were generally encompassed by ice, he was advised to keep close to the southern land; which, however, it must be remembered, consisted of still larger islands, and not of the continent itself.　He had, however, the choice of passing up Queen's Channel, between North Devon and Cornwallis' Isles, and so round the north of all, should the sea appear to be more open there, or southward towards the mainland, if he could find a passage.

When this expedition started, it was not expected that news could be received for nearly two years after entering the ice.　Lieutenant Griffiths, of the ' Barretto' transport, left 'all well and in good spirits :' and the ' Prince of Wales' whaling-vessel saw them shortly afterwards moored to an iceberg in the middle of Baffin's Bay : but from that time a dead silence ensued.

It was a terrible silence, without doubt, to the private friends of the party; but, for the first two years, only the expected time of suspense.

When, however, the allotted time had fully expired, this suspense, we know, rapidly grew into a fearful anxiety, and, in some hearts, even to agony.

But Sir John Ross had returned after all hope concerning him had been given up, and why might not Sir John Franklin ?

So, by the beginning of 1848, it was fully determined that search must be made; and made not only quickly, but thoroughly.

In three directions it was to be made; and volunteers for the service were not wanting. Sir John was too well known, and too much beloved, for that; and his old companion, Dr. (now Sir John) Richardson, was among the first to offer himself.

He proposed to go, and was sent in the direction which he knew best—that straight over from New York, across by the old trading route, and so down to the Mackenzie's mouth, to examine the coast eastward, in case the missing party should have made their way so far south. And in company with him went Dr. Rae, lately the conductor of an important expedition sent out by the Hudson's Bay Company.

At the same time two other parties were to search in the Polar Sea; one entering it by Behring's Straits, where they were to arrive by the 1st July, and the other following exactly in Sir John's own wake, and so proceeding to meet the former.

The 'Herald' and 'Plover,' under Captain Kellett and Commander Moore, were the vessels destined to enter by the west; and the 'Enterprise' and 'Investigator,' under Sir James Ross and Captain Bird, were those ordered to enter by Lancaster Sound: and this last was, perhaps, the most important of the three expeditions.

It was hoped that Sir J. Richardson might possibly make the voyage in one season; but, in case of not doing so, he was directed to make deposits of pemmican at various points, for the use of a party to be sent southward from the ships, by Sir James Ross, next spring.

One winter only was to be passed away from home in any case, and that was to be at Great Bear Lake.

At the delta of the Mackenzie's mouth bottles were to be buried in a circle, from the point of a broad arrow painted on the signal-post; and land-marks were to be painted white or red, or with black stripes.

Sir John Richardson was at this time sixty-two years of age; but still full of ardour and energy, and of love for his old friend, he pushed on his way so rapidly that, in three months, he had reached the sea.

The openings between those large islands on the northern side of the narrow channel which bounds a good part of the northern coast, namely, Banks' Land, Wollaston, Prince of Wales' and King William's Lands, were to him, he tells us, very full of interest. And as Sir John Franklin's instructions had been to steer south-west after passing Cape Walker, he felt convinced that the ships were pro-bably blocked up in one of these passages.

The first point, however, to be ascertained was whether any ships had passed along the coast; and this, during a voyage between the Mackenzie and Coppermine Rivers, he was pretty well able to settle in the negative, through his frequent communications with the Esquimaux.

The remaining part of the examination he was obliged to leave to Dr. Rae, who had volunteered to search the passage, as Sir James Richardson's time was expired; and he was, therefore, compelled to return to England.

Let us now follow the second expedition.

Its commander, Captain Kellett, was with his vessel, the 'Herald,' at Oahu, in the Sandwich Isles, when it was planned at home; and there the 'Plover,' a miserable sailer, had to join him.

It was August before the two ships met; and, therefore, too late to think of proceeding that year: so the 'Plover' wintered in a Kamptschatkan port; and in June the 'Herald' joined her at Chamisso Island, in the bottom of Kotzebue's Sound. There they were joined also by a yacht, named the 'Nancy Dawson,' which belonged to Robert Shedden, Esq., a wealthy gentleman, who happened to be in China when he heard of the expedition, and resolved to turn aside from his pleasure-trip round the globe to join it.

By July 20th they had passed Behring's Straits, and were in sight of Cape Lisburne. There, boats were put off to examine the coast, and hold intercourse with the natives, who soon began fearlessly to visit the ships, and seemed well-disposed. Seals, walruses, and whales, were blowing, grunting, and barking all around; and immense flocks of ducks were also seen.

Icy Cape was next passed, the old point which had been so seldom attained; and it was hoped that the 'Plover' might winter in Wainwright Bay beyond it; but the water was found too shallow.

Four boats were now put out: and they and the ships weighed anchor in company. A fog soon, however, came on, and they were separated for a time, and seem to have got out of their direct course; for hereabouts, but far to the northward, two little islands were discovered by Captain Kellett, which were called the Herald and the Plover.

Some of the boats were, however, sent on to make their way to some of the stations on the Mackenzie River, but as soon as winter approached the 'Plover,' which was a depôt ship, went into a good anchoring to await the return of the boats, while the 'Herald' was obliged, according to her instructions, to return to the south, in company with Mr. Shedden and his yacht.

This latter gentleman fell a victim to his exertions, and died on the homeward voyage.

Sir James Ross had, meantime, left England in June, 1848, with the two splendid vessels, 'Enterprise' and 'Investigator,' each at his own special request being provided with a launch fitted with a small engine and screw. He preferred this plan to that of having the machinery attached to the vessels themselves. Now the quantity of work appointed to this able commander was certainly very considerable. All the coasts, north and south of Lancaster Sound, Barrow's Straits, and Wellington Channel, were to be thoroughly explored by the 'Enterprise;' and, meantime, the 'Investigator' was to be left to winter in some harbour of North Somerset, in order to be ready to examine, next spring, the shores of that ice-bound country and Boothia, sending her steam launch to meet the whaling-vessels and to forward despatches home.

When the 'Enterprise' reached either Winter Harbour or Banks' Land, parties were to be started in all directions to continue the search. Of this vessel Sir James Ross himself took the command, and with it he seems to have purposed remaining out alone, even after the second winter, should he not previously have met with the desired success. But when news of this scheme reached the Admiralty in a letter sent home by a whaling-vessel, they immediately sent out further supplies, in order to enable the 'Investigator' to remain, and so prevent so venturesome a proceeding.

The large reward of 20,000*l.* was offered to any successful party; Lady Franklin adding to this 3000*l.* more: but these offers were made too late to be carried on that year to the various crews.

It was in the end of 1849, when the anxiety felt for the missing vessels was becoming intense, that two gleams of hope flashed across our country, and as quickly disappeared.

The first was the rumour of news received by means of a sealed bottle, which had been picked up in Davis's Strait, and brought home. When opened, however, it was found to contain only tidings of a still earlier date than those last received.

But before people had recovered from this disappointment, the ' True Love' whaler arrived, whose captain had learnt from a brother captain that an Esquimaux had, on board his ship, sketched four vessels beset in the ice, in an inlet supposed to be Regent's Inlet; and two of these ships he described as shut up for four years, the others for one only.

It may be imagined how eager many would be to verify this report; but the captain was only able to tell them that a solid bar of ice had prevented his doing so himself.

It was a mysterious matter; but the Admiralty soon discovered many inconsistencies in the story, which has since proved to have been an entirely false one.

Sir James Ross made his investigation most carefully, firing guns every half hour, and keeping up a scrutinising examination with glasses when near any shore; for they hoped, and constantly expected, he says, to see those of whom they were in search.

In Possession Bay they landed, and found the papers left there in 1819 by Sir Edward Parry still legible!

At Cape York a very conspicuous mark was fixed up, with a paper of written instructions as to where their missing friends might find them or the depôts of food. Rockets and blue-lights were used as signals during the night, and everywhere papers were distributed, begging Sir J. Franklin's party, if possible, to make for Port Leopold in North Somerset, where a large depôt of provisions was to be provided. And there the two ships had to winter!

It is not difficult to picture to ourselves the disappointed feeling of vexation with which the crews had at last to settle down to an all but inactive state. One thing, however, they did during the whole time. Many foxes visited them, and for these

Drifting in the Pack.

traps were set; and because these creatures roam over a vast extent of country after food, copper collars were fastened round their necks, on which were engraved notices of the position of the ships and stores.

Early in spring many land journeys were made, and as soon as possible they tried to push westward; but in vain.

Scarcely had they got free from the dangerous shores of North Somerset than the ships were caught in a drifting pack, and fairly swept with it back into Baffin's Bay. It was, in fact, a narrow escape from destruction; and with his enfeebled crews Sir James Ross was forced to give up the search and return to England, earnestly hoping that Sir John Richardson had been more successful.

This hope was, however, dissipated two days afterwards, when he also arrived.

The failure of the three expeditions could not but cast a sad gloom over the public mind. There was no disposition, notwithstanding, to give up the search; and, in a few months, the 'Enterprise' and 'Investigator' were again in readiness to accompany the 'Plover' on another voyage, by way of Behring's Straits.

The time was now approaching when the labours of many brave men, during a lengthened course of years, were to be brought at length to a successful termination. That result, and that alone, we may safely say, could ever have settled the minds of Englishmen; and yet, after all, it was expedited by the melancholy disappearance of one of her bravest sons.

Sir John Franklin had gone forth in 1845, ardently hoping to be the favoured man; and though not permitted to return to tell his story, he yet, as now appears, succeeded: while, had he never gone out, this North-west Passage might still be a thing to be sought for.

Never, certainly, had those icy seas been so industriously and thoroughly searched; for never had there been such a motive for searching them: and thus it came to pass that ' the matter which was so near Sir John Franklin's heart' came at length to be settled.

Nor was there any difficulty, at that time, in finding men or leaders for these searching voyages; for England was then very rich in men and officers, well qualified both to direct and carry them out.

Each previous voyage had been a school, of which the results were now to be seen.

In fact, there were so many volunteers that Government could not employ them all; and many private voyages were therefore planned: so that, from 1850 to 1854, Barrow's Straits and Wellington Channel became quite an inhabited region of the globe.

Captain Austen was there with his two sailing and two steam-vessels, wintering at the extreme south-west of Cornwallis' Island. His was a Government expedition.

Captains Penny and Stewart were there from the merchant-service, in a port of Wellington Channel, with ' the Lady Franklin' and ' Sophia,' equipped by private means; Sir John Ross himself was there, in the neighbourhood of Regent's Inlet, with his yacht; and the ' Prince Albert,' fitted out at Lady Franklin's expense, and commanded by Captain Kennedy, was there too: while, not far off, were the American

Captains Haven and Griffin, and their vessels, sent by the United States to lend their aid.

In the expedition of 1848, under Sir James Ross, there had sailed two lieutenants, who were soon to become distinguished men—the one as the solver of the old problem; the other as the finder of the relics of the missing party. The latter, Lieutenant M‘Clintock, was now with Captain Austen: while the former, Captain M‘Clure, was engaged in an expedition of which we shall have to speak almost immediately.

But first, let us take a glance at Captain Austen's proceedings.

Previous to his arrival, he tells us, Captain Penny had discovered, on Beechey Island, at the entrance of Wellington Channel, three sailors' graves, and an immense number of cases of preserved meats; apparently discarded because they had turned putrid. And from these things the captain gathered that, at some time or other, this spot had been the wintering-place of his unfortunate countrymen; as, indeed, we now know to have been the case; while the quantity of the abandoned food raised very melancholy apprehensions as to the state of their provisions.

Having passed the winter as comfortably as they could, Captain Austen prepared for active operations early in spring; and on the 15th of April, fourteen sledges, manned by 104 men, and victualled for six weeks, started off in all directions; after having first united in prayer for the success of their undertakings.

THE THREE TOMBS AT BEECHEY ISLAND.

The sledges were drawn by some of the men, two officers walking in front to point out the direction : but these and the men had to be changed every half-hour, because they could not longer support the intense glare of the sun on the ice. When, however, the wind was strong, the sledges were borne along

A Sledge Journey.

by means of the tent-curtains, which were transformed into sails.

Their sufferings from cold were intense, and the health of many suffered greatly in consequence. The wine froze in the bottles; and when sufficiently thawed to allow of its being drunk, all kinds of precautions had to be used by the men to avoid leaving part of their lips attached to the bottle.

Coffee was found to warm them more than anything else; but, by some of the parties, the best antidote against cold, namely, fresh meat, was not once obtained.

Some were attacked by ophthalmia; some got their limbs frost-bitten: and one officer, George Malcome, commander of the sledge 'Excellent,' actually died on duty.

Lieutenant M'Clintock's party visited Melville Island, and found themselves better off. It proved, indeed, just the privileged spot of the animal creation in the Arctic Regions which Parry had described it. Bears, rein-deer, musk-oxen, foxes, hares, and ptarmigans, abounded there; and though it was only May, the snow had melted from many slopes, and mosses and green turf appeared on them instead.

In Bushman's Cove many indications of Parry's residence still remained; and in Winter Harbour they found the rock engraved by him in 1820, to which they added a record of their own visit.

Meantime Captain Penny's party were in the same manner exploring the coasts of Wellington Channel; but with no better success. And by the end of 1851, the strength of all the crews being exhausted, Captain Austen, Captain Penny, and Sir John Ross, returned to England; while the American vessels would gladly also have gone: but they, after being made the playthings of wind and storm, to such an extent that they could keep neither fire nor lights on board, at length became

frozen in, and could not escape from their imprisonment for the next ten months.

The 'Prince Albert' (Captain Kennedy) had,
meantime, been prevented by the ice from communicating with the other vessels. It had been fixed
in the entrance of Regent's Inlet, and had wintered in Batty's Bay, whence excursions had been
made around North Somerset, and the little
strait thus discovered which separates that country
from Boothia, and which, strangely enough, had
been passed unperceived by both the Captains
Ross.

This little strait was named after Bellot, an ardent young Frenchman, who had entreated to be
allowed to join the expedition, and who proved a
most valuable assistant.

This unfortunate young officer was engaged also
in the expeditions of 1852, and perished among the
ice over which he was travelling in a sledge, in the
following manner:—

Several vessels were then out, under the command of Captain (afterwards Sir Edward) Belcher,
pursuing their investigations in all directions. The
'Phœnix' was afterwards sent from England with
despatches to Captain Belcher, who was then very
far north. To carry these on over the ice was a
dangerous service; but Lieutenant Bellot volunteered. He started with a sledge and four men: but
one day the ice cracked, and left him and two of
the men alone on one piece, which drifted fast away.
He attempted to cheer his companions, and to cross

again over some narrow part in order to make their situation known.

It was blowing a violent storm; but after waiting a little for his return, and listening in vain for his answer to their shouts, the men followed, and perceived on the opposite side nothing but his staff lying on the ice; its master being, no doubt, far below under the dreadful masses. Without food or fire, the others spent twenty-four hours on this dreary island of ice before they succeeded, as they did at last, in crossing and regaining their companions.

CHAPTER XIV.

SIR ROBERT M'CLURE'S VOYAGE.

NEVER, perhaps, did this country show greater earnestness about anything than it did in this search after the Franklin expedition.

Sir James Ross only returned late in 1849 with his two ships; and yet, by the 10th of January, 1850, the 'Enterprise' and 'Investigator' were once more putting to sea, under the command of Captain Richard Collinson and Commander Robert Le Mesurier M'Clure; the former having gained a reputation in China, and the latter, as well as his vessel, having only recently returned with Sir James Ross.

He was promoted for his good services during that voyage, and gladly turned back again to resume the work, though he had only spent a few months in England.

A long and tedious sail of six months lay before the two vessels before they could begin their Arctic work; for whilst others were searching in the eastern, and now well-known openings, these were once more to try a course which had never yet succeeded, and along which no large ship had ever passed: though, of late years, as we have seen, some boats had done so. They were to enter by Behring's Straits, and return home, if possible, from west to east, passing from ocean to ocean by any openings that they could find.

Accordingly, having first been sent into dock to repair the injuries which they had sustained, the noble ships were liberally furnished with everything that could possibly facilitate their work; gunpowder for blasting the ice, poles, hatchets, and ice-saws, and a sharp-pointed machine of about fourteen pounds weight, attached by a tackle and fall to the extreme end of the bowsprit; which, being worked on deck, and allowed to drop suddenly, would penetrate any ordinary ice, and so open a passage for the ships. They had also provisions for three years; and finally left Plymouth on the 20th of January.

We shall, however, have only to do with the 'Investigator' in this chapter. She, being a slow sailer, could not keep up with her consort; and when she reached the Straits of Magellan, she found that the 'Enterprise' had already passed, having been towed through by H. M. S. V. 'Gorgon,' which had received orders to be in readiness for that purpose, and was now prepared to take them on. They were, however, mortified to find that, as the 'Enterprise' had taken all the bullocks, there was no chance of fresh meat until they reached the Sandwich Islands.

Soon after rounding Cape Horn they met with their consort lying at anchor in Fortescue Bay; but, being soon separated in a gale, they met no more during the voyage: but the idea that the 'Enterprise' was ahead, continually urged the Captain of the 'Investigator' to hurry on.

Before reaching the Sandwich Isles a leak in the bread-room was discovered, and more than a thousand pounds of biscuit found to be mouldy; but at Honolulu they were happily able to replenish their stores, the work of getting these on board being generously undertaken by the crew of another vessel lying there, in order that the seamen of the 'Investigator' might have a holiday; and during their stay in the beautiful island of Oahu the men had free leave to go where they would.

The 'Enterprise' had already called there, and passed on. In eager haste to overtake his superior officer, Commander M'Clure anxiously looked out for the shortest passage to the straits, every day being now precious.

The old course was to run to the north-west, across the north-east trade-wind, and into the Asiatic coast; then, with the westerly winds, to run along that shore, and so keep clear of the dangerous channels between the Aleutian Isles. But M'Clure had heard of a shorter route; and by the advice of an intelligent sailor, whom he met at Honolulu, he resolved to run directly northward. He was hastened also by a rumour in the island of Captain Collinson's intention to take the 'Plover' on into the ice, and leave the 'Investigator' in her place.

Through fogs of unusual density, therefore, he

still proceeded under a press of sail, until, in Kotzebue Sound, they were greeted by the 'Plover' herself.
This vessel, which, as we have said, was used as
a depôt ship, had received orders to remain in
that capacity for the assistance of this expedition
somewhere near the entrance to the ice. She
had not seen the 'Enterprise' pass; but they
supposed that this was owing to the dense fogs:
the 'Investigator,' therefore, continued her course
through the straits, and to Cape Lisburne, which
had been fixed on by Captain Collinson as the next
rendezvous. All letters were, however, first transferred to the 'Plover,' and with them M'Clure's
despatch, explaining his intentions should he have
to proceed alone.

He wrote in his journal the same night,—'I
consider that we have said adieu to the world for the
next two years. May that arm which has conducted
us so far in safety still continue its protection upon
a service where all else is weakness indeed!'

All the implements for dealing with ice were now
brought on deck; and by the 31st of July they fell
in with the 'Herald,' which annually came that
way to replenish the 'Plover,' and to communicate
with her, and whose captain was now cruising there
in the hope of falling in with Sir John Franklin;
and whilst so occupied, Captain Kellett soon after
discovered not only a small group of islands, but
an extensive land, very much to the north of any
hitherto seen in that direction. But neither had he
seen the 'Enterprise;' and so, after receiving three

new volunteers and further supplies on board, Captain M'Clure determined to proceed alone.

He entered the ice on the 2nd of August, and fell in with an immense herd of walruses, some of which were so large as to be supposed to weigh 35 cwt., and the ice rose two feet when they moved off a mass of it. The men would have shot some of them, but witnessing the affection evinced between the mothers and their great babes, Captain M'Clure's feelings were touched, and he forbade it.

After running on some way he discovered that his vessel was in a *cul-de-sac*, and having to turn back once more, he again sighted the ' Plover' off Wainwright Inlet.

Point Barrow was their next landmark, and that once past, all the men felt that they were now really on their way home, having thoroughly rounded this eastern coast, and reached a point which no large vessel had previously succeeded in gaining.

Gladly would they have steered their course directly across for Melville Island ; but the ice northward was perfectly impregnable, and they, therefore, had no other way than to get into the space between the continent and the heavy ice, which is called ' land-water.'

The Esquimaux had spoken to Dr. Richardson of an open sea off Mackenzie River ; so for this sea they made with all the haste which numerous hummocks of ice and heavy fogs would allow. To have mastered the difficulty of reaching the Arctic Ocean from the Pacific was a great triumph ; and in the utmost excitement both men and officers laboured on, sometimes sailing in a dense fog, and at others towing the ship with all the boats ahead, while that dreary coast was continually enlivened by loud songs and hearty cheers. It was important now to obtain some intercourse with the natives, in order that they might learn from them whether Franklin's ships had passed.

The 'Investigator' in tow on the Ice.

The first were met with at Point Pitt, about 120 miles east of Point Barrow, where some men had been sent ashore with an officer to erect a cairn, and place a notice there of the 'Investigator's' voyage.

They had with them an excellent interpreter, Mr. Mierching, who had for many years been a

Moravian missionary among the Esquimaux of Labrador, and was therefore well acquainted with their habits and the best method of getting into their confidence.

These three men whom they now met were at first very timid, but gained courage when the friendly act of rubbing noses had been performed. Their astonishment at the sight of the vessel with its 'three great moving trees' was unbounded, and they could find no name for it, except 'oomiack,' or large canoe.

Captain M‘Clure obtained from these people the best encouragement regarding his voyage, for they spoke of a continuous open channel of water all the way to the east. He left with them a letter to be given to any Europeans who might visit the coast. This letter reached England at length, but not till after the first despatches from the expedition had been received.

He told them that he was looking for a lost brother, and made them promise to be kind to any Europeans who might visit them hereafter.

Working slowly along this coast, which is a low monotonous plain, variegated at that season with moss, grass, and flowers, and broken here and there by fine sheets of water, they kept a constant look out for any trace of Franklin's crew, and frequently received visits from the natives. But of any land to the northward they could hear nothing: the seal-skin kajaks could not go so far; and the ice forbade any progress up the inlets. The ' Investigators' tried by all possible means to spread the intelligence of their visit as far as the natives travelled, by giving them presents of knives and looking-glasses, on which the ship's name was engraved.

Tobacco was found a very good trading medium; and everywhere the people seemed peaceable and friendly. This difference in their manners from those of the natives met by Franklin was probably owing entirely to Mr. Mierching's influence.

The navigation along this coast was very dangerous; and fogs, rapid currents, and shoals, sometimes hidden by floes of ice, kept the commander in a constant state of anxiety.

At last the 'Investigator' became completely beset,—grounded, and was only got afloat again by their transferring the deck stores to the boats, one of which capsized in the operation, and thus they lost eleven casks of salt meat.

As far as the eye could reach northward, the ice was driven close together in immense masses; the edge of which looked like a line of chalk cliffs. And yet, while they found it difficult to keep clear of this packed ice, the atmosphere became heavy and sultry, dark clouds gathered, and a thunderstorm came on; the first, Commander M'Clure tells us, that he had ever seen in so high a latitude, namely, 70° N.

It was hard work t get along, and only accomplished by dint of towing and warping pretty constantly: though, whenever the wind served, the sails were hoisted again, and the 'Investigator' urged to encounters with the ice, which set all the ship's bells ringing.

Although now only the 17th of August, even the open sea was beginning to be coated over with ice. Next day they passed Flaxman's Island, and began to feel the influence of the Mackenzie River on the ocean; for, even at this distance, the outpouring of so large a body of water had repelled the main body of ice so far to the northward that M'Clure felt tempted to run straight across in the direction of Banks' Land. He soon, however, discovered his mistake, and a fatal one it had nearly proved; for, after apparently making good progress, they found that the ship was, as it were, in a kind of trap, amid the packed ice, and the fearful thought that this might close behind them, and so shut them in for ever, urged the necessity of immediately retracing their way. But they had run ninety miles into this mass of stupendous hummocks, deceived by the passage of open water in the midst of it, and by the pitching motion of the ship; and perhaps not a man on board ever felt more grateful in his life than when once more the 'Investigator' was steering her course along the coast. They found the sea across the wide angle of the Mackenzie's mouth comparatively clear, and passed Richard's Island on the eastern side of the river on the 22nd, keeping a strict look out, as we may be sure, and yet utterly unaware that a boat's crew from Lieutenant Pullen's vessel were only a few miles off!

They passed each other unseen; and undiscouraged, therefore, by the report which Lieutenant Pullen would certainly have given of the state of the ice near the next prominent point, Cape Bathurst, M'Clure passed on; and by the beginning of September had rounded that point, and, sweeping along Franklin's Bay, reached Parry Point by the 6th, and

View of Cape Bathurst

next day had crossed the channel and landed at a point of Banks' Land, which they named Nelson's Point.

Not knowing, however, that this was a part of Banks' Land, they gave it the name of Baring's Island, after Sir Francis Baring, then first Lord of the Admiralty; which name it has since borne.

It was a rocky and picturesque coast on which they had landed, and many traces of rein-deer and hares were visible; while wild geese were even then soaring overhead. But late in the season though it was, the sea to the north-east was still open; and they continued, therefore, working round the coast, up the strait now known as Prince of Wales's, or M‘Clure's, knowing well that hours, and not days now, would probably end the season for Arctic work.

Land soon after seen on the eastward, was hastily named Prince Albert's Land; and on the 9th September, 1850, the observations taken showed them to be only sixty miles from Melville Sound.

It is impossible to imagine the eager excitement that then prevailed on board. ‘Only give us time,’ they said, ‘and we must make the North-west Passage ;’ and the Captain writes in his journal that he could not describe his anxious feelings. ‘Can it be possible,’ he says, ‘that this water communicates with Barrow's Straits, and shall prove the long-sought North-west Passage? Can it be that so humble a creature as I am will be permitted to perform what has baffled the talented and wise for hundreds of years? But all praise be ascribed unto Him who hath conducted us so far in safety. His ways are not our ways, nor the means that He uses within our comprehension. The wisdom of the world is foolishness with Him.’

‘Oh, for another week of summer weather!’ was, notwithstanding, the cry of all on board. ‘Then we might finish the work this year.’ But no: ducks

were already flying southward; and winter was,
therefore, certainly begun: besides, ice began to
block them in.   Now, on the 16th, they were only
thirty miles from the open sea; but a heavy pack
of ice blocked up the entrance of the strait, and the
'Investigator' was carried back twenty-four miles
in three days.   There it remained stationary; and

'Investigator,' near Baring's Island.

the question then had to be decided whether they
should return to the south, or remain to winter in
the pack.

The latter plan was one which had never been
tried, and which had been pronounced to be certain
destruction by many great authorities on the matter.
And yet, to lose a single mile of Arctic work seemed

so great a loss that it was, at length, decided on. But the ice moved so incessantly that, for a considerable time, no firm spot could be found to which to attach the ship, so that the curtains might be nailed down over her to protect them from the nipping, northern blasts.

Not until the 10th of October did the ice finally settle down; and the harassing anxiety which Commander M'Clure underwent whilst still uncertain whether the vessel could be kept safe amidst its buffetings, was terrible.

At one time it seemed as if she must be wrecked; and all hands were occupied in preparing to assist her should she strike.

The sun was now making each day a smaller and a smaller arch in the heavens, preparatory to taking his leave for many weeks; but the aurora was also beginning to shine out with wondrous brilliancy, and this formed a very considerable substitute for his light, though not for his heat.

Both men and officers were, notwithstanding the danger of their position, in the best of health and spirits; and Captain Parry's plans were once more followed as regarded devices for their amusement and employment.

Rambles on the ice became frequent. On one occasion Captain M'Clure and a party had nearly lost their lives in this way, having wandered far from the ship and lost their way.

Much of the preserved meats which had been brought with them became putrid also, in consequence of injuries received by the tins during the buffetings which the ship had undergone; and there was already a danger of suffering from want of food.

On the 22nd of October, the Captain determined on attempting to reach the sea by means of sledges; and leaving the ship under the command of Lieutenant Haswell, he started off himself with a party of men. It would be too long a story to describe all the hardships which they endured on this journey from cold, hunger, and, above all, from thirst. Frequently the pemmican was frozen when they stopped for a meal; and sometimes no water could be obtained to slake their thirst; and the snow which surrounded them being composed of salt-water, only added to their sufferings. But at night, when the tent was pitched and the candles lighted, the Captain would read them a tale out of 'Chambers' Miscellany,' whilst they mended their torn garments and boots; and so the troubles of the day were forgotten.

At length, on the 26th of October, on ascending a small hill, the sight which they longed to see burst upon them. There were the two coasts of Banks' and Prince Albert's Lands clearly defined on either side; so there could no longer be any doubt as to the water communication all the way up the strait into that broad piece of water known as Melville Sound, or Strait, on which Parry had sailed some thirty years before. *The passage was therefore discovered;* so, once safely back in their native land without loss of ship or crew, and Captain M'Clure's voyage would not have been a fruitless one!

Encamping that night on Russell's Point they lighted a small bonfire, made of a broken sledge and dwarf willow, and enjoyed an extra glass of grog in celebration of the event.

One strange thing happened during the winter passed by the 'Investigator' near Princess Royal's Island, which must be related; while others — because similar to what has been often described in these pages — are passed by; and it is this. A man named John Eames was walking out on the floe, towards the end of January, when, to his utter surprise, he met a small herd of rein-deer. No animals had been seen for a long time; and he, like all the rest of the world, believed that every living creature had long ago migrated southwards.

John Eames' tale was good news at the ship: too good almost to be true! but there were many ready to go and see. Hunters sallied forth in all directions; but to no purpose; for no other deer were to be found — as Captain M'Clure thought, because there was not light enough to see them.

Later travellers also have thought with him; and the subject having been pursued, much doubt has been thrown on the subject of these migrations of the animal creation.

The great object of the expedition, namely, the search for Sir John Franklin, was not meantime forgotten; and no sooner did the sun re-appear, and the weather begin to break a little, than sledge-parties were arranged to go in search. And very gallantly did the men bear the, to them, strange sledge-drawing work — the frost-bites, and numberless dangers and hardships of the journey; each in the hope of stumbling on some poor, lost fellow-countryman. Banks' or Baring's Land was regularly examined, and found to be an island; Prince Albert's Land was crossed as far as to a deep inlet in Wollaston's Land, and eagerly those at the ship watched for the open water, which should enable them to proceed on their voyage.

Meantime, during all these months, no human beings had been seen, nor any other trace of them discovered, except some very old and moss-grown ruins of former Esquimaux dwellings. But now Lieutenant Haslar, on his return from his southern journey, met with a few, from whom they learnt that Wollaston and Victoria Lands were united; a fact which was not previously known.

Captain M‘Clure took great interest in these poor, desolate, and yet often merry-hearted, children of the north, who, since the lull in Arctic discovery, have been thought but little of in Christian lands; and in his journal he more than once expresses his wish that many missionaries, like Mr. Mierching, could be sent among them; as well as that the Hudson's Bay Company could be brought to recognise their duty with regard to them, as representing the British Government in so vast a territory.

Spring passed, summer came, and early in July the floe began to break up. On board the 'Investigator' there was great anticipation regarding that completion of the voyage, which they fondly believed to be close at hand. But the breaking up of the ice

ESQUIMAUX DANCING.

only renewed the old dangers of the last autumn. Again, by no possible means, could the 'Investigator' approach the open sea nearer than a distance of twenty-five miles.

At length, therefore, seeing that the season would soon once more close in, Captain M'Clure determined to return to the mouth of the strait, and, coasting round Banks' Land, attempt the passage that way. Accordingly the ship was put about; and after a number of hair-breadth escapes she succeeded in reaching the north-east point of Banks' Land, where she was again beset.

While waiting to proceed, the officers landed, and, rambling into the interior, discovered a great number of fossil trees, which evidently formed a part of some ancient forest. They found also many lakes, some of which were full of fish.

Struggling along this coast they at length fairly arrived on the shore of Melville Sound, beyond Capes M'Clure and Austen. But the poor, brave vessel's voyage, was nearly at an end. In attempting to pass through some narrow passage between the cliffs and the old ice, the 'Investigator' one night ran ashore on a steep bank. It was only by dint of the most violent exertions that she could be floated again, and got into harbour in a large bay; which, in gratitude for their deliverance, was named 'the Bay of Mercy.' Here the second winter was passed, and passed on shorter rations; this having now become necessary, in consequence of their precarious situation. Happily, however, the land was found to teem with rein-deer and hares; the former of which went in herds of sometimes a hundred and fifty at a time.

The second Christmas-day was, therefore, a merry one, in spite of the dreary situation of the crew and the howling of the numerous wolves which infested that land. Indeed, years afterwards some of the petty officers of the ship declared that they had never passed a merrier one. The doctor also had but four trifling cases on his sick list; and the sporting, which was renewed as early as possible in 1852, helped to preserve this comfortable state of things.

One non-commissioned officer greatly distinguished himself as a sportsman during this season, and was found also to be a man ' good at need' on other occasions. This was Sergeant Woon, an instance of whose generous bravery may here be given. There was a coloured man among the crew, who had gone out sporting, wounded a deer, and then lost his way in a fog. Fatigued and half-frozen, the poor fellow lost his presence of mind, and wandered about until he happened to be discovered by Sergeant Woon. But the horror of his situation had quite taken possession of the man's mind. He fell into fits, and could not be reassured by either promise or encouragement of any kind. Induced at last to try and walk a little, he soon sank again on the ground, bleeding at the nose and mouth, and writhing in convulsions. It was evidently vain to think of his saving himself: so he must either be abandoned as the prey of wolves, or Sergeant Woon must drag him home. But he was a heavy man, and the sergeant had to carry his own musket, with which he dared not part. He hesitated not, however, but slinging the latter over his shoulder, and taking the man's arms round his neck, he set out towards the ship.

He gained some relief by rolling the poor fellow down every ravine, and thus succeeded in getting to within a mile of the ship; then, finding his own strength utterly fail, he tried once more the effect of entreaties, that the man would try and arouse himself, but the only reply was a request to be left alone to die.

Nothing remained, therefore, but to lay him down in the deep snow, and start off himself for assistance, which, happily, he soon met. But when the party who accompanied Woon returned to where he had left his companion, they found him stiff and rigid, with his mouth so tightly closed that it had to be violently forced open in order to administer restoratives. His life was saved after all; and seldom perhaps has any life been saved under such circumstances.

Early in April, Captain M'Clure determined on crossing the ice in a sledge, and paying a visit to Melville Island, where he hoped to find some of Captain Austen's ships, which might, he thought, be able to give them assistance. By the 28th they reached the spot where Parry had left his monumental stone; but, to their bitter disappointment, they read also thereon the addition inscribed by Lieutenant M'Clintock, who had conducted to the spot one of the sledge-parties sent on by Captain Austen.

This hope having, therefore, vanished, they returned again to the ship, where all were still well, and found that to their stock of provisions had been added during their absence twenty head of fine deer. Mercy Bay had proved, indeed, a good harbour

Melville Island.

for them, and had sometimes yielded them three fresh meals a-day. And yet, by the 10th of May, scurvy had made its unwelcome appearance among the men : and notwithstanding all the care of the doctor and captain, it continued to make progress.

The next summer was a dreary one, and less game was shot, so that not until the stock of venison was exhausted did Sergeant Woon succeed in shooting some fine musk-oxen, whose flesh yielded 647 lbs. of good food, for which all were grateful.

Until nearly the end of August there was not even a hope of getting the ship into open water; and that hope soon died out by the closing up again of the one narrow open lead of water which had appeared, and by the falling of the temperature.

It now became a pressing question whether or not the ship should be abandoned; as it was doubtful how long the crew could hold out on their present store of provisions, and all were thinner and weaker than they used to be.

Captain M'Clure, however, determined himself to stick by the ship to the very last; so, after due deliberation, he assembled his men, and told them that in April two parties should go home — one *viâ* the Mackenzie River, and the other by Beechey Island, where Captain Austen's notice at Melville Isle told them they would find provisions, and a boat with which they might gain the Danish settlements of Greenland. Meantime he would stay himself, with thirty of the strongest men, spend a fourth winter, and then retreat on Lancaster Sound, should no help have previously come to them.

All the men acquiesced cheerfully in this arrangement, and so, much in the same manner as before, passed this third winter; except, we must add, that less game was caught than during the last.

When much hard work had to be done on their present short rations hunger was felt, it is true; but when once shut in during the actual winter, and with little to do, the health of the crew, to some extent, improved, and the most praiseworthy good-humour still reigned on board.

April came; the preparations for the two journeys had gone on, and all was now ready. The poor sickly fellows were trying to brace themselves up for the journeys, which were certainly their only hope of escape—though a poor one it was, after all; and those to be left had been giving into their comrades' charge the letters to wives, mothers, or friends, who probably were even then mourning them as dead; while their iron-hearted captain had been endeavouring to cheer up the spirits of his whole crew, just then depressed by the occurrence of the first death, when the most extraordinary and entire change in the state of affairs took place.

The captain and first lieutenant were walking near the ship, and talking of the possibility of digging a grave for the poor fellow who had just died, in ground which was so hard frozen, when suddenly a man was perceived coming towards them, who appeared unlike any of their own men. Feeling certain, however, that no others were near, and supposing that some one had been trying on a new travelling dress, they continued to advance while still conversing together. A strange figure he was, with a face black as ebony, gesticulating like an Esquimaux, and shouting in a manner which brought the two officers to a stand-still.

At length the young fellow came near enough for them to hear his words.

'I'm Lieutenant Prim, late of the 'Herald,' and now in the 'Resolute.' Captain Kellet is in her at Dease's Island.'

And such a rush took place, and such a grasping of hands followed, as probably Lieutenant Prim would never forget. The news spread like wild-fire; sick men leapt from their beds; workmen dropped their tools; and all pressed forward to learn how relief had come, and to meet the two dog-sledges which were following on their visitor's steps.

We must now explain how all this was brought about.

Captains Ross, Austen, and Penny had been unsuccessful in their efforts, as has been stated some pages back; but Lady Franklin could not be satisfied, nor could she rest until another expedition was resolved upon. There were also now, not one, but two missing expeditions to search after, and others to be anxious about beside Sir John and his gallant crew. Others, therefore, besides herself, were urging this matter on, and amongst them, Mr. Cresswell, whose son was with Commander M'Clure.

This gentleman not only rightly judged of the course taken by the 'Investigator,' but also as correctly conjectured whereabouts she then lay, as well as that some of her crew would visit Melville Island. His letter addressed to the Admiralty decided the matter; and it was determined to send out four more ships, under the command of Captain Belcher;

two of which were to proceed up Wellington Channels and two direct to Melville Island.   These
latter vessels were commanded by Captains Kellett
and M'Clintock, and very promptly they fulfilled
their task.   They went, and formed a depôt, but
found no cairn or notice of M'Clure's party having
preceded them, and unable to do more that season,
they returned to winter quarters; but were no sooner
settled down, than Captain Kellett began to send out
parties to scour the country.

One of these visited Winter Harbour, and on a
close inspection of Parry's famous sandstone rock a
new inscription met their astonished eyes; and they
could scarcely credit their senses when they read of
Commander M'Clure's visit, of his having really
accomplished the passage, and of his present position.

It was, however, too late to proceed that season;
and they feared that before they could reach Mercy
Bay in the spring, the crew of the 'Investigator'
would already have left it by some other way.   We
have seen that the relief was, notwithstanding, in
time, and that by this means the lives of many brave
men were probably saved.

The sledge-journeys might now be abandoned,
and almost the first thought was how the good
news could be most quickly forwarded to England.

It was soon decided to send Lieutenant Cresswell on to Beechey Isle, with this view; and there,
fortunately, the 'Phœnix' happened to touch, so
that he very soon had the honour of presenting his
despatches.

It was on the 7th of October, 1853, that the tidings thus reached the Board of the Admiralty.

Having now obtained supplies for his men, Commander M'Clure earnestly desired to remain with his vessel until she could be got out of the ice.

But he felt obliged, before coming to any decision, to submit the matter of the men's health to a medical examination, and the report was so unfavourable that he felt himself compelled to abandon the vessel and return home with all his men.

When this much-enduring crew and its commander reached England, they found the nation almost engrossed with the Russian war; and many of them, therefore, felt that the honours which they received were hardly proportioned to the sufferings which they had undergone, or to what they had accomplished.

Commander M'Clure, however, received his commission at once, and it was dated back from the day of the great discovery; as were also those of some of his officers. Nor was it long before Her Majesty conferred on him the customary honour of knighthood.

The question next to be taken into consideration, was that of the reward of 10,000*l.*, offered by Government to the first finders of the passage. And it might have been expected that this would have been immediately decided in favour of the ' Investigator's' crew. But a letter addressed to the Government by Lady Franklin, who was naturally jealous for her husband's fame, caused some little delay. She argued that, until his papers came to hand and his course had been traced out, it would be impossible to decide to whom this honour belonged.

This plea was admitted, and after passing a high encomium on the courage and zeal shown by Sir Robert M'Clure and his men, a committee of the House of Commons at length decided that the 'Investigator's' crew having discovered *a* north-west passage, merited the 10,000*l.* as their just reward.

The uncertainty of Arctic voyages was afterwards shown by the result of Captain Collinson's voyage. His ship, the 'Enterprise,' notwithstanding her superior sailing qualities, did not succeed in rounding Point Barrow during the same season as did her consort.

The next year he followed exactly in the 'Investigator's' track, as far as to the Prince of Wales' Straits, but neither was he able to carry his vessel that way into the ocean. He wintered in 1851 on the western coast of Prince Albert's Land, and in 1852 in Cambridge Bay, to the north of Dease's Strait, and while exploring the eastern coast of Victoria Land he came on traces of Dr. Rae's expedition of the previous year, and also bought from the Esquimaux some articles which he believed to have belonged to the 'Erebus' and 'Terror.' Captain Collinson returned by the same way that he had come, after passing a third winter on the north coast of America.

It was, of course, for the assistance of his vessel, as well as of that of her consort, and the Franklin expedition, that the four ships under the command of Sir Edward Belcher and Captain Kellett had been sent out from England. These had all, more or less, got into difficulties; but as they were nothing compared with what other crews had endured, the surprise of the 'Investigators' was great indeed, when they found that, contrary to the opinion of all his officers, and in spite of the remonstrances of Captain Kellett, Sir Edward Belcher was determined to abandon all four vessels, as well as the 'Investigator,' and crowding all the men on board of three depôt and store-ships, to return at once to England.

The result of such a step was, of course, that a general feeling of gloom and depression filled the minds of all interested in the still missing crews; and a court-martial sat to examine into this conduct of Sir Edward Belcher.

Just at this moment, however, news arrived from a quarter whence they were least expected. Dr. Rae, lately the companion of Richardson, having been appointed by the Hudson's Bay Company in 1853 to complete the survey of the western shore of Boothia, fell in with a party of Esquimaux in Pelly Bay, which lies in the south of the gulf of Akkolee; and from one of them he learnt that a party of *Kabloonas* —white men—had died of hunger a long way to the west of where he then was, and beyond a great river. But the man said that he had never been there himself, and could not travel with them so far. Dr. Rae pursued his inquiries, and elicited from different persons other particulars, which led him to believe that the river spoken of was no other than Back's, or the Great Fish River, and also that these unfortunate persons were certainly a part of Franklin's expedition.

When first seen they were about forty in number, and headed by a man who seemed to be an officer; they were dragging a boat and sledges southward over the ice. They could not speak the Esquimaux language well enough to be understood; but by signs they made the natives understand that their ships had been crushed by the ice, and that they were going where they hoped to find deer. This was about the year 1850; and later in the same season, but before the breaking up of the ice, some graves were found by the Esquimaux, and about thirty corpses, some in a tent, others under a boat, and others scattered about. But the most dreadful fact of all was, that from the mutilated state of some of the bodies, as well as from the contents of the cooking-vessels, there was reason to believe that the unhappy men had been reduced even to cannibalism. At the same time there was nothing to lead Dr. Rae to suppose that any violence had been offered to them by the natives; although some of the articles thrown away by the white men were in their possession; and Dr. Rae purchased several things of them: amongst others, a silver star, on which were engraved the words 'Sir John Franklin.' No writings or papers of any kind had come to hand; and many were the treasures supposed to be still lying on the desert ice. While, therefore, to Dr. Rae and his men, was adjudged the promised reward of 10,000*l.* as the first discoverers of some traces of the expedition, a very general desire was felt to pursue the research still further.

Before, however, we go on to relate the successful termination of this deeply interesting inquiry, we must turn aside for a while to speak of an American expedition, which came first in order of time, and which, besides, was one of the most extraordinary and daring on record.

CHAPTER XV.

DR. KANE'S EXPEDITION.

DR. ELISHA KANE, who, under Lieutenant De Haven, had sailed three years before in the first Grinnell expedition, was appointed by the American Admiralty to the command of a new Arctic expedition in 1853.

It had for its object, like the first, the discovery of Sir John Franklin's crews; and though chiefly supported by Mr. Grinnell, it was also very greatly assisted by the generous donations of the well-known Mr. Peabody of London.

The plan proposed was to sail straight up Baffin's Bay, and thus enter the Arctic Ocean through what was called Smith's Sound; and this idea seems to have originated with Dr. Kane himself, whose mind, since his first voyage, had been constantly occupied with the matter.

He thought that he should thus more quickly reach the ocean; that he should have *terra firma* as the basis of his operations; animal life to sustain travelling parties; and the co-operation of Esquimaux almost to the extreme north, as it was known that settlements of them were to be found even as high as Whale Sound.

In the 'Advance' brig, and accompanied by only seventeen men, including officers, Dr. Kane therefore left New York on the 30th May, 1853. Of these, Mr. Brooks was the first officer, Mr. Hayes was the surgeon, and Mr. Sontag the astronomer; a Dane, named Carl Petersen, undertook to act as interpreter; and on reaching Greenland, an Esquimaux, called Hans Christian, was engaged as a hunter, after having first shown his skill by spearing a bird on the wing.

In eighteen days the 'Advance' arrived at Newfoundland, and there obtained some stores of fresh beef to add to their rather slender stock. The Governor, also, made them the valuable present of a team of Newfoundland dogs.

From Newfoundland they steered for the Greenland harbour of Fishernaes, which is situated on the south-west coast, and is famous both for its dry and healthy climate and for its cod-fisheries. Here their arrival was quite an event; and, accordingly, the whole population came out to receive them. The officers were hospitably entertained by Mr. Lassen, the governor of the place; and from thence Dr. Kane went to visit Lichtenfels, the ancient seat of Greenland missions, of which he had read much. The old house seemed to have been built in the time of Hans Egede himself. It was a sober, old-fashioned building; and he tells us, that 'it was almost with feelings of devotion' that he approached it. The inmates appeared to be frugal in their habits, and very poor; yet of so independent a spirit that they could scarcely be prevailed on to accept a small present of potatoes. They were, however, people of some education and intelligence.

Much of this Greenland coast is very picturesque, especially during the summer season.

The Danish settlements have been, for the most part, fixed on remarkable points; and each one is famous for some article of trade. Cliffs, which sometimes assume the grandest forms, and which are composed of variously coloured strata of earth and rocks, with sometimes a glimpse of the red snow between their chasms, edge the coast; while all the back country seems to be one great expanse of glaciers, which here and there shed off their mighty icebergs into the sea. To these, for want of anything more secure, they were at times obliged to fasten the vessel, in order to avoid being beset in the ice; yet it proved, on one occasion, but a sorry alternative.

After eight hours' hard labour in heaving, planting ice-anchors, and so on, they had scarcely succeeded in, as they thought, securing the ship, when a series of loud, cracking sounds above her, and the dropping of a shower of small pieces of ice, excited alarm; and only just time had they to get free again when the whole face of the berg fell, 'crashing like near artillery.' On the 5th of August they passed the crimson cliffs noticed by Sir John Ross, and perceived them even at ten miles off. Next day they reached Hakluyt's Island, with its tall spire of gneiss, which forms a valuable landmark for a long distance round. 'It would,' Dr. Kane observes, 'have formed a fine study of colour for an artist, being covered with this crimson snow, interspersed with lovely green patches of moss, and now and then a piece of the bare brown sandstone.'

On the 7th they passed Cape Alexander, and when fairly within Smith's Sound began to make *caches* of provisions in various places, to facilitate their future onward march, and to build cairns as signs by which others might, if necessary, follow them. Signs of winter were already visible; and though determined to push as far to the north that season as possible, Dr. Kane felt that one place must be stored, to serve as a retreat in case of necessity, and he selected Littleton Island for the purpose. On it the lifeboat, provisions, and a few blankets, were left, while a further depôt was made on the mainland.

Greatly to their surprise, traces of human beings were visible even here; and from some tombs various little implements were carried away as specimens of native ingenuity. Esquimaux, not being able to dig graves for their dead, place them in a sitting posture in little cairns, and these they hold too sacred to be disturbed.

Keeping to his purpose, Dr. Kane resolutely pressed on amid floes and icebergs, which almost hourly threatened the party with destruction; and towards the end of the month a storm came on, which greatly increased their danger. For many days the gale blew on; and when at last it subsided, most of the men were for returning to winter in the south.

It was all that their captain could do to persuade them to persevere for a while longer, and then to establish themselves in the most available spot, in order that they might be ready for work when spring came. At length he determined on proceeding in a boat, with a few men, in order to judge whereabouts would be the best wintering ground ; and he chose Messrs. Brooks, Sontag, Bonsall, M'Gary, Riley, Blake, and Morton, to form the crew of the 'Forlorn Hope,' as being some of the strongest and most daring of his companions. Besides the clothes that they wore, they had buffalo-robes for sleeping-dresses, while each carried his girdle full of woollen socks, and a tin cup, with a sheath-knife at the belt ; and a soup-pot and lamp were taken for the mess in general.

After a time the icy belt round the coast became impracticable, and the boat had to be hauled up under the shelter of a hummock, while they pushed on in the sledge.

No place, however, was found so eligible as the bay in which the 'Advance' lay, so it was resolved to winter in Rensselaer Harbour. Hitherto it had been one constant blaze of daylight; but now the heavens began to wear more sober tints, and a few stars appeared. The change was very agreeable at first. It was expected that the sun would disappear in this latitude about the 10th of October, and much work had to be done during the daylight that remained, as it was advisable to empty the hold, and deposit its contents in Butler Island. Besides this, they were already at a loss about winter provisions, as no game had been seen in Smith's Sound, and they had come out entirely without the preserved meats generally used; so that all their salt meat had to be *unsalted* by a twelve hours' immersion in an adjoining fresh-water pond, on which the icy covering had to be broken for that purpose. The salt fish and pickled cabbage were treated in like manner.

Here, then, in this harbour of Rensselaer, in the midst of some little islands, which protected her from the violent assaults of moving masses of the ice, the ' Advance' was soon frozen in, and her crew had to resign themselves to the long dark winter which would soon come on them, in a more northerly latitude than any previously reached by a European, except in Spitzbergen, where the climate is much modified by the circumstance of its consisting of islands, and also by the influence of the Gulf Stream, which reaches even those shores.

All the rest of the daylight was occupied in making *caches* of provisions; for it was Dr. Kane's plan to have a chain of these depôts, from each of which, unencumbered by heavy loads, he hoped to travel far in different directions.

The journeys were to be performed in sledges drawn by dogs, of which he had a number, both Esquimaux and Newfoundland. The latter he employed himself in training to draw in a regular harness, two a-breast, guided by the voice alone, without the whip; and six made a powerful team. The sledge was made of American hickory, carefully

jointed in its various parts by thongs of seal-skin, so
that it had no stiff hinges, but yielded to the least
inequality of surface.   It proved a very satisfactory
little carriage, and was named ' Little Willie.'

The Esquimaux dogs, which were in a half-wild
state, and much resembled wolves, were kept for the
long tough journeys, in which their patient en-
durance, their speed, and their sagacity, proved
invaluable.   A larger sledge was used for the heavy
parties, which was named ' Faith.'

To drive an Esquimaux team is a serious affair,
and so fatiguing that Esquimaux drivers travel in
couples, and change continually.   The whip used is
of seal-hide, six yards long, with a very short handle
of only sixteen inches.   It must be used with a
masterly sweep, and the driver must be able to hit
any particular dog, and to accompany the stroke
with a resounding crack, bringing the whip clearly
back again; which, of course, is not easy, as it
is apt to get entangled among the dogs and lines;
and sometimes in travelling over the ice the sledge
will come to immense rents and fissures, which
have to be leapt by the whole team.   On one occasion the poor dogs failed, and all fell in, so that
their drivers had to cut the traces and haul them
out, which was done with difficulty.   Another time
one of the drivers was flung out, and narrowly
escaped being drawn under the ice by the rapid tide.

This winter was, indeed, a dark one ; and in Dr.
Kane's journal we read neither of snow-blink nor
aurora lights as substitutes for the sun, though the

moon and stars often shone out with wonderful brilliancy. This was only in fine weather, however; at other times it was absolutely dark; and men and dogs alike felt the depressing influence of so long a night. Many of the latter soon died, indeed, from an anomalous disease, produced, Dr. Kane says he firmly believes, by no other cause. This disease seemed to be entirely mental, and no amount of anxious care availed to save the valuable creatures. It began with a kind of epilepsy, which was soon followed by a state of lunacy, or rather idiocy. The poor animals would bark frenziedly at nothing, walk about in straight or curved lines with the utmost perseverance, move about in the most senseless manner, and then relapse into hours of moody silence. Generally symptoms of lock-jaw came on before they died.

By the time when perpetual daylight had succeeded to this perpetual night, only six dogs remained of the nine Newfoundlands and thirty-five Esquimaux; and the men were many of them suffering from scurvy, and generally debilitated. They had occupied themselves as best they could by lamp or moonlight, some in writing, some in drawing or making maps, some in ship-work or in attending to the business of *freshening* the meats; others in working up the skins into various articles of clothing; others in writing up the journals or books of observations; while chess and other games often finished the monotonous days.

The cold, as may be imagined, had been intense,

the thermometers ranging from 60° to 75° below
zero; and they had but a scanty supply of fuel.   By
the 21st of January only did they reach 'the state of
mitigated darkness,' which made the midnight of
Sir Edward Parry in lat. 74° 47', so that such a
winter was probably never passed by any Europeans.

As soon as the outline of the coast became once
more visible, the ice-foot, or belt as Kane prefers to
call it, was perceived to have undergone many
changes.   This ice-belt consists of an immense zone
of ice, which extends all along the shores from the
Arctic circle to the extreme north; and in the
highest latitudes, though somewhat reduced in thick-
ness in summer, it never disappears.   It served our
travellers for a kind of high road, and was at some
seasons a tolerably level one.

Sledge-parties began to go out and return as
soon as the spring appeared; and in the end of
March preparations were making for a general
advance, when the appearance of three of their
number, who had been absent, startled the workers
in the cabin.   These were Messrs. Sontag, Ohlsen,
and Petersen, who, swollen and haggard, and scarcely
able to speak, hurriedly told their alarming story.
Four of their companions were still in the ice,
unable to come on, being frozen and disabled: they
had risked their lives to bring the news, but could
not describe the spot or the direction in which they
might be found, and were evidently sinking fast
themselves.   It was felt that not an instant must be
lost; so, while a hasty meal was being got ready, and

DR. KANE AND HIS COMPANIONS IN THEIR WINTER CABIN

' Little Willie,' a tent, &c. prepared, Ohlsen, the most conscious of the party, having had some refreshment, was strapped on to the sledge in a fur bag, wrapped in dog-skins and eider-down ; and Dr. Kane with nine men set out.

The temperature was 75° below zero, and they knew not which way to go. Mr. Ohlsen fell asleep almost immediately, but soon awoke in a confused state of mind, and could give no help. There was nothing for it but to abandon the sledge and disperse in search of footprints; but it was absolutely requisite to keep constantly moving in order to avoid freezing; and so they continued for some hours, till Mr. Ohlsen, being a little recovered, was liberated from his bag and set on his feet : but now some others of the party were seized with trembling fits and short breath, and Kane himself fainted twice upon the snow. And so for eighteen hours, without food, they wandered on, until suddenly Kane exclaimed that he thought he saw a broad sledge-track. They followed it, and soon came, first to footsteps, then to a small American flag hung on a hummock, and then to the tent close by, where lay in the darkness the four poor fellows stretched on their backs, whose burst of gratitude was felt fully to repay every one for the twenty-one hours' march.

The tent would only hold eight men ; so those of the fifteen who could not squeeze in were obliged to keep from freezing by incessant exercise. A two-hours' sleep for each of the two parties was all the halt that could be managed ; and then the sick were carefully sewed up in furs and packed in a bed of buffalo robes, the whole being tightly lashed together and covered over so as only just to leave breathing-room ; and the party started back again. Strange to say, they marched on for six hours cheerfully ; but at the end of that time all began to feel a most alarming failure of strength ; and some of the poor fellows even entreated to be allowed to sleep.. No efforts or commands indeed sufficed to hinder it ; so, with much difficulty, for they had scarcely strength enough left, the tent was pitched, and all who could be crowded in were left under Mr. M'Gary's charge, Kane himself, with one companion, pushing on to the half-way tent, in order to thaw water and pemmican by the time the others came up. For four hours these two walked on, never suffering themselves to cease talking, that they might keep themselves awake, yet scarcely knowing what they said or did, or why they took any particular direction. In fact, neither of them was in his right senses ; and when they reached the tent they just crawled into their sleeping-bags, and slept on dreamily for the next three hours. When Dr. Kane awoke, his long beard was frozen to his buffalo-skin ; and his companion had to cut him out with his jack-knife. The others came up in due time much better, and after partaking of the food which had been prepared, all proceeded again on their way, and now comfortably, under a clear sun and without wind.

It was desperate work, notwithstanding, to perform the rest of the journey. They lost their strength

and their self-control; and to assuage their thirst
could not resist eating snow, though it *burnt* and
blistered their mouths, and caused many to become
speechless. When they reached the brig, none of
them were in a sane condition; but all, under ju-
dicious treatment, recovered, except two, who died
in spite of every effort to save them. Some, however, were obliged to have parts of their feet ampu-
tated. One of the poor fellows who died was seized
with lock-jaw on the day before his death. It was
whilst watching beside him that they received their
first visit from the Esquimaux. ' People holloaing
ashore!' cried the deck-watch; and there they were
truly, dotting the snow in considerable numbers,
and vociferating, ' *Hoah, ha, ha!*' ' *Ka, kăāh!*'
' *Ka, kăāh!*' but in no friendly tones: indeed their
violent gesticulations were at first alarming. It was
soon perceived, however, that no weapons were in
their hands; and Dr. Kane therefore, calling Petersen
to be his interpreter, went forth unarmed to parley
with them.

A tall, powerful fellow, with a swarthy skin and
jet-black eyes, came forward to meet him; and
others, at his signal, soon crowded round, seemingly
in a perfectly peaceable mood; so, after awhile,
many were admitted on board ship. They had
sledges drawn by dogs, which they managed admirably, and were a very strong set of men, some
of them able to combat singly with the Polar bear.

The first who came was named Metek; he was
dressed in a sort of fur-hooded jacket, with bear-

skin breeches, and boots in which were concealed knives. He and his companions remained for a considerable time on board, examining everything; stealing whatever they could, and laughing loudly at the ignorance of the white men, because they could not understand their language. They saw a great

Metek.

deal of these people that winter; and though at first they were shy and suspicious, yet they afterwards became the firm friends of the whites, Dr. Kane taking care, from the first, to impress them, by every possible means, with an idea of his own and his companions' superior strength, in order to keep up a salutary awe in their minds.

As soon as the ice broke up a little the Esquimaux took their departure: but they were afterwards met with again. In fact, it was sometimes found advisable to follow in their track; as they always knew where food was to be had. The whole country was, indeed, as well known to them as a sheep-walk is to a shepherd; they noted every change of wind, or season; studied the heavenly bodies; and could even predict certain changes in the weather: while their advice about hunts was often invaluable. The flesh of the walrus seemed to form their principal food: but more to the south they also procured whales and sea-unicorns.

During the summer many parties were sent out from the bay in which the 'Advance' was imprisoned; one, led by Mr. Bonsall and Mr. M'Gary, was sent to endeavour to surmount an enormous glacier, named after Humboldt, which lay at twelve days' journey from the brig, in a large bay, which they named after Mr. Peabody: but that proved perfectly impracticable; besides which, as the disagreeable discovery was then made that the bears had been committing great depredation on the depôts which they had made on the way, they could not remain out long.

These creatures also more than once interrupted their progress during their marches: and on one occasion a monstrous fellow, to their great disgust, paid them a visit in the tent when all were asleep, after a long day's journey. A scratching noise on the snow outside first disturbed Mr. M'Gary; and rousing himself, he perceived that the bear was walking round the tent. A loud cry aroused his companions; but not before the creature had, to their horror, presented himself at the entrance, where he stood quietly surveying the inmates. There was an instant blaze of paper torches, their only weapons of defence, all their arms having been left in the sledge; but of these Mr. Bear took no notice whatever, though they were thrust under his nose. In this terrible dilemma, a man named Tom Hickey saved them all, by first making a hole in the tent with his clasp knife, out of which he contrived to squeeze himself: then seizing one of the supports of the tent, he gave the beast such a vigorous blow on the nose with it that he was glad to retreat. On this, Tom, pursuing his advantage, rushed to the sledge, and snatching up a gun, returned to the charge. In another instant the brute's head was pierced through with a ball, and all were safe. It was the last time that they slept unarmed in a tent.

Another excursion was made by Mr. Morton and Hans Christian towards the north. This was the most remarkable of all their journeys. Travelling over the ice, which in some places was found to be so unsafe that the dogs had to be coaxed along, they passed Peabody Bay, and a curious natural minaret, which had been named Tennyson's Monument, and got among bergs which stood so closely together as to obstruct all view in front. These past, they soon

KENNEDY CHANNEL.

perceived land on the western side; and named the passage Kennedy Channel.

Here they encountered a bear and her cub, and a fierce combat ensued between her and the dogs. The old one was at last killed by a shot from Hans; and the little one then so fiercely defended its mother's body from the dogs, that it was obliged to be despatched with stones.

On this journey they reached their most northerly

Pack's Cape, in Kennedy Channel.

point, and named it Mount Parry. Here, with patriotic pride, they hoisted the American flag, and saluted it. Dr. Kane believed the water here to be open sea: a part of the Arctic Ocean, in fact.

The summer was wearing away, and still the ice did not break up: so that anxious fears were felt lest another winter should have to be passed at Rensselaer Harbour, as their health was greatly weakened;

and they had neither fuel nor provisions to enable them safely to do so. But Dr. Kane could not as yet think of deserting the brig, and therefore formed a plan for communicating with Sir Edward Belcher's squadron on Beechey Island. He started with five of the strongest men in an open boat; a kind of navigation especially dreaded in the open sea by experienced seamen; but they soon encountered storms, such as they had not been prepared for. The ice also blocked them in ; and it was found impossible even to reach Cape Parry : so there was no alternative but to return to the brig and put up a beacon, in case any rescue-party should be looking for them.

On arriving at the brig, however, it was found that many thought an escape overland possible that year ; and broken down by scurvy as they were, without provisions, or hope of provisions, suited to their circumstances, Dr. Kane felt that he had no right to control the men in this matter, and therefore determined to allow each one to act for himself. The result was that eight determined to stay, and nine to go. These latter went with an assurance given that, should they wish to return, they would be welcomed back. They remained away several months — long and weary months, too, they must have been — and at length, after having suffered what it would fill a volume to describe, they were obliged to go back to their comrades.

Those who remained endeavoured to accommodate themselves to circumstances, and to adopt the

HOISTING THE AMERICAN FLAG.

habits of the Esquimaux — filth and extravagance
excepted.   They thus tried whether white men
could live like these people; but the experiment
could not be called a successful one.

A place called Etah was the regular haunt of the
Esquimaux; and there our party often visited them,
and became acquainted with Metek and his relations;
Accomodah, his fat young son; Paulik, his nephew;
and many others with curious names, and still more
curious ways.

Dr. Kane once went even so far as to enter one
of their tents, and throw himself down amongst the
heap of human beings to sleep. The hut was, indeed,
so hot, that sleep came naturally to him.   It was
but seven feet by six, and contained thirteen persons,
some of whom — that is, the women — were cooking,
each in her 'kothok,' slices of meat cut from a
walrus.

Dr. Kane was always saluted as 'Nalegak,' or
Great Chief, wherever he went: and so pleased were
they with this visit, that they almost deafened him
with shouts.

A woman, whose name he translates as Mrs.
Eider-duck, constituted herself his attendant, and
prepared his breakfast—a lump of boiled blubber
and a choice cut of meat.

These poor children of the North differ most
wonderfully from those who have become civilized
and christianized, as the southern tribes have.

If they have no laws, they are certainly bound
by their own peculiar customs; which have, no

doubt, been those of their ancestors from time immemorial. One of these singular customs is, that of holding weeping meetings, not only for the death of a friend, but for that of a dog, the failure of a hunt, the breaking of a walrus-line, or any other calamity.

Mrs. Eider-duck.

They hold their angekoks, or magic-men, in great esteem. These angekoks are the general counsellors in time of trouble; in sickness they *powwow*, or prescribe; and when death follows, they direct as to the manner in which grief is to be shown. A husband, for instance, after burying his wife, may be obliged always to wear his nessak, or hood, or forbidden to eat some kind of food, or even to abstain from seal or walrus-hunting for a year. They seem to have but little that can be called religious belief of any kind, though they evidently do believe in certain supernatural influences.

When they were once thoroughly persuaded of the superior powers of the whites, a treaty between the two parties was proposed by Dr. Kane, in which it was stipulated that certain mutual kindnesses should be exchanged, and no harm done by either to the other party. This treaty was solemnly ratified; and, to the honour of the natives, strictly kept.

We cannot follow the poor travellers through the sufferings of this winter. Getting sometimes a supply of the eider-ducks, sometimes some walrus-flesh, sometimes a little fish, but often wanting food, they struggled through, though not without further losses by death. But when the next June came, there was no doubt as to the duty of abandoning the vessel, and attempting the long and perilous voyage back in boats. When preparing for departure, they received much assistance from their Esquimaux friends, who evidently took leave of them with sincere sorrow. Hans, indeed, had already deserted to them; and it is not improbable that they tempted him away.

Dr. Kane says also, that he and his companions had received so many kindnesses from them, and had got to know them individually so well, that, as he took leave, his heart warmed towards them.

Every birth, marriage, or death, which had happened of late in this tribe, though scattered over some six hundred miles, had been discussed and reported to him; for every man knows every other in this tribe: so that scarcely one seemed a stranger to their famishing visitors. The poor people took the greatest pains to instruct them which would be the safest and shortest route; and on the 18th of June the three boats started. Not, however, until Dr. Kane had told them what he knew of their southern brethren, of their wonderful and their far happier condition, and tried to persuade them to march southward, season by season, until they joined them.

To this parting address they listened with intense interest, and in their turn tried to persuade him to come back some day, and carry a boat-load of them to the stations; and a happy result of his stay among them would it indeed be should these poor people ever follow Dr. Kane's advice.

It was a long and weary journey for half-famished and enfeebled men — that along the Greenland coast. Plenty of birds were seen, it is true, flying about the rocks along the shores; but it was not often possible to reach them, and they suffered much for want of fresh meat. Once they were all nearly lost in a sudden break up of the ice, when they were out searching for game: so nearly, indeed, that it seemed a miracle that any escaped.

At length Cape Dudley Digges came in sight; and, utterly worn out, they put in for a few days' holiday in a lovely spot, abounding in animal and vegetable life, which they called Weary-man's Rest. Here, surrounded by all kinds of natural remedies for the scurvy, they gave themselves up to enjoyment; and when they put to sea again it was in much recruited health and strength. But their troubles soon returned, and want of food brought on a kind of low fever, accompanied with swollen feet, which made the labour of towing almost intolerable to them.

The large, open, and dangerous Bay of Melville had yet to be crossed, and in boats so leaky that they required constant baling to keep them afloat. And though worn out by day, yet the men could not sleep when their turns came to take rest. This was the worst symptom of all; and their commander's hopes of escape consequently grew very faint.

Just, however, when things looked black indeed, some large animal was seen floating, apparently asleep, on a small patch of ice. It was taken at first for a walrus, but proved to be a seal. Nothing of the kind had been seen for some time, and the sight inspired something like hope. Drawing stockings over the oars to act as mufflers, both the boats' crews neared the animal in perfect silence, and in such an intense state of excitement that they could scarcely move their oars. Their lives depended on the capture of this creature; and when they saw him rear his head, despair was ready to seize them.

But they were already within rifle-shot, and the captain gave the signal to fire. Petersen, in his anxiety, could with difficulty steady his gun; and the instant the shot was fired the creature made a movement, as if about to plunge. But his head fell helplessly on one side; and, with a frantic yell of delight, the men urged the boats upon the floes, and rushed forward to carry the seal to a safer spot. To use Dr. Kane's words, ' they ran, over the floe, crying, and laughing, and brandishing their knives. It was not five minutes before every man was sucking his bloody fingers, or mouthing long strips of raw blubber.'

That night a fire was made of two planks taken from one of the boats, and they had a grand feast, not an ounce of the creature being lost. This supply saved them; and it saved their poor dogs, too : for the two remaining ones had been brought with them in case of extremity, though not a man liked to think of killing them.

By the 1st of August they were approaching the Devil's Thumb, in the ordinary whaling-ground on the southern side of the bay. They then passed the Duck Islands; and, coming close to Upernavik, prepared once more to land on the firm earth.

Petersen soon recognised a native whom he knew. It was Carlie Mossyn, who had come up in the Fraulein Flaischer to get the year's supply of blubber from Kingatok; and of course he was full of news—such news as he got from the whalers, and relating chiefly to the Crimean War.

Of America he knew little, he said, as Americans have no whalers on that coast. He only knew that, about a fortnight before, two vessels had gone up into the ice to seek Dr. Kane's party. He could tell them, however, what interested them as much as anything, namely, that Dr. Rae had found traces of Sir John Franklin's expedition nearly a thousand miles to the south of where they had been seeking him. This he knew, because his pastor had read it in a German paper. So, after being eighty-four days in the open air, Dr. Kane and his companions landed, and that night 'drank coffee *before* many a hospitable dwelling;' for they could not remain long within the four walls of a house without a distressing sense of suffocation.

CHAPTER XVI.

SIR LEOPOLD M'CLINTOCK'S VOYAGE, AND DISCOVERY OF THE RELICS OF THE FRANKLIN EXPEDITION.

THE discovery of the three graves at Beechey Island by Captains Penny and Ommanney in 1850, and the report sent home by Dr. Rae in 1854, were, up to that date, the only clues which had been obtained of the course of the lost expedition. On the receipt of the first intelligence the English Government had redoubled its efforts, and continued to send out more and more ships. But Dr. Rae's information had the contrary effect, as it seemed to destroy all hopes of saving life; and when Lady Franklin earnestly intreated that this new track might be followed up, the reply was, on this ground, a negative one. The British Government did not consider it right to risk more lives, or to spend more treasure, in this perilous enterprise; and her petition was consequently rejected.

She, however, viewed the matter in a different light, and considered it as a sacred duty to rescue, if not the lives of her husband and his companions, yet at least their reputation from oblivion.

She had already greatly impoverished herself by the large expenses which she had incurred in this cause; yet she hesitated not on receiving this answer, but at once determined to take the matter into her own hands.

The 'Fox,' a screw-yacht, was purchased by her, and placed under the command of Captain M'Clintock, who had already so greatly distinguished himself in the voyages of Sir James Ross and Captain Austen; and whose heart, as he himself tells us, was most thoroughly in the work.

Lady Franklin was not, however, left to bear the pecuniary burden alone; for many eminent and scientific men shared in her enthusiasm, and amongst them was Sir Roderick Murchison.

A large sum was consequently soon raised; and, by the 1st of July, 1857, the 'Fox' was getting to sea, having previously undergone a thorough refitting and preparation for the voyage.

Volunteers had been so numerous, that it was only difficult to make a selection; and the crew of men and officers was really a picked one, although but twenty-five in number. Lieutenant Hobson, already a tried man in Arctic work, was the second officer; and Captain Allan Young went as sailing-master, and contributed also largely to the expense. He had but just returned in ill-health from the Crimea, yet he went solely as a volunteer. Dr. Walker went as surgeon, naturalist, and photographer; while Carl Petersen, who had only a few days before returned to his own country from Dr.

Kane's expedition, in which he had suffered so much, came to join this one at the invitation of Sir Roderick Murchison.

The ship was, likewise, well and wisely stocked with provisions, including plenty of vegetables, pickles, lemon-juice, and pale ale; and Government liberally contributed towards these supplies, besides giving arms, ammunition, and various Arctic instruments, when once the thing was started.

Lady Franklin herself, accompanied by her niece, Miss Sophia Cracroft, went on board shortly before they sailed, and received three hearty cheers on quitting the vessel. In less than a fortnight the 'Fox' was off the southern coast of Greenland; and there, contrary to their intention, they were obliged to put into the harbour of Frederickshaab, in order to send home by a Danish vessel, soon leaving that port, one of the men, who had begun to show signs of diseased lungs. And thus Captain M'Clintock had an opportunity of getting better acquainted with this country, and with its inhabitants, both Danish and Esquimaux.

The whole population, he tells us, amounts only to about 7000 souls, of whom 1000 are Danes. These latter, in fact, possess all the habitable parts of the country, although without dispossessing its original inhabitants. The latter still maintain their independence and their laws, but are cared for and instructed by the Danes, to whom they are really attached. At each station there is a Lutheran pastor, doctor, and schoolmaster, of whose advice

and instructions these poor people have the benefit,
without any payment whatever being required.   In
times of famine, also, they are supplied with provisions: but spirits are strictly forbidden.

Is not this the right way of occupying a heathen
country; and a way which, as Captain M'Clintock
remarks, we English should do well to imitate?
Yet the Esquimaux of Labrador, and all the Hudson's
Bay territory, would hardly bear witness to the same
kind of treatment.

The 'Fox' soon proceeded on its northern voyage, and reached the Moravian settlement of Lichtenfels, and the sunny little cove of Fishernaes,
to both of which Dr. Kane had so lately paid a visit.
At the latter place boys brought handfuls of large
rough garnets, which they gladly exchanged for bis-
cuits.   Here, too, Captain M'Clintock was conducted
by Petersen to see the entrance of an Esquimaux hut,
all the inmates of which were, as they would have
said, in bed; but, as the captain remarks, 'Going
to bed here only means lying down with your clothes
on, upon a rein-deer skin, wherever you can find room,
and pulling another fur robe over you.'

Godhaab, or New Hernhutt, still the seat of a
Moravian mission, also received a visit; and four
missionaries, unpaid by Government, were found to
be labouring there.

The Danish home-bound vessel having been met
here, the invalid, the letters, and the pilot, who was
Hans Christian's brother, were soon sent on board
of her; and the 'Fox' again weighed anchor.   Pro-

ceeding up Disco Fiord, they found it in all the
beauty of its summer dress,—the blue campanulas
and other wild-flowers spread profusely over the
rocky slopes, and game of many sorts abounding
in the neighbourhood. This place is famous for
its salmon-trout fisheries, of which fish a large
supply was brought off to the ship in kajaks. A

Baffin's Bay by Moonlight.

young Esquimaux dog-driver, named Christian, also
volunteered, and was accepted in that capacity.
He was soon in the hands of the crew, undergoing a
thorough scrubbing and cropping, and when dressed
in his new sailor's clothes, he looked very well contented with himself.

A fresh supply of coal was taken on board in
Waygatt Strait, which our readers will remember

separates the isle of Disco from the main land.
Here the scenery is described as very grand. They
had still to complete their number of dogs, and
stood in need of some other things; so Petersen's
knowledge of the resources of the country, in which
he had lived for twelve years, was found very ser-
viceable. At Upernavik he was welcomed as an
old friend; and the visit of a friend, whether old or
new, is always a pleasant event in those lonely parts.

The last traces of civilization were seen here;
and now they had to choose between the different
routes across Baffin's Bay.

A pack of ice, caused by the breaking up of the
main body in spring, always obstructs the passage
from east to west, even in summer. This must be
sailed round either on the north or south, or a
vessel must push through the middle of it; and now,
failing in the southern and middle courses, Captain
M'Clintock steered northwards.

They were in Melville Bay, which Dr. Kane had
so recently crossed; and one vast glacier extended
along the coast for 40 or 50 miles, while innumerable
icebergs were glittering in the sunlight and ren-
dering the navigation almost impossible. It was
late in the season, too, and soon the yacht was completely beset in the pack; and to the captain's great
mortification, there was every appearance of her
being forced to winter there. They were in a
dangerous part, too, and exposed to many storms;
and when he thought of Lady Franklin's disappointed hopes, the delay seemed almost unbearable.

In these feelings of their captain, the men, fortunately, did not participate. They had all that they wanted, and, with the usual thoughtlessness of sailors, made themselves quite happy with the various diversions within their reach.

Bear-hunts and seal-hunts formed part of these; and Petersen and Christian diligently practised the Esquimaux method of attracting the latter,—scraping the ice so as to make a noise like that produced by a seal with its flipper; then putting one end of a pole into the water, they made all kinds of grunting noises, like those which the seal itself makes.

Like other Esquimaux, Christian would carry his kajak on his head, and drag a seal after him when he came back from hunting.

They had also a barrel-organ on board, which had been presented by the Prince Consort to the vessel which bore his name, and which Lady Franklin had sent out in 1851. This was its third winter in the ice; and it served greatly to amuse the men, especially Christian, who had never seen such a thing before.

So September passed away; but no change in the ice came sufficient to allow of the ship's passage through it, and the preparations for winter went on the more rapidly as the dismal prospect became a certainty.

On the 1st of November the sun paid them its last visit; and on the 5th, in order to vary the monotony, the crew kept Guy Fawkes' day on the ice in great style.

In the beginning of the next month, however, the

BURIAL IN THE ICE.

daily routine of ship life was broken in a sadder way, for a death occurred among the crew, not by illness, but as the result of an accident. Scott, the engine-driver (for the 'Fox' was provided with a steam-engine in case of need), fell down a hatchway, and received such injuries from the fall that his death occurred two days after. Captain M'Clintock describes the scene at this funeral, at which he had to officiate, as one which could never be forgotten by those who witnessed it.

The moon was shining at the time, and apparently not alone. A halo encircled it, through which passed a broad streak of light, which stretched along the horizon, and above the first halo appeared parts of two others. Six paraselenæ, or mock moons, appeared in the heavens at the same time. Yet the sky was dark and murky, and the cold intense, when the little procession descended from the deck, where most of the service had been read, and while the ship's colours were set half-mast high, and her bell tolled mournfully, proceeded by the light of torches to the spot where a hole was cut in the ice. Thus was the body committed to the deep.

Petersen proved himself a very interesting companion during this weary winter; having, of course, endless stores of information about the country, the Esquimaux, and the animals of the region: but he was not called upon to exercise his office of interpreter, as no natives came near the ship.

In March the strong gales caused movements to take place in the ice, in which the 'Fox' got nipped, and was often in imminent danger. Then the pack began to drift, and she with it, until, by the 26th of April, she had actually repassed Davis's Straits, and was once more opposite to Fishernaes, but some way out at sea! It is, perhaps, one of the most remarkable drifts ever known; and though eight months had thus passed uselessly, yet it was with great thankfulness that her captain found his vessel safely free from the 'villainous pack,' and his crew safe after all the terrific perils of that long run.

They then steered for Holsteinborg, one of the best places for obtaining rein-deer, in order to refit and refresh the crew. We must pass over the time of that delightful though short summer holiday in Greenland. Soon they were again steaming northward, and after narrowly escaping shipwreck, and then being again caught in the pack, they succeeded by the middle of July in reaching the entrance of Lancaster Sound. They had on their way, while opposite to the crimson cliffs and Arctic highlands, received a visit from some of these poor highlanders, who instantly recognized Petersen, having lived at Etah, and seen him there with Dr. Kane. They told them that Hans was married, and living at Whale Sound, but would gladly go southward if he had a kajak or dogs, as he suffered much from want where he was.

It was probably in consequence of a letter of Dr. Kane's that the Danish Greenland Company, pitying the condition of these poor people, now requested Captain M'Clintock to bring them all, that is, a hundred and twenty people, down to the southern settlements: a thing which, he says, he would gladly have done, had not duty called him elsewhere.

As a pack of ice lay across the entrance to the Sound, he steered now for Pond's Bay, to the southeast of it, and there had another opportunity of sending home letters by the 'Diana' whaling-vessel.

Here they met an old native woman and a boy, who were subjected to a close cross-examination as to wrecks, ships, and white people; but they declared that they knew of none ever having come there: and yet they knew well enough about the depôt of provisions at Navy Board Inlet, which is the next on the north of this coast, and which some of their tribe seem to have robbed. The old woman traced for them a chart of the coast line, and the next day, being less excited, she remembered a wreck on the coast when she was a girl, about forty-five miles to the northward — a piece of which wreck was afterwards brought on board and found to be English oak.

As no further information could be obtained from her, they determined on going on to visit her tribe, taking her and her boy with them as pilots; and while on board she drew for them another chart, which fully displayed her geographical powers. She told them that she was a widow, and that her daughter was married and living at Igloolik, which turned out to be the same that Parry had visited; for she spoke of a ship which had wintered there, and of one of the crew's dying, whose name was

Allah, or Ellah, — Parry's ice-master, Mr. Elder, no doubt, who died and was buried at Igloolik.   She spoke, too, of another wreck, which happened before her first child was born.

No information could, however, be gained from any of her tribe regarding those whom they sought, nor of any wrecks westward, though all these people were questioned both separately and together.   The name of their village is Kaparōk-to-lik, a mere strip of land surrounded by glaciers.   They were very poorly off, as there is little game in this locality, and less wood; and they constantly repeated '*Pilletay*—Give me,' in a whining tone.   On the return of the captain to the ship, which had been nearly crushed during the absence of the party, some of these people came in their kajaks, with whalebone and narwhals' horns to barter.   They remained on board some time, drew more charts, and spoke of two other wrecks a day's journey southward, which they had visited five winters ago: but they all agreed that it was a long time since they took place; and it was considered likely that these were the wrecks of two whalers mentioned in Parry's narrative.

This tribe had yearly communication with another, probably the Akkolee people, from whom they had heard of some white people who came in two boats, and spent a winter in snow-huts: but none of these died; therefore these were, most likely, Dr. Rae and his party.

They now steamed on through Lancaster Sound to Beechey Island depôt; and here a marble tablet sent out by Lady Franklin was erected, close to one recording the deaths of those who died in Sir Edward Belcher's expedition, and also to another to the memory of the young Frenchman, Lieutenant Bellot.

Lady Franklin's ran as follows :—

To the Memory of
FRANKLIN,
CROZIER, FITZJAMES,
AND ALL THEIR
GALLANT OFFICERS AND FAITHFUL COMPANIONS
WHO HAVE SUFFERED AND PERISHED
IN THE CAUSE OF SCIENCE AND
THE SERVICE OF THEIR COUNTRY,

This Tablet
IS ERECTED NEAR THE SPOT WHERE THEY PASSED
THEIR FIRST ARCTIC WINTER, AND WHENCE
THEY ISSUED FORTH TO CONQUER
DIFFICULTIES OR TO DIE.
IT COMMEMORATES THE GRIEF OF THEIR ADMIRING
COUNTRYMEN AND FRIENDS, AND THE ANGUISH,
SUBDUED BY FAITH, OF HER WHO HAS
LOST, IN THE HEROIC LEADER OF
THE EXPEDITION, THE MOST
DEVOTED AND AFFECTIONATE OF
HUSBANDS.

———

' AND SO HE BRINGETH THEM UNTO THE HAVEN WHERE
THEY WOULD BE.'
1855.

Twelve days later than this, in 1850, Captain M'Clintock had been on board the 'Assistance' when Captain Ommanney landed, because a cairn had attracted his notice, and thus discovered the three graves.

On the 18th of August the ‘Fox’ ran easily down Peel Sound, between North Somerset and Prince of Wales’ Island, and attempted to pass by the passage of Bellot Strait into the Gulf of Boothia;

Bellot Strait.

but the ice not suffering the ship to proceed, they turned out again and made for Port Leopold.

Passing down North Somerset on the east, they once more tried Bellot Strait from that side; a barrier, however, still stopped them in the middle of it, nor was it until the fifth attempt that they succeeded. On a point a little north of this Captain M‘Clintock had stood, just nine years before, with Sir James Ross;

and he now thought, as he had done then, that a wide channel southward certainly existed, that is, the one now known as Victoria Strait. All this country had then to be explored; and Captain Young started in a sledge to seek a route from Brentford Bay to the Western Sea. But this he reported impracticable. Three separate sledge-routes were then planned, which were to be led by the Captain, Lieutenant Hobson, and Captain Young.

The first was to go to the Great Fish River, examining the shores of King William's Land; the second, the western side of Boothia to the Magnetic Pole; and the third, the shores of Prince of Wales' Land. They were to be absent from sixty to seventy days, and to start in March, the earliest time they thought possible. Meantime the ship remained in a creek, which they named Port Kennedy, in the neighbourhood of this little strait, for her winter quarters; but her crew were not to be long inactive.

Travelling parties in all directions went out to examine the country, and to endeavour to meet with Esquimaux, from whom the desired information might possibly be extracted. They lost their engineer this winter by a fit of apoplexy; and thus their numbers were reduced to twenty-four, and they had no one left to manage the engine.

It was a severe season; but they had plenty of occupation in preparing for their journeys after the turn of the year. And, profiting by experience, all sorts of improvements were made in the wearing apparel, in order the better to enable travellers to stand exposure to wind and weather. Face-covers and light over-all dresses, called snow-repellers, were made to keep off the drifting snow; and every article was tried and tested by preparatory walks.

The little light calico tents, to hold six persons, and which weighed, including poles, only $18\frac{1}{2}$ lbs., were altered and strengthened: and warm sleeping-bags and tent-robes were made. The cooking utensils, those for carrying food, and other articles, were also thoroughly tested and repaired; and, in short, everything was done to enable them to begin their excursions with or soon after the reappearance of the sun, and to pursue them in a temperature which would, in the course of four or five months, vary from fifty degrees below zero to about the same number above it.

They got away earlier than any previous travellers; but Captain M'Clintock's party were somewhat retarded in their progress, by the dogs' sufferings from cold. They became lame, and sometimes fell down in fits; so that he was unwillingly obliged to lighten the loads more than once. They travelled till dusk, and then built themselves a snow-hut, in which they passed the night. It took two hours to erect these structures; and even then the tent was put over them to roof them in, as they could not spare time for the arched dome.

On the 1st of March they arrived at the Magnetic Pole; and there, to the captain's great joy, he saw four natives approaching. None had previously been seen, which had caused him to fear that the journey would be fruitless.

These natives did not appear at all surprised at the sight of whites; and, by means of Petersen, a conversation was at once begun, though the English party were careful not to get too soon on the true object of their visit.

One of the men had a naval button on his dress, which he explained to have come from some white people, who were starved on an island where there are salmon: by which they meant an island in a river; and they added, that they had got their iron knives in the same way.

Another man had been to Repulse Bay, and had seen seven members of Rae's party.

Captain M'Clintock went on with these people to their village, and in half-an-hour they built him a good snow-hut. He then told them that he wished to barter with them, and especially to buy all the articles belonging to the starved whites.

So next morning the whole population of the village, consisting of forty-five people, came out, and readily sold silver spoons; a silver medal, which had belonged to Mr. A. M'Donald, assistant-surgeon; part of a gold chain, several buttons, knives, and bows and arrows, made of different parts of the wreck.

None of these people had seen the whites, though one man said he had seen the bones of some of them; and Petersen understood from him that a boat had been crushed by the ice.

Another man told him that a ship with three masts had been crushed by the ice, out in the sea, westward of King William's Island; but not until all the crew had landed safely. He said, also, that the ship sank; and so nothing was got from her. All their spoils came from the island in the river.

An old man also sketched on the snow the coast-line, near where the ship sank; but Captain M'Clintock could make nothing of it.

Thus Dr. Rae's statements were confirmed, and one ship accounted for; but no papers whatever were yet obtained, nor was anything heard of the other vessel. The old people all remembered the visit of the ' Victory;' one of them, an old man named Ooblooria, turning out, in fact, to be the same individual whom Sir James Ross had employed as a guide. He en-quired after Sir James, by his Esquimaux name of Agglugga. And Captain M'Clintock, in his turn, asked after the man for whom a wooden leg had been made by the carpenter of that vessel; but he got no direct answer, though his daughter was pointed out to him. Petersen explained that this proved the man to be dead, as the Esquimaux never like to speak of departed friends.

This tribe seemed to be well off; they were clean and well-dressed, stout and hearty people, and very friendly: but, like the rest of their nation, terrible thieves. They have a great partiality for needles; and one woman, in order to obtain more, pulled her naked infant out of its fur-bag, though the temperature was 60° below freezing, and held it up before the captain; begging in this way for one for her child.

Having got all the information which they could obtain from these people, Captain M'Clintock returned to the ' Fox,' where he found Captain Young, who had also got back. All were eager to start again, and Dr. Walker soon took out one party: while Captain Young went with another to Fury Beach, where many valuable supplies yet remained. He found that preserved vegetables and soups, left there in 1825, yet remained good; and the party supped off them! They also brought away some sugar. But many of them were seized with snow-blindness on the journey, and had to be led home.

These were, however, only preparatory trips. The three great journeys did not commence till the 2nd of April, when Dr. Walker remained in charge of the ship. When they returned, the precious document had been obtained which tells of the fate of the gallant crews.

The sledges started, each with their gay silk banners flying, while the yacht hoisted her flag: and, by the 20th of April, Captain M'Clintock had again met with his old acquaintances of February last, who were out seal-hunting.

Entering their huts, which were of a more elaborate form than usual, and contained more apartments than the former ones, they found many articles which had evidently once belonged to an English ship, and also heard that *two* ships had been seen by the natives of King William's Island, one of which sank in deep water, while the other was stranded on the shore at a place called Oot-loo-lik; and that it was from this wreck that they got most of their wood.

It was a young man, however, who let out this

piece of information; the old one had previously said nothing about it. The young one also spoke of having heard of the body of a very large man being found on board this wreck. They both said that it was in the autumn when the crews deserted the ship and went away to the large river, and that in the next winter their bones were found on its banks. But the old man also gave the unpleasant information of one of the depôts having been, plundered by some of his countrymen, who had followed their homeward track; which piece of news prevented them from making any further depôts among these people.

Captain M'Clintock had travelled in company with Lieutenant Hobson so far; and they went on together to Cape Victoria, the south-west point of Boothia, where they separated, the former proceeding on towards the south, while the latter marched across the ice to Cape Felix, the north-west point of King William's Island, the plan being that Lieutenant Hobson was to search for the wreck, and Captain M'Clintock for the relics of the Fish River party.

Crossing over then from Boothia to King William's Island, Captain M'Clintock once more met with natives, who, though they seemed never before to have seen white people, were perfectly friendly and ready to trade. These also knew about this wreck, of which, they said, little now remained, as their countrymen had carried much of it away.

They sold more plate, bearing the crests or initials of Franklin, Crozier, Fairholme, and M'Donald, and offered a heavy sledge made of a large piece of carved wood; but this was too heavy to be carried away. 'It was five days' journey to the wreck,' they said, and there had been *many books;* but the weather had long ago destroyed them.

An old woman also spoke of the white men who dropped down and died as they travelled to the river, of whom she said some were buried, and some were not; but as to the number of these poor fellows, nothing could be ascertained.

Captain M'Clintock, it should be remembered, was examining all round the eastern part of this large island. He soon came to a bay which he named 'Latrobe,' after the esteemed Moravian friend of Sir John Franklin, and on the 10th of May reached Booth Point, the south-eastern extremity, where they only met two or three old people who were too frightened to give any information. On the 12th they crossed over to Point Ogle, on the continent, and just at the mouth of Back's River. Down this they journeyed as far as Montreal Island, but were obliged to travel by night to escape snow-blindness. No relics were, however, obtained there; so they crossed over to the mainland, and examined the shores of Duncan Point with as little success.

Ogle peninsula was next searched, and a cairn found there taken down and rebuilt; but nothing was discovered. They were now on their return journey, and on the very shores on which the unfortunate crews must have marched. But the sledges kept on the sea-ice close to the shore, while the men narrowly looked out for any trace of relics.

It was on the 25th of May that Captain M'Clintock came on a very painful one, namely, the skeleton of a slight young man, who from his dress, and especially the loose bow-knot in which his handkerchief was tied, was judged to have been a steward or officer's servant; but the face and limbs had been gnawed away or broken by wild beasts. Near him was found a frozen pocket-book, a clothes-brush, and pocket horn-comb; all which articles, had the Esquimaux discovered him, would have been stolen. The poor young fellow seems to have fallen down exhausted,—probably fell asleep, and so died. Nothing but deserted native huts were found along the south coast of King William's Island, to which they now bent their steps, making for Point Herschel, in Washington Bay, where it had been arranged that Hobson should leave a note.

A cairn built by Simpson stands conspicuously on the summit of this cape, at about 150 feet above the sea. It now appears that the retreating parties must have passed this point, travelling as they did round the west of King William's Island; and therefore it was natural to expect records here, where this cairn was built ready to their hands. They might even have recorded here the *discovery of the North-west Passage.*

A very careful search was therefore immediately instituted. The cairn was taken down stone by stone, and all the ground broken up with a pickaxe. The appearance of any cairn will always tell whether it has been taken down and rebuilt, and some signs of this having been done were perceived on one side; yet with the bitterest disappointment they were compelled at last to turn away without finding the records which it seemed impossible to believe were not there.

Nevertheless, the interesting discovery was close at hand. It had already, in fact, been made by Lieutenant Hobson, who had been at a spot a few miles farther on, where his note, left in a new cairn built by himself, was found.

He had discovered the record so long and anxiously sought, not at Cape Herschel, but at Point Victory, on the north-west of the island—the spot where the ships were deserted. It was written on one of the printed forms supplied to all the Arctic ships, and was soldered up in a thin tin cylinder; and a duplicate was also found in Back Bay, but without further information. The paper ran thus:—

'*28th of May*, 1847.—H. M. ships "Erebus" and "Terror" wintered in the ice, in lat. 70° 5′ N.; long. 98° 23′ W.

'Having wintered in 1846-7 at Beechey Island, in lat. 74° 43′ 28″ N., long. 91° 39′ 15″ W., after having ascended Wellington Channel to lat. 77°, and returned by the west side of Cornwallis Island.

' Sir John Franklin commanding the expedition.

' All well.

' Party consisting of 2 officers and 6 men left the ships on Monday, 24th May, 1847.

' GM. GORE, Lieut.

' CHAS. F. DES VŒUX, Mate.'

The first date is evidently an error, as they had

by their own showing passed two winters in the ice; and the first must therefore have been that of 1845–6. They had accomplished the passage when this was written in good spirits, having descended southwards by the channel now known as Franklin's, between Prince of Wales' Land and North Somerset, and Boothia, into a sea which was well known. But a short time changed all their prospects, and a few months afterwards another hand had added round the margin the following melancholy tidings:—

'*April* 25, 1848.—H. M. ships "Terror" and "Erebus" were deserted on the 22d of April, 5 leagues W.N.W. of this, having been beset since 12th September, 1846. The officers and crews, consisting of 105 souls, under the command of Capt. T. R. M. Crozier, landed here in lat. 69° 37′ 42″ N., long. 98° 41′ W. Sir John Franklin died on the 11th of June, 1847, and the total loss by deaths in the expedition has been to this date 9 officers and 15 men.

(Signed)   ' T. R. M. CROZIER,
              ' Captain and Senior Officer.'
(Signed)   ' JAMES FITZJAMES,
                 ' Captain H. M. S. " Erebus."

And start (on) to-morrow, 26th, for Back's Fish River.'

There was also another addition, by a third hand :—

' This paper was found by Lieutenant Irving, under the cairn supposed to have been built by Sir James Ross in 1831, four miles to the northward, where it had been deposited by the late Commander Gore in June 1847. Sir James Ross' pillar has not, however, been found, and the paper is transferred to this position, which is that in which Sir James Ross' pillar was erected.'

Such news stimulated M'Clintock's party to press on, as did also the shortness of their provisions.

They reached the western point of the island on the 29th of May, and named it after Captain Crozier; and on the next day they came to a large boat, of which Lieutenant Hobson had also spoken. This boat contained an immense quantity of clothing, though not one article bore its owner's name; but the first sight showed them what turned their attention from everything else; namely, parts of two human skeletons. It was a sight which struck them all with horror; but no part of the skull of either was found which could lead to the identification of the persons, for they had both been the food of wolves.

A pair of worked slippers lay near to one; and by the other, five watches. But the search for journals or pocket-books was again vain; five or six small books only were found—all devotional ones, except the *Vicar of Wakefield*. A small Bible also lay there, in which were whole passages underlined, and many marginal notes; and there were, besides, the covers of a New Testament and Prayer-book. No food was found in this boat, except tea and chocolate; but of other articles there was an immense variety, including plate, with the well-known crests of many of the unfortunate officers. This boat, which rested on a sledge, was about fifty miles from Point Victory, and seventy miles from the first skeleton found. It was directed towards the ships, as if returning to them. Perhaps a party had gone forward for fresh supplies, leaving these two in charge of the boat, and had not been able to return.

Captain M‘Clintock now, naturally, was chiefly anxious to find the wreck itself; but no sign of her was to be seen: nor did he find any other relics. Hobson found two other cairns, and other interesting articles, and everything that could be carried was borne away. Strange to say, however, out of all the immense heap of clothing, no memorandum of any kind was found in the pockets. Yet Esquimaux could hardly have visited these parts, or all would have been taken away. Captain M‘Clintock thought, that if Sir John Franklin had known of a passage eastward of King William's Island, he would have taken it and escaped all the disasters which befell him and his crew; but his chart told him of none such.

Both the searching parties now returned to the 'Fox.' Indeed, it was high time that Lieutenant Hobson did so, as he was too ill even to stand alone, on his arrival, from the effects of scurvy. But, happily, Christian had shot some ducks, which, with preserved potatoe, milk, strong ale, and lemon-juice, proved the best medicine for him; and he soon began to amend. One man, the steward, had died from this disease during their absence; but the rest were tolerably well.

Captain Young had, meantime, discovered a passage between Victoria and Prince of Wales' Lands. He had come back in bad health; and, contrary to the doctor's opinion, had gone out again. As, therefore, there was much cause for anxiety about him, Captain M‘Clintock himself now set off in search of him.   He was found at last in a terribly reduced state: and all returned to recruit by a liberal indulgence in all the good things on board ship.

Every one knows what it is to have important news to communicate, and how impatient persons in such a position are of every obstacle.   And no one will wonder that, in the present instance, a third winter in the ice was much dreaded.

On the breaking up of the ice the steam was got up, and, with the help of the two stokers, Captain M‘Clintock found that he could work the engine himself.   This was a great relief; and a greater still was it when, on the 10th, a passage cleared in the ice, and they were really able to start.   On the 17th they passed Fury Beach, and were soon after off Port Leopold, and then out in open sea.   By the 28th they reached the Danish harbour of God-haven, where the two Esquimaux were discharged; and on the 21st of September Captain M‘Clintock reached London, and was able to report the result of his voyage at the Admiralty.   There he learnt that instead of 138 men, as had been supposed, only 134 sailed in the ‘Erebus’ and ‘Terror,’ and that of these, five had returned invalided before they entered the ice.   He thinks that it is wholly unlikely that any persons could have escaped death by taking refuge among the Esquimaux, as there were very few on the island, and these, generally, were so ready to give information that, had they helped the poor whites, they would certainly have spoken of it.

The relics which were brought home were deposited at the United Service Institution, and it is needless to state, that those who brought them were received everywhere with the hearty welcome which they so well deserved.

Arctic medals were given to all who had not previously received them.   Lieutenant Hobson was informed that he would shortly be promoted; and her Majesty, in due time, bestowed on Captain M‘Clintock the honour of knighthood, with which his predecessors had so uniformly been rewarded.

By the discovery of Barrow's Straits, Sir Edward Parry may be said to have unlocked the door through which, by different routes, Sir John Franklin, Sir Robert M‘Clure, and Sir Leopold M‘Clintock, · have each shown us a way into the Pacific.   These ways are, however, so barred up by natural obstacles as to be practically useless; but the service itself has proved so valuable a training for British sailors in times of peace : through it we have been introduced to so many lands and peoples formerly unknown, and it has led to such discoveries in the realms of science, that the time, talent, and treasure which it has cost, cannot be said to have been thrown away.

LONDON:

STRANGEWAYS & WALDEN, Printers, Castle St. Leicester Sq.